EARTH:
Giants, Golems, & Gargoyles

Edited by

Rhonda Parrish

EARTH:
Giants, Golems, & Gargoyles

Edited by

Rhonda Parrish

TYCHE BOOKS LTD.

Earth: Giants, Golems, & Gargoyles
Edited by Rhonda Parrish
Copyright © 2019

Published by Tyche Books Ltd.
Calgary, Alberta, Canada
www.TycheBooks.com

Cover Art by Ashley Walters
Cover Layout by Indigo Chick Design
Interior Layout by Ryah Deines
Editorial by Rhonda Parrish

First Tyche Books Ltd Edition 2019
Print ISBN: 978-1-989407-05-9
Ebook ISBN: 978-1-989407-06-6

This book was funded in part by a grant from the Alberta Media Fund.

Dedicated to Jo.
As always.
Thank you for being my rock.

Contents

Introduction

By Rhonda Parrish

IT TOOK ME two tries to write this Introduction. I don't mean that I wrote an Introduction and then this is the revised version. I don't even mean that I had a false start when I began writing this and needed to start over again (though I had several). I mean, I wrote the Introduction and included it in the manuscript when I handed it in to my publisher. Then, when it came time to do copyedits I read over what I'd written and cringed. It was a mess.

So this is take two. Hopefully it goes better.

The reason I struggled so much to write this Introduction is because of just how big the topic is. Fire was reasonably easy to talk about, most everyone knows what fire is, what it represents, and how it has impacted human evolution, so I only needed to touch on that and then move on to fiery creatures. Earth, on the other hand, is a whole different thing. First of all, earth is not just an element, it's also a planet. It's our home. And it's in trouble.

Not only had I not really taken that into account when I began to write the Introduction, I hadn't even really taken it into account when I wrote the call for submissions for this anthology. Or pitched the anthology series to the publisher in the first place. But the people who submitted to this anthology did.

When I originally approached Tyche Books with the idea for this anthology series, earth was meant to be the first element we tackled (rather than fire), and the title I proposed for the book was Guardians: Giants, Golems and Gargoyles. I imagined stories of gargoyles mounted on rooftops warding off evil spirits, and golems crafted from mud and magic to protect their creators. And giants... well, giants weren't necessarily protective of humans but they could be, and the alliteration worked.

As the idea and the series evolved we dropped the "guardians" idea from the title, but it was definitely always there, tucked away in the corner of my mind. And now, as I write this and look over the Table of Contents I can still see that guardian theme, but not only in the way I'd first imagined. The planet is in need of guardians even more so than we are but, because we are interconnected, protecting it protects us too.

It's true, some of these stories contain earthly creatures who exist—wholly or in part—to protect and serve humans (whether they like it or not), but another kind of guardian is also very much present—people protecting the earth (or the Earth).

And while some of the stories are epic in scale, some are smaller, more personal dramas, and there are a couple that are just good, earthy fun.

These ideas of guarded vs. guardian and global dramas vs. personal ones vs. light-hearted fun were absolutely not front of mind as I put this anthology together, but I am very happy with the way they balanced out.

Because our current reality is one of climate change, islands of plastic, and vanishing species, but it's also one of incredible scientific innovation, new power sources, and strong grassroots efforts to preserve the environment. And in this reality, some of us (*cough* me *cough*) need a similar mix in order to stay productive and sane.

It's important to look at the large scale issues threatening our world, and the smaller scale ones surrounding our communities and families, but if we don't take some time out to notice and enjoy the good things, the beautiful things, the silly things, not only can we lose our sense of balance, but we can forget the reasons those bigger things matter.

Or perhaps that's just me. But I don't think so.

Either way, this anthology has that. We've got dark stories, light stories, big stories, small stories . . . we've got lush forests and burned out swaths of devastation. Volcanoes and, well, giant penises. Heart and humour. A big ole diverse ecosystem of stories.

Kind of like this planet. But book-shaped.

It's no wonder I had trouble trying to figure out how to introduce you to it.

Rhonda Parrish
Edmonton
6/12/2019

Grin of Stone: A Political Rant

Jane Yolen

That gargoyle, church born,
full of Sunday sanctity,
incense filling flared nostrils,
screech of stone claws on slate roof
out-shouting the downstairs singers of soul.
If you want to know his heart,
check that grin of stone.
Just because he lives above the righteous
like the butcher above his shop,
does not mean he has given away
the last laugh, does not mean
he will not slaughter what he admires
does not mean he will not anoint his meat
with the church's own holy oil.

The Enforcer

Chadwick Ginther

FRANK WALKED PAST St. Mary's Cemetery on his way home from the vendor every night, carrying his usual two-four for later, and king can for the road. It'd never stood out to him more than any other boneyard but tonight something prickled at the edges of his vision.

The shadows were *wrong*.

Frank squinted closer, wondering if some drunks had kicked over headstones for shits and giggles. No, headstones weren't knocked over, they were *gone*. Frank didn't like mysteries, especially when his boss—Winnipeg's local necromancer—was away on a job.

He muttered, "Well, shit," took the gate lock in a meaty, dead hand, snapped it, and headed in.

There was no sound other than wind rustling through leaves, and distant traffic. A shadow rose behind Frank in the moonlight. He spun around. A huge shape made of dirt with patches of grass-like hair, and wearing tombstones like hockey pads, reared back to drive him into the ground.

He dropped his beer and rolled away. An earthen hand, bigger than Frank's entire body, slammed down on the case, shattering the contents.

"Aw, fuck."

The vendor was closed now.

He kicked a marble stone, dead centre, cracking it in half. The thing howled like a cement mixer starting up. Frank didn't know if he'd hurt it. Or if it *could* be hurt.

Tombstones slid over its body as the earth churned. Obelisk-shaped grave markers slid from the dirt where its hands should've been. Another swing. Frank caught the first obelisk, braced his feet, and wrenched. There was a sucking sound, like pulling a fence post from wet clay, and it came free.

Frank slammed his makeshift club through the dirt, severing the thing's other wrist. The second obelisk dropped and the thing swelled, absorbing more graves, replacing the cracked tombstones. Frank slugged it again, but it swallowed him like a mudslide. The earth flowed around him, but still felt like it'd been packed hard.

He had no leverage but he dug and scratched. The thing's form shifted around him, keeping him trapped. Nothing to punch. Nothing to kick. He didn't need to breathe, or he'd have already suffocated. He hit something solid. It wasn't dirt. Had to be important. A coffin, or casket. Frank knew the feel. He doubted it was empty.

Frank clenched tight to a pallbearer's handle and tore it free with a grunt. Dirt poured into the coffin and Frank plunged his hand inside with it. There *was* a body inside. Frank fumbled for the skull and crushed it in a meaty hand. It felt wet. Fresh. The dirt parted around him, and the golem dissipated, like it'd been dumped by a truck, leaving an unembalmed body among scattered tombstones, earth, and coffin remnants.

He glimpsed someone in a wide-brimmed hat and long duster getting into a big, dark car. Only a necromancer thought that look rocked. He dug himself out from his shallow grave of loose earth as red taillights grew fainter in the dark, and disappeared.

FRANK DIDN'T WANT to stick around to clean up the mess. He didn't hear sirens yet, and if he did, the cops would want no fucking part of him. Part. He grunted a mirthless laugh. Frank was made of parts.

A composite man.

The only unbound composite man in the world, his boss'd told him. His body formed from a dead platoon sewn into an approximation of humanity, and imbued with power beyond the grave. He didn't eat. Didn't sleep. He could outrun a car and lift a truck. And his name wasn't really Frank. None of the guys that formed him had been named Frank. Not Francis. Not Franklin. Not Benjamin *en francais*. It was just what he'd been called, first as a joke, then, later, he'd claimed it not knowing anything else.

Frank wasn't a soldier anymore, not professionally anyway, but he was still a beater of ass every chance he got. Mostly because feeling every stitch in his artificial body kept him in an exceptionally bad mood.

He didn't know what the fuck to make of tonight. Frank was muscle, not a detective. He kicked in doors where directed, he didn't try to figure out who'd gone through an already open one. He didn't consider himself stupid, but he *was* a brute. A blunt instrument. Things tended to crawl out of the woodwork when a necromancer wasn't watching, and he needed to make sure his boss had a city to come home to.

He took out the burner phone she'd given him and called her favourite mortician. Woj kept odd hours too. Hazard of the job. And his coke habit. Some people weren't meant to deal with the world's weirdness.

Woj picked up after two rings.

"Hey, Pretty Boy. I need a pick up. You good to roll?"

A pause, then, "Good*ish*."

"When can you be at my place?"

Woj sighed. "Twenty minutes?"

"See you in ten."

FRANK WAITED IN the shadows beside his three-storey walkup, nursing the one beer that'd miraculously survived the earth-thing's attack, and staring impatiently at the Safeway across the street. He didn't know where to begin, but he knew how. Kick the shit out of enough troublemakers and they'll point you in the direction you're looking for.

Woj's hearse stopped in front of the building, and inched forward until it wasn't directly under a streetlight. Frank hustled in.

Everybody was a fucking pretty boy next to Frank, but Tom Wojciechowski took it to the extreme. Prick could've been in the movies. The mortician's hair was either artfully mussed or he'd passed out with gel in. Frank didn't know if the stubble was because his hands were too shaky to shave, but there was no white powder traces in the bristle, or rye on his breath. Frank assumed he'd been working when he'd got the call.

Woj asked, "Where to?"

"Downtown."

FRANK HOPPED OUT of the hearse by a Tim Hortons across from Winnipeg Square. "Keep circling in case I need a pickup."

"What's open this time of night?"

"If you don't know, you don't need to know and you don't wanna know."

Winnipeg Square was an underground concourse and shopping mall serving the city's business community. For folk who brag about their winters, Winnipeggers would do anything to avoid the wind and cold.

If you knew where to look, you'd find The Red Circus down there. It was Lollapalooza for the skeletal sort. Assuming you were welcome. If you weren't, shit happens everywhere, and it would definitely happen to you there. Frank peered over his shoulder, touched the blood red bricks next to a door marked "No Admittance," and tugged the door open.

Ten feet down a cinder block hallway was a second door. As the entrance swung shut behind him with a click and crunch, Frank knew he stood in a potential kill zone. He smirked. He'd like to see her try.

A peephole slid open; four eyes stared back at him from one face. A high-pitched voice demanded, "What do you want?"

"What do you think I want, Blinky? I want a fucking drink."

No point in telling the doorman why he was really there. He'd get shut down. Start some shit though, and Camilla would come to him. Maybe with answers. The Red Circus wasn't Switzerland for the Graveside crew, there was no neutrality, no peace accords. Camilla didn't care if people scrapped here. Largely because she used host's prerogative to eat the losers. A policy that kept most people in line.

Blinky opened the door. It'd been a while since Frank had

been to The Red Circus. They'd expanded. He was arguably the most human-looking being in the joint. Frank had seen shit that would give nightmares nightmares in his day. Even before he'd started working Graveside. The Red Circus though . . . it was as if the fuckers here *needed* to be a whole 'nother fucking level. A few folks lounged around without their skin, wearing it like some rich prick named Carlton would wear a sweater, walking skeletons grinned at him as they clattered by, and one guy's chest cavity had been replaced with a bug zapper. An insect cloud followed him, swarming and dying, one by one by one.

At a table in the nearest corner, a deer man with a bloody muzzle nibbled at something that *could*, at a glance, be taken for steak. Frank doubted it was beef. Further in, a dandy who blended human and fox, eyed him with golden eyes full of fuckery.

Frank didn't give two shits about any of them, other than whether they'd try and piss in his cornflakes. More likely to get in his face were the three fish-belly-white guys by the bar in matching black suits, and faces extruded from a mould. They worked for the local information broker and were no friends of Frank.

Frank sidled up to the bar and ignored them. If they wanted to fire the first round, fine by him, it'd mean he could see Camilla sooner. The shelves behind the bar were filled with glass bottles with no labels and liquid of wildly poisonous hues. Frank let out a long breath, his lips vibrating. Whatever he ordered, he doubted he'd be bored for long.

"Gimme a Standard," Frank said.

The bartender, a woman with a goat's head growing from her shoulder, pulled a face, and the goat bleated in irritation. "Right away."

She lifted a cellar trap door and the goat's rectangular pupils watched Frank the entire time the woman's back was turned until she disappeared. When she came back, she set down a dusty can without opening it. Folks preferred opening their own drinks in this kinda place.

Frank cracked the tab and relished the hiss. He was a good dozen beers behind where he'd wanted to be by now. He peeled a five from his money clip, slapped it on the bar, and took a long pull of his beer. Two of the suits plonked down beside Frank, knocking his shoulders. They stank of formaldehyde and cigarettes.

Motherfucker. Frank swallowed his anger. Wrong play. He burped instead. "You should fucking know better than to sit next to me."

The suits straightened their ties. Apparently they wanted their asses beat.

Frank grabbed the first suit's tie and jerked, cracking their jaw against the bar, shattering bone. Frank spun and kicked the second suit off his stool, while throwing the first guy over his shoulder by the tie and into the third. The second suit stood, drawing a blade. Frank kicked him in the face and the suit's neck cracked loudly. He flopped, boneless, to the floor.

Fighting got whatever passed for blood in Frank's veins pumping. In those moments he could feel his heart. Feel *alive.* He wrapped the tie around the first suit's neck like a garrotte, and pinned the third with a knee to the sternum.

"Nickel's worth of free advice. Don't wear a tie to fight. Fuckwad."

A light touch on Frank's shoulder from behind made his entire body stiffen and he stole a glance while the suits moaned and gasped.

"Been a while, Frank," Camilla said. She found a bit of grave dirt hiding in his collar with a jagged fingernail, and slipped it over her tongue like a minty breath strip. "St. Mary's. Very tasty."

"Not long enough."

"And yet, here you are."

Frank grunted, released the suit's tie, grabbed his beer, and took a sip. "Yup."

The woman smiled with shark-like teeth, row upon row, disappearing into shadow. Dead eyes, cloudy as the first piss of the morning, hungered. A ghoul. In Winnipeg, *the* ghoul.

Frank had always figured ghouls were pieces of shit wrapped in human clothes. They fed on memories and hopes as much as bodies. The rare undead *not* created by necromancers, and even *they* refused to work with them. Probably because the ravenous pricks would eat all their raw materials.

"Your employer usually keeps you looming. You must want something."

Frank's cheek twitched. He'd hoped he wasn't that transparent. "I wanted a beer but then these shits got delusions of grandeur."

Camilla looked to the bartender. "Audrey, another for our guest. One for me as well. Call my pack to . . . escort these three out."

Audrey nodded, no trace of snark on either face this time.

Frank didn't like asking questions about what necromancers were up to, because nobody liked the answers. *Why the fuck would you stick twenty different dead soldiers together to make me?* Frank knew the answer to that one, *power*, but it didn't stop him from asking the question damn near daily.

"Got slammed by a walking grave."

"Grave golem," Camilla said without hesitation. "I could taste the magic animating the dirt."

"Who's controlling it?"

"Something for something and nothing for nothing, my friend." She smiled her shark-like grin. "And I've already given you something."

Figures. "What do you want?"

"What do you offer?"

They could go back and forth all night. Frank drained his beer and signalled for another. The bartender's goat head screamed at him, but the rest of her went to the cellar without complaint.

"My blood would kill most folks. Poison, they say. Not to you, I imagine."

"I have a *robust* constitution," Camilla said with a laugh. She rolled the bottom edge of her can over the bar and finished it. "I'm intrigued. What's in this deal for you?"

Frank smiled. Suspicion was good. The faster she leapt at the offer, the less likely he could trust her. Camilla probably still had an angle—she was crooked as a dog's hind leg, but he doubted she wanted him dead. Or deader, anyway. He'd have to convince her.

"Just a name. The golem's creator. And where to find him."

"You're so precious." She patted his cheek and it took all his will not to break her hand. "I could. Eat. You. Up. I don't know his true name, or where he is at the moment, but in my circle, they call him Digger."

Digger. Perfect. Another round arrived. The bartender set an empty shot glass beside it.

"You've felt it," Camilla said. "The call of the void."

Frank didn't answer.

"I think you have. You have supped with death. And you want another taste."

Frank bit his cheek. Hard. And spat in the glass. "There's *your* first taste."

HE KNEW WHAT he faced. Golems had creators. The grave golem wasn't the problem. The man in the hat, "Digger," *he* was the problem. Frank didn't need to wait long for Woj's pick up.

"The first thing a rogue necromancer does is seek out their own mortician."

"Well it's not me," Woj said defensively.

"Protest much?" Frank said.

"Why do you have to drag me along?" Woj asked.

"You need to nut up, Snowman, if you want to ride with me."

"First: I *don't* want to ride with you. Second: It's my car. You're riding with *me*."

"That's the spirit." Frank cocked a finger pistol. "You're a shady mortician—"

"That's what my card says," Woj said dryly.

"Ha, fucking ha. I figured you'd know where to start."

"We're businesses. We compete for clients. Sunside. Graveside. We don't exactly play poker with each other."

"You know the locals, yeah? Who's the worst of the bunch?"

Woj sighed. "I have an idea."

THE FIRST TWO morticians seemed Jake. As Jake as could be, given they tried to sell Frank spare parts he didn't need. Frank grew angrier at the thought, but those two wouldn't be working any funerals today. Their offer, and his visit to Camilla got him thinking. Of who he'd been. Why he'd been made. Maybe he wasn't so different from the golem. Dead flesh instead of dead earth. He tapped the dash hard enough to make Woj wince.

Frank didn't know how his squad had been chosen, or why, but he remembered what they were chosen *for*. Dark shit. The kinda stuff that'd make a billy goat puke.

He didn't remember much of what they'd made him do.

Thankfully. The boss said his new consciousness hadn't fully formed. Still, he knew he'd done it. His memories of the old lives he'd lived were scattered. Images mostly. The worst were always the families. Intimate flashes, love and happiness he knew he'd never see again.

Damn near nothing could hurt him, so nothing could kill him. So far. In the meantime, he worked for a necromancer better than the rest. Tried to do good. As much good as one could in their world.

Woj interrupted his brooding. "My life went to shit once I ended up working Graveside too."

"You want shit? I remember dying twenty times. Twenty goddamned times. I don't know which memories are me—" Frank tapped his head– "and which belong to some other dead guy I'm made outta. Christ, I don't know if I should cheer for the Leafs or the Habs."

"I cheer for the Devils."

"Fuck you."

"Look, I recognize the face you're pulling. I've been there."

"Bullshit."

Woj kept talking. "The nightmares for me are the worst. The powerlessness. I want to fight back. But when I reach for courage, it's just not there. I'm . . . empty."

Frank snorted. "You let me in the car. Brave in my book."

Woj chuckled mirthlessly. "That's not brave. Brave would've been telling you to go fuck yourself and find a different ride."

"No," Frank said. "*That* would've been stupid."

DAYLIGHT CREPT INTO the sky. Frank pulled a hat low over his mismatched eyes and a bandana over his jaw. The first two morticians may have been a bust, the third, however, based in Winnipeg's west end, had a black 1970 Cadillac Eldorado parked outside with out-of-province plates. Frank watched the mortician's assistants—a man and a woman—shuffle folding chairs around, wearing jackets that matched the business's purple awning.

Woj whistled at the car. "Now there's a ride."

"Yeah, nothing like having your car scream 'I'm an evil necromancer.'"

Woj shuddered at the word necromancer. "I can't go in there

with you."

"You'd only get in my way."

Frank's door was half open before Woj said, "They're not open yet."

"They'll open for me."

A tall, lean stringy-haired guy dressed as a Wild West undertaker walked past the window, complete with dirty shovel and leather side bag. "There's our guy."

"Who?"

Now Frank was doubly sure. Necromancer invisibility lets them run around wearing their robes and cloaks and being gother-than-goth without drawing any mortal side eye; 1880s undertaker complete with duster and wide-brimmed hat was just the kinda look those fuckers would go for. That, and walking around downtown Winnipeg carrying a fucking bloody shovel and nobody being the fucking wiser. Nobody but Frank. Their invisibility didn't work so well on him.

"What guy?" Woj repeated.

Frank gestured toward the undertaker. "The invisible numbnuts."

Woj shivered, but got the point. "What if another golem's in there?"

Frank shrugged. "Doubt there's enough dust bunnies in there to make one and we're a good ways from a graveyard."

"Your funeral."

"Heh." He nodded at Woj. "Keep the car running. I'm going in."

Frank jerked the funeral home's door open, snapping the dead bolt and pins. The mortician, a suited woman in her fifties, scrambled behind Digger while her purple-jacketed assistants yelped and skittered behind her.

"Catch you pricks at a bad time?"

Digger hurled a handful of earth from his bag at Frank. "Stop!"

Frank stopped dead. He tried to wipe his face, tried to advance, and couldn't. Digger's spade lit up, blinding bright, and Frank's stitches glowed to match it.

"You thought you couldn't be hurt? Couldn't be stopped?" Digger dropped his bag and backhanded Frank with the shovel, knocking him prone. "You believe you're immune to magic.

There are ways to control you. Your body belongs to the earth. To me. Go to sleep."

Frank had a brief moment to be thankful Woj wasn't there to say I told you so, and the lights went out.

IT'D BEEN A long fucking time since Frank'd had his bell rung.

When he blinked the cobwebs away he was inside a mausoleum. Alone. No sign of Woj. And the place was warded. He could tell by the faint itchy sensation on his skin. Wards didn't mean much to him. Most necromancer magic disappeared off him like a fart in the wind. He hurled himself at the door. It held.

"Shoulda known. If he could knock me out, he could keep me in."

Frank gave the door another kick to be certain. May as well have kicked a bank vault. He stewed, pacing the confines for what felt like an hour. His watch said it'd been ten minutes. After another ten, the door creaked open. Digger flashed him a yellow-toothed grin.

"Your friend had quite the lead foot." The grin stretched. "Had."

"Son of a bitch."

Digger brushed Frank's shoulder with his shovel. It was a light touch—a ghost's whisper—and he shuddered as if he was covered in bugs. Creeping, crawling bugs, trying to burrow into his body. His mind. His soul. He felt . . . sifted.

Torn apart into his constituent parts. No, not parts. People. Frank felt them all now, in a way he hadn't since he'd first woken in that cult hidey-hole back in Afghanistan. They'd been roaring in his brain then. Now . . . they were quieter. And yet, more distinct.

"Come," Digger said, turning and walking away.

Frank followed, dragged as if tethered to the shovel. He didn't recognize the boneyard they'd dragged him to, but it was dark again. Memories bubbled and popped out of his mind as he walked, silent. Helpless. The sensation made Frank think Digger was hunting for something specific. Memories and experiences were discarded as quickly as they were encountered. Digger knew what he wanted and hadn't found it yet.

But what?

Why?

Digger didn't care who he'd been before he'd been made. And didn't care who he was now, only what he'd been when he'd first woken. A fine distinction. Only one time period interested Digger: the span after his creation when he had been bound. Digger wanted to see how he'd been made. And controlled. How he could make Frank *his*.

Clever. Frank was surprised he'd noticed.

He wanted Frank to be hollow. A shell. No better than a grave golem. Frank's fist clenched. He strained to slow his steps. Break the tether; regain control. He couldn't. His limbs were numb. Frank clawed for a memory. Any memory. A kid on a bike. His kid? Or him? A smiling woman, a proud man. Every snapshot of a past life he saved meant three others lost.

He'd thought nothing could kill him. Maybe what Digger wanted for him *would* be better. The supernatural power that'd infused him kept him going. His heart beat once per minute—if that—pushing the poison his bugeating creators had given him for blood through his veins. His stitches hurt. His mind hurt. His soul *hurt*. And he didn't know why, or how, he could still feel any of it.

Digger stopped at a spiralling circle of stones. Behind the circle, a freshly filled grave dashed any confidence Woj had gotten away. A coffin had roughly ten minutes to five and a half hours of air. Assuming a buried person didn't panic. At least, that's what the boss had told Frank. But Woj was also the panicky sort which changed the numbers, and not to the good.

"Kneel."

Frank knelt. The mortician and her assistants laid out the stones, adding to the circle, after scratching symbols on them.

"Grave golems don't last. Or, rather, the bodies I build them around don't last. Their power is based on their host's spirit, and with your power? I have more permanent plans for you."

"Those plans better involve taking my boots off before I shove my foot up your ass."

Digger smiled and let dirt trickle through his fingers and back into his bag. "I tracked your first death. Blood-drenched earth, that. I could still feel the pain."

"Fuck you."

Digger tossed dirt at Frank while he spoke. "These stones came from cairns belonging to soldiers. Warriors without name now. With you, there's no necromancer who could match me. No city I couldn't take. No score I couldn't settle."

When Frank's entire body was dusted with the ground of his first death, Digger dropped a cairn stone at Frank's feet. The runic bullshit they'd scratched on it didn't mean shit to him but the stone wobbled and danced, clattering up Frank's body and stopping on his chest at an impossible angle. It shouldn't have held there, but it did. Another stone joined the first, then another.

There were many more to go.

FRESHLY REINTERRED IN a living cairn, Frank knew what came after death. He knew what waited in that dark. And there was no angelic choir, no pointy-tailed red devils either. Once Digger made him a blank slate, Frank wasn't coming back. He'd be a slave. A tool.

A memory struck him like dust in his eye. A voice, half-forgotten. Frank held on to the words by mouthing the words Camilla had said, "You've felt the call of the void."

Yeah, he had. Damn near every day. Working helped. Responsibility. Purpose. He'd had that in all his previous lives in the military. He'd been left in charge. Watching the gates.

And you fucked it up.

Purpose twisted in Frank's guts, opening a loathing torrent. Hate. Directed, as usual, at himself. The desire to be done. Finished. He tried to feel his heartbeat, sighed when he couldn't.

Purpose.

Woj was probably already dead. Buried.

Frank felt buried too. *Was* buried.

Dead.

Dead, so many times over.

The stitches in his arms burned.

His only thought: he needed to fight.

He remembered how to fight.

He was *made* to fight.

"You wanna feel alive, go find somebody to hit," Frank muttered to the stones.

Digger wanted to take him back to when he'd been created? Fine. There was nothing he hated more than the cultists who'd made him. Frank's nose filled with the stink of gunpowder, his ears twitched from phantom reports. Blood. Screams. Sensory overload. They'd been ambushed. He never saw who did it but he remembered his makers' grins, siblings to Digger's smile. They were the same. Except Frank's creators were dead, and Digger wasn't.

Yet.

His chest ached, heart thudding.

Alive.

Time to kick some ass.

Frank tore a rock off his chest. It came free with a squelch, as if he'd ripped out an eye, and he hurled it at the mortician. Her chants stopped with a thud, and she crumbled to the ground. Frank charged Digger, dropping rocks like an old bridge.

He swung a haymaker and Digger redirected the strike. The fucker was strong for someone so sinewy. Maybe the shovel and undertaker getup wasn't for show. Didn't matter. Frank was stronger.

"You're gonna need to dig a lot more graves before you can jerk me around, pal."

He hurled Digger across the graveyard. The necromancer yelled as he flew but didn't drop his shovel. Digger grunted when he hit ground, but before Frank could follow, the mortician's assistants were on him.

Frank snarled and grabbed the closest—the man—by the clavicle and squeezed. It cracked and he screamed and dropped. Out of the fight. His co-worker yelled and charged Frank with a rune-carved rock. Frank reared back and headbutted her stone as she swung, shattering it. He repeated the action with her nose. Broke that too. Blood gushed and she punched him anyway. Frank broke her wrist and tossed her aside.

"Get over here," he yelled at Digger. "We ain't done."

Digger smiled, and Frank saw where he'd tossed the necromancer: onto the freshly filled grave. Digger drove his glowing shovel into the turned earth and pushed himself to his feet. A new golem, smaller than the first, rose in front of him.

"Oh, fuck. *C'mon.*"

The earthen wave crested, slamming him to the ground and

grave dirt filled Frank's mouth. He gagged, but didn't choke. One benefit to being mostly dead: he didn't need to breathe. It was as if he were swimming underwater. At night. With no fucking moon in the goddamned sky. Every way he pulled himself, the earth resisted him. Woj was in here somewhere, and judging from how fresh the first golem's body had been, the longer Frank struggled, the more likely Woj would need to hire someone to preside over his own funeral.

The smaller golem had a harder time containing Frank entirely; his head poked out of the dirt and Digger slammed the shovel into Frank's head. His ears rang from the impact and he grunted. That'd hurt. Shouldn't have hurt. Maybe he'd finally found the thing to kill a dead man but he couldn't quit yet. Not to this loser.

Digger reared back for another swing and Frank caught the shovel's haft on its downward arc. The blade cut into his forearm. Frank didn't bleed, not really, what pulsed through his body wasn't blood. Some fucking alchemical cocktail. But the cut *hurt*. Frank growled as Digger tried to tug the shovel away. Frank dragged himself out of the grave golem instead.

Frank wrenched the shovel free, spun it, and slammed it into Digger. The necromancer yelped and folded over the shovel's haft. Frank swung again. Digger wailed when the shovel snapped over his back, and lay motionless. The shovel's light faded.

The grave golem fell away to nothing. Frank dropped to his knees and dug in a fury, hurling earth wherever it landed. He dug the coffin from the dirt, jerked the nailed lid free, and hauled out a sweaty, drained—but alive—Woj.

Not sure what else to do with Digger, Frank tossed him into the coffin, rummaged through his coat, and pounded the nails back in with a closed fist.

"I need a drink," Woj whispered.

Frank tossed him the keys to Digger's Eldorado. "Ever been to The Red Circus?"

Wings of Stone

Kevin Cockle

"GRAMPA, ARE GIANTS real?" she had asked, long ago. But that was how it was now, when she visited him. The silence invited introspection, and the past seemed closer, with years scaling to hours in the confines of his private room.

"No," he had said, towering over her six-year-old self like a giant in spite of himself. She remembered the cigarette in his hand; how bad that was, because it was illegal in parks. She remembered the river running to their right; the clear blue sky; the hot white light of the sun. "Actually it depends," he continued, as he almost always did. "What do you mean by 'giant'?"

"Like . . . " she stretched her arms up as high as they would go, affecting a monstrous gait. "Super tall!"

"How tall?"

"Twenty meters!"

"And what do they look like, these giants?"

"Like people, only super tall."

"But the same shape? Just bigger?"

"Yah."

"Nope—that doesn't happen. At least not in our configuration space."

"Config . . ."

"Configuration. C'mon, don't be a little kid. You want to know about giants, you have to be able to say 'configuration'."

"Congfigerashun."

"Close enough."

"You okay, Beth?" The rumbling bass from the doorway interrupted her thoughts. Her Gun-Boat, Vince, checking in. Speaking of giants. His massive bulk backlit by the hallway lighting filled the threshold, and in the shadows of his face, the low green light of his HUD eye-coverlets glowed. Part man, part machine, part animal neuronics-overlay, part counter-terrorism platform, part bodyguard, part test-bed, Vince was a first-gen Gun-Boat, and still one of the most reliable. Beth had had a hand in programming the neural network interface with his nervous system. She had known for sometime that her nickname amongst the lab techs was Dr. Frankenstein, and supposed that the label would have been inevitable for anyone in her position. It didn't bother her, but she resented the implications for Vince, and the others of his kind.

"It's been over an hour," Vince concluded by way of explanation. He was monitoring her vitals as a matter of course; knew she was tired.

"Yes. I'm wool-gathering tonight, I'm afraid. A few more minutes, Vince." The Gun-Boat nodded his tiger's skull and resumed his position in the hall.

Hospital rooms were never silent. Beth could hear the burble of a water tank and the intermittent clicking of electronic diagnostics. In the low light, her grandfather seemed made of stone, the great hooked nose in profile, the prominent brow seemingly chiselled in granite. They had positioned him in his wheelchair, looking out the window at a panoramic view of the Rockies in the distance. His hooded gaze was baleful, unwavering. He was reptilian in his stillness. He was an unnerving combination of fragility and authority; his brooding presence seemed more appropriate for the walls of some gothic castle than a palliative ward.

She placed her hand atop his, feeling the stony cool of his skin. The jagged saw-tooth pattern of his knobbed knuckles further reinforced his statuesque appearance.

They had sat on a bench together, all those years ago, on that day she had wondered about giants, and he had drawn her attention to a bridge spanning the nearby Bow River.

"You can't just scale-up a human being—in human proportions—to twenty meters tall," he had said. Six years old or sixty, it made no difference to Grampa, once he got going. "The problem is the bones."

"Bones?"

"The length and width of bones scale differently with size. If you had bones of the same width, but one was twice as long? The force needed to buckle the longer bone would be four times less than the short bone. A super tall giant couldn't keep his human proportions or his legs would snap."

Beth had had a re-vision of the movie she'd seen, with the giants lying on a plain in front of their castle, screaming in agony from broken bone-shards pushing through bloodied skin. Years later, that subjective edit would be the only recollection she had of the film.

"Now, see that bridge?" Grampa continued. "See the columns supporting that bridge? How wide and thick they are at the base? That's the aspect ratio you need to support massive weight. When you push on the Earth, it pushes on you. Forces are neat that way: they always occur in pairs."

When he'd said "aspect," Beth had thought of some dish mom usually made for Thanksgiving, but sensed that wasn't right. Even then she'd had good instincts.

"So giants can't happen in our universe, Beth, but here's the thing: in our universe, *giants appear to us as bridges!* If you transform our coordinates to some other con . . . work with me . . . con . . . "

"Configuration!"

"Yes—some other configuration space—our bridges become giants in that other universe. Isn't that a kick?"

Beth had agreed that it was. Looking back, she recognized it as her first introduction to linear algebra, candy-coated with a soft outer shell of magic. Just one of many seeds Grampa had planted over the years.

You really are wool-gathering tonight, Beth smiled to herself. It was getting late—only reason she'd been allowed to stay was because of who she was, and what Vince was. Grampa might have been proud of that much at least. She could smoke in any damn park she wanted. *Well, let's be honest,* Beth chided herself. *He wouldn't be* that *proud of what you've become.*

In those little-girl days, she'd been all about magic and fantasy, castles and crowns. "Want to be able to predict the future?" Grampa would ask. "Learn physics."

"Physics?"

"Math—same thing. In our universe, it's what we have instead of magic."

"In our configuration space."

"Now yer gettin' it."

Slowly but surely, his prodding had taken effect. She'd wanted to be able to predict the future, wanted magic to be real so badly. And it was odd that it would be Grampa who had kept pushing her towards the sciences. Edward Wellan was a Professor Emeritus of English Literature after all, not an engineer or physicist or computer scientist. Beth had eventually come to realize that this was the least of the man's many contradictions. "When I was your age," he would say. "English was a respected degree. You could make a buck off it. You're not going to have that option, kiddo." Even he had had no idea how right he would be.

Grampa never attended family Christmas or other get-togethers. No one ever talked about him. When Beth saw him, it was when her mom—Ed's daughter—took Beth round to his apartment downtown, and her mom never stayed to visit. One day one summer, when they were at Prince's Island park just a few blocks from his home, and he had said his usual piece: "Ask me a good question," she'd responded with: "Why don't you live with Gramma anymore?" She was a little older then, no longer believed in giants or flying horses, but she hadn't really been old enough to ask an adult that question. They both knew it, which is why he'd given her that wry nod before answering. His acknowledgment that the question had been good.

"Well, sweetie," he began, squinting off into the treeline as he chose his words, "I'm not really welcome there anymore. I left your Grandmother, which would be bad enough, but what made it unforgivable is that I left her for a man."

"A man?"

"Yes. So you see, not only did I break marriage vows to her, but I broke a promise I'd made to her as well. I said I was one thing, but became another over time. She's right to feel the way she does. They all are."

"But what man? Do I know him? Where is he?"

"Actually, you know, I left him as well. For a woman, oddly enough. The thing is, Beth, it was wrong of me to be married. Irresponsible. We all have a responsibility to know who and what we are, and if we misrepresent those things, we own the lie. It's the only way to live, but it's hard, kiddo, so most of us don't get it exactly right."

"So you're like a shape-shifter."

He'd smiled at that. "Indeed," he'd said.

One of the close-support drones flew into Beth's line of sight, like a firefly against the night sky. Vince's cybernetic-intuition controlled the drone array, giving him complete tactical control of the local battle-space. The drones—meaning Vince— monitored cell communications around Beth, kept watch on her in the visible spectrum and infra-red, noted and assessed any approaching objects within several hundred meters of her position. Becoming aware of the security made her aware of her prosthetic leg, artificial left eye, and facial scarring—wounds she'd suffered when an assassin's bomb had destroyed her first lab. She hadn't been the target back then, but she surely would be now. Hence the personal Gun-Boat, usually reserved for heads of state or corporate luminaries.

As her star had risen, Edward's had fallen. She was in Advanced Placement grad school as a teen at Cal-Tech when she'd heard the news that the University of Calgary had shuttered its humanities departments. She'd been on the short list for the Fields Medal when he'd been arrested that first time, protesting the corporate annexation of aboriginal land outside Calgary. He was becoming dangerous, erratic, bitter, unemployable. He was on no-fly lists and placed under regular surveillance. He was the sort of contact one couldn't afford to have in the new Alberta, or the old America. That rare crackpot who could get and keep the attention of crowds.

It had been dicey, sticking her neck out for him in the early days, before she'd become "Dr. Frankenstein"; before she'd had Gun-Boat clout. She'd send bail money, food money, sometimes rent, and through it all, all the risks she'd taken, he'd never bother to disguise his resentment. "How could you work for the defence department?" he'd say on Skype, heedless of who might be listening.

"Are you eating?" she'd say. Not his idea of a good question. He'd never been one for deflection.

She'd always been struck by the complex symmetries between them. His restless bisexual appetites; her sedentary asexuality. His ability to captivate the attention of strangers; her near invisibility in crowds. His rawboned physicality; her avian refinement. His failure or refusal to occupy any designated silo; her lifelong focus which had resulted in the Gun-Boat program, and its world-shattering applications. Together they expressed some weird conservation law—some mysterious quantity kept in perfect balance between them.

What will happen when you're gone, she wondered, looking at his impassive face. *What happens when the Earth stops pushing back?*

He was, she realized, her closest, most profound relationship. Her mother had contracted the H1AV90 strain: Beth hadn't been able to make the two-week deathbed-vigil. Her father had died on the QE2: Beth hadn't been able to attend the funeral. Her work had become too important, too all-consuming. As she became one of the central components of a modern-day Manhattan Project so her connections to the outside world began to atrophy and die. At least, the work was a large part of the reason for her isolation. The other part was that she knew exactly who and what she was and hadn't wanted to lie about it.

Yet on the eve of her greatest achievement, the culmination of her life's work, here she was, sitting beside the frozen catatonic shell of her grandfather. Feeling what it had been to be a little girl again; sensing how things might have played out differently.

She'd found him in a dying forestry town just north of Merritt, British Columbia. He'd lost the ability to balance on ladders and lived in darkness since he couldn't change lightbulbs. Neighbours fed him, but no one bathed him, cut his toenails, and such. He'd been unrecognizable to her, but he'd recognized her. It was that moment that had broken her heart; the fact that of all the things he had forgotten, she was the one thing that was still real to him. He didn't fight relocation only because she'd been there to take him away. That lack of fight had been the final straw though, the moment of relaxation that allowed his mind to drift. Once she'd gotten him cleaned up, settled, and secure, he was gone.

"I'm going to push a button tomorrow that's going to change everything," she said quietly, rubbing her grandfather's knuckles with her thumb. "Gun-Boat 2.0: 'Oracle'. You told me if I wanted to predict the future—if I wanted to do magic—I needed to learn math. Mission accomplished, Grampa."

She wondered if he would have hated what she was about to do; assigned some probability to the affirmative. But human beings couldn't keep going on as they had been. There needed to be legitimate authority again; order to which people could and would consent. "Oracle" would give them that. And once Oracle was up and running, Beth could begin her own fade. The n-dimensional cost-function harnessing enhanced human intuition to predict "price" was the solution matrix that would change the world. After that transformation, she wouldn't be needed. Indeed, after that, she and the core members of her team might be too dangerous to be allowed to go on living at all. Vince may already have been tasked to transition from bodyguard to executioner at the proper signal. *So be it*, she thought. If it came to that, she was ready. She'd been bearing a titanic weight most of her adult life, and her bones were brittle.

They were headed to a new configuration space, she realized. There would be a giant, a leviathan, the likes of which no one had ever before imagined. In its colossal wake, there would be peace.

She imagined her grandfather in that new universe, transformed into a grim sentinel crouching on a parapet.

Watching over the world she had made.

Taking to the air on wings of stone.

Soil, Native and Otherwise

Damascus Mincemeyer

DAVE'S FIRST DAY on the job didn't start the way he wanted it to. He began by showing up twenty minutes late after getting snared in a traffic jam on the interstate, and then he'd gone to the wrong administrative building and spent half the morning being shuffled from one manager to another until someone finally directed him to Earthworks' Transportation Department. When he at long last met his actual supervisor face-to-face, Dave thought the man was going to blow a gasket, but instead Mr. Higgins only laughed and shook his head.

"Don't worry about it, kid," he said as they walked down the hall from Higgins' office to the elevator. "This place is so damn big it's easy to get turned around," he sighed as they descended three floors. "But that's the nature of the beast. Corporate keeps pushing for more, so we have to keep expanding the facility to Godzilla-sized proportions. Tell you the truth, I've gotten lost in here more than a few times myself."

The elevator opened with a hissing rush of cool air into a long corridor leading out to a vast warehouse, row after row of towering metal shelves extending back as far as Dave could see. Everywhere there were workers in hard hats crawling on ladders and operating forklifts, raising and lowering shipping containers of various sizes from the shelves while yellow-vested floor managers choreographed the commotion like police officers directing traffic. Higgins popped a stick of gum in his mouth, looking back to Dave.

"Well, here it is, the lifeblood of Earthworks Shipping Inc." His voice had a droll bite to it. "Don't let the excitement kick you in the ass."

They went further into the warehouse, the temperature so chilly Dave shivered despite the late June heat. Higgins didn't seem to notice, barking orders to everyone around him like a blue-collar dictator before Dave asked, "What exactly is it you do here? I mean, not *you* specifically, but what's the *company* do?"

Higgins peered at him. "You mean no one's told you?"

Dave shook his head. "Not even when I interviewed."

"And you never thought to ask?" Higgins stopped, running a hand through thinning hair. "How old are you, kid?"

"Twenty-one."

"College kid?"

Dave nodded. Higgins continued. "So I suppose it's safe to say you were really out to pick up extra beer-swilling cash when you applied for this gig, right? No, don't answer that. I don't care. I only care that you're capable enough to do the job, but if you don't even know what it is we do, my faith in you is already seriously lacking." He gestured to the buzzing warehouse. "Earthworks ships one thing, and ships it better than anyone else." Higgins led Dave to the nearest shelf, rolling one of the containers from its perch. It was similar to a steel footlocker, thirty inches long and rectangular; along the front was a jumble of numerical information and bar codes, the words FRANCE/BOURGOGNE-FRANCHE-COMTE printed above them. Higgins unfastened the metal clasps on the container's lid and flipped it up.

Dave peeked inside, frowning. *"Dirt?* You ship dirt?"

Higgins pulled a handful of rich, black earth from the full container, crumbling it between his fingers. "You got it, kid. Dirt's our stock and trade. Well, *soil,* technically. Corporate discourages us from saying *dirt.* Sullies the company image, I suppose."

Dave looked up and down the shelves around him, then to

the seemingly endless aisles throughout the warehouse, wondering how many containers were there before he glanced back to Higgins. "So all of these boxes are filled with . . . dirt?"

"*Soil.*"

"Right. *Soil.* Sorry. But . . . *why?*"

Higgins wiped his hands on his pants. "Because there's money to be made, that's why. There's a need out there that Earthworks meets. Admittedly it's a niche market, but one that's proved extremely lucrative. Our client list is just *bursting.*" When Higgins saw Dave's face droop into confusion, he pulled the youth forward by the arm, closer to the open, earth-filled locker. "See, it's like this, kid. Our Acquisitions Department sends crews around the world—everywhere you can imagine, to every country, on every continent—to excavate soil deposits and ship the samples back here, where they're catalogued and separated by country and region," he pointed to the container's label. "See, this particular shipment comes from the Burgundy region in France, and that's what's important to note, because while we have multiple samples of French soil in the warehouse, each comes from a different region," he motioned to the containers directly adjacent to the one he'd pulled out. "This one's from Normandy, and the one over there's from the Centre-Loire Valley. All from France, but different regions, and *that's* where your job comes in."

Higgins turned, snapping a command to one of the floor managers, who disappeared into the depths of the warehouse, returning a few minutes later with a pistol-shaped hand-held scanner, a small screen and keypad on its flat-topped surface. The supervisor slapped the thing into Dave's hand like an old-time gunslinger, pivoting him back to the containers. "When we receive a shipment, you have to scan the barcode as A.A.U.—Arrival At Unit—which logs the proper national and regional information into our main on-site server. *But* here's the tricky part, and where you've got to watch yourself. A lot of times the barcodes or shipping numbers will be scratched or scuffed-up in transport and the scanners won't pick 'em up, so you've got to plug them in manually. You've got to be careful, though, to get the codes *exact* because that's how we make sure each container is sent to the right destination when it ships out again," he smiled, gesturing to the scanner Dave gripped. "Go on, give it a test shot. See how it feels."

Dave scanned the open container's barcode, and the screen lit up with a quick burst of data. He read the information aloud. "France/Bourgogne-Franche-Comte: FR-77584938."

"Bingo, kid. Now all you have to do is send the info to the server and go on to the next one."

"That's *it?*"

"Well, *yeah,*" Higgins closed the container, sliding it back into its proper place on the shelves. "The job's not rocket science. But there's thousands of these damn things coming and going every day so don't think it's easy. Be careful. Corporate will come down like a guillotine on the whole department if something gets fouled up, and I'm primed for early retirement in two years and don't want to lose that benefits package for shit. We clear?"

"Crystal."

"Good." Higgins slapped Dave on the back. "Now I suggest you get to work."

DAVE'S LIFE SLIPPED into a comfortable routine as the weeks rattled by. Up at six for a breakfast of cold pizza or shrimp ramen washed down with some Red Bull. On the road by seven, battling his way to Earthworks by quarter-to-eight. Clock in until noon, then lunch from the vending machines in the hall, resuming work until four-thirty. Some fast food after that, then pool and beer with his fraternity brothers and maybe a text to his ex-girlfriend for an attempted hook-up on Saturday night. Unconscious by three or four in the morning. Wash. Rinse. Repeat.

He didn't mind the *work* part of the daily cycle, even if he found scanning containers of exotic foreign soil screamingly, insanely, stiflingly dull. The gap times in-between the junk food excuses for meals made Dave's brain swim with numbers to the point that, if not for the brews chugged after-hours, he would've had difficulty sleeping from the constant stream of codes marching behind his eyelids. It was, as Higgins had said, deceptively simple work—easy, boring but astoundingly repetitive. There were times when Dave held onto his scanner so long he thought he'd grown a new, unwelcome appendage when he wasn't looking.

Oddities remained, however, to occasionally break the monotony. One was the sheer size of the Earthworks facility, which still proved daunting to Dave even as August rolled around. After the debacle on that first day, he was determined not to get lost again, but inevitably he found himself wandering down halls and exiting the elevator to floors he'd never seen and departments he didn't know existed. Another was the reverential way employees—all of them, from forklift operators to janitors to supervisors—spoke of Earthworks' corporate heads. It wasn't a case of rampant brown-nosing, but rather one where everyone went out of their way to express their satisfaction with the company executives with nauseating regularity, even if, to Dave, there was an obvious fear behind it all, as if one misspoken word would end careers.

The most consistent struggle, though, was with the cold. The Transportation Department was a constant humidity-controlled icebox at all times, and Dave took to wearing sweaters in the warehouse no matter how hot it was outside. That familiar cranial-penetrating chill was making life unbearable Dave's fourth Monday morning on the job; too much weekend excess had taken a toll on Dave's head that no amount of coffee or Tylenol would touch, and he felt like a beaten boxer and drowning swimmer all at once. His sinuses were pounding, muscles aching, and that shivering wasn't helping one damn bit. After half an hour of scanning, his misery was so great, he wanted to crawl into the nearest soil container, close the lid, put a headstone on top, and be done with it.

One of the floor managers informed him of a newly delivered shipment, and after a hike through the warehouse, Dave came to a dozen freshly unloaded Lithuanian soil lockers, stacked high enough he had to climb one of the rolling ladders to gain access to them all. Most scanned easily, but the higher he climbed, the more dismal the condition of the containers became. Several had been damaged in shipping, the metal dented and the barcodes all but scraped off. The catalogue numbers remained mostly legible, and Dave pounded the information into his scanner's keypad before descending to the warehouse floor.

It wasn't until later in the week that he had the first inkling something was wrong. On Thursday morning Mr. Higgins was waiting near the elevator, a worried look on his face and chomping a fresh stick of gum so vigorously Dave thought he was going to chew through his cheeks. At first inquiry Higgins didn't reveal much, but around lunchtime he assembled all the floor managers and inventory scanners in his office.

"There was a discrepancy located by our tech guys in some of the inventory identifier data. It's probably just a glitch in the system, but until we find out for sure, Mr. Stephenson thought it best for me to tell everyone to be extra vigilant when cataloguing and to double-check their work from earlier in the week."

After dismissing the gathering, Dave went to leave when the supervisor stopped him. "You're doing a good job, kid. You've really impressed me. You really have," Higgins said, surprising Dave. "I'm even thinking of suggesting you to Mr. Stephenson for an open managerial position we've got once this data mess is straightened out. Be some extra change in your pocket. Some extra beer on tap, am I right?"

Higgins smiled, slapped Dave on the back, and left, but despite the compliment something in Higgins' tone was unsettling. Until then, Dave had only heard of Mr. Stephenson, the plant's executive director, in hushed whispers from other employees, and the uneasy way Higgins spoke the name in relation to his own somehow worried him.

Dave took his break in the department's computer room, re-running the inventory data from his scanner through the system while he snacked on his vending-machine lunch. If he'd thought scanning barcodes once was a banal affair, going over the unending series of twisting numerical information twice was boredom bordering on cruelty. When he was just about to nod off, a sudden *ping!* followed by a flash of red roused his attention. An on-screen code-error pop-up box winked on and off, and when Dave saw the information sprawled across the computer, he almost choked on his potato chips.

"Inventory code incompatibility," he read aloud. "Lithuania/Aukstaitija: LI-11485736. Lithuania/Samogitia: LI-11485737."

He compared them again. Save for that single numeral at the end of each sequence they were identical. That was it. One number. He stared at the screen. The error warning was still blinking, but after re-reading the two numbers again, he closed the error box out and leaned nervously back in the chair. Higgins had warned him the consequences of mis-shipment were severe, but how dire could the situation really be? It wasn't like he'd purposely typed the incorrect code. He'd just been tired and hungover and made a simple mistake. And after all, despite being from different regions, both soil lots were still Lithuanian. Were people really *that* persnickety about *soil?*

Despite the cozy rationalizations his brain concocted, Dave's worry, childish as it was, revolved about others finding out. Earthworks may have been an oddball place to work, but it sure as hell beat burger-flipping.

The information regarding the error had been time-and-date stamped on the computer, which meant that if *he* could backtrack the mistake to himself, it wouldn't be too long before the I.T. workers did the same. Dragging the file to the computer's recycle bin, Dave's finger hovered over the delete button before he finally pressed it, and the incriminating evidence disappeared like some digital legerdemain.

The following day, however, Dave was surprised to find the warehouse shut down and all the employees sitting idly around.

"Tech guys narrowed down the source of the problem to our department," Higgins told them after an hour's wait. "And it *wasn't* a system glitch. Someone screwed up. They're just not sure who. *Yet.*" He paused, gum chomping, a grim look on his face. "So it's like this: the family of one of our clients is threatening legal action over this little foul-up, and Mr. Stephenson decided to temporarily close Transport until further notice, which isn't something Corporate wants to see done. So if anyone here knows what happened and why, now's the time to speak up. Money and jobs are on the line, people. Think about it."

The assembly was as quiet as a funeral mass, blank, uncomfortable stares spreading around the room. Dave was as silent as everybody else, though deep down he didn't know if his reticence stemmed from guilt, cowardice, or plain, naked fear. After a few minutes, Higgins nodded his head. "All right then. That's the way it is. Everyone's dismissed for now. Might as well go home for the day."

As the crowd dispersed Dave made a beeline for the exit

hoping to avoid Higgins, but the supervisor caught him near the door. Though he was smiling, Dave sensed the aggravation bubbling just beneath Higgins' surface.

"Is there something bothering you, kid?" he asked. "You looked like ten tons were weighing you down back there."

Dave squirmed. "No, I'm good," he hesitated, then: "I just don't understand what the big deal is about this inventory mishap. It can't be *that* serious, can it?"

"It *can* be, and it *is*. It's like I said, our client's family is threatening to end their business dealings with us."

Dave furrowed his brow. "So? Don't you have *thousands* of clients?"

Higgins shook his head. "You don't understand. A client *died* due to company negligence. That's what's got everyone in such an uproar."

"Are you seriously trying to tell me someone *died* from receiving the wrong soil shipment? Who dies from *that?*"

The supervisor peered at Dave. "You have figured out who our clients *are*, haven't you?"

"No."

Higgins sighed. *"Vampires,* kid. Our clients? They're vampires."

Dave cocked an eyebrow. *"Vampires?* Are you nuts? Vampires aren't real."

"And believe me, they want people to keep thinking that, too," Higgins said. "But the sunglasses-after-midnight crowd's an actual population demographic, and that's the market we cater to."

Dave still thought Higgins was crazy, but the more he mulled it over, the more unsure he became. Was the possibility of the undead really *that* far-fetched? He'd believed in Bigfoot and the Loch Ness Monster as a kid. Dracula? Why not? He looked at his boss. "But I thought vampires only lived in, like, old castles and cemeteries in Transylvania and places like that."

"Yeah, five-hundred years ago," Higgins snarked. "But this is a twenty-four-hour global economy we live in. For everyone. Even vampires."

"But why soil?"

"Jesus, haven't you ever heard that old saw about a vampire needing to sleep on his native soil? Well, it's true. And that's the niche Earthworks fills. I mean, how's a modern-day internationally business-oriented bloodsucker supposed to globe-trot when he's hampered with having to cart around a coffin's worth of dirt from his hometown? That's why we've got soil from every region on earth here, and that's why it's so important to make sure each order is correct before it ships. Sure, to you and me there's no difference if a clump of mud's from Brooklyn or The Bronx, they're both New York City, right? But to a vamp it just might mean the difference between another century above ground or taking that short train ride to the underworld." Worry squashed Higgins' brow. "And that's what Corporate is so upset about. Vampires, they're powerful. Influential. They can pull strings and shut us down like that," he snapped his fingers. "And if any fault is shown on our part here in Transport, there's going to be hell to pay, believe you me."

"But this kind of thing's had to have happened before, right?"

"Sure. But it still puts a black mark on Earthworks' reliability record. I mean, if word of this incident gets out, it could ruin our reputation completely," Higgins sighed again. "The good thing is there's been suggestions by the client's family that an out-of-court settlement is a possibility."

"That's a relief," Dave said, though any comfort was dashed when Higgins spoke again.

"But you mark my words, kid—when it's figured out who's responsible for this mess, they'll wish they'd never been born."

DAVE'S UNEASE SEEPED into his weekend, marring the schedule he'd grown so accustomed to. He opted out of burgers, beer, and billiards with his frat mates in favour of a microwave entree he couldn't finish and time spent perusing the internet, devouring every spare scrap about both vampires and Earthworks itself. Neither inquiry proved especially fruitful. Vampires had done an excellent job of disguising themselves behind a pop-cultural smokescreen to the point where unearthing anything substantial about the *real* undead untainted by dark, seductive romantic archetypes was virtually impossible. Earthworks' online presence likewise in no way suggested their involvement in shadowy, unearthly dealings, though Dave hadn't expected there would be; nothing would kill prospective business growth faster than trumpeting links to the frightful things that went bump in the night.

He tried to relax, reminding himself that he'd already disposed of his mistake, but when he passed on a Saturday night booty-call from his ex-girlfriend, even his frat brothers took notice of his unusual behaviour. When he finally spilled the beans—*sans* vampires—it was to Mark, the fraternity's resident computer-head, but the reaction Dave received wasn't hopeful.

"You can't really delete anything from a computer," Mark told him. "The information is just removed from the hard drive to a back-up area out of the way so it won't keep eating memory. Any halfway decent geek can recover it, but if it's been backed-up to the company's server it wouldn't matter anyway. What you need to do is go into *that* and overwrite the data with zero-fill to truly eliminate it."

Dave didn't understand half of what Mark proceeded to explain; it was a complex scheme involving ones and zeroes that made Dave's head swirl. But with the notes he'd taken, he made the trip to Earthworks Monday morning determined to clear himself from suspicion once and for all.

The plant's I.T. department took Dave half an hour to find. All the workers had yet to arrive, and there was only one employee in the area. When the man left to use the restroom Dave made his move, plopping down behind a computer terminal, fingers nervously clattering away at the keyboard, feeling every bit the international spy his ten-year-old self had wanted to be.

He never knew if he came close to overwriting the information or not because before he finished filling in the first line of code there was the wailing of a security alarm, a winking red light out in the hall, and the computer froze, a message reading SYSTEM BREACH frantically flashing on-screen in bold letters.

Dave froze; outside the room there was the sound of stampeding boots, and before he could even scoot the chair back, a squad of blue-clad security guards swarmed in, tossing him to the floor. Face pressed down hard on the tile, he saw Higgins enter the room.

"Morning, kid," the supervisor said. "Knew you'd be coming in." When he saw Dave struggling to speak, Higgins knelt beside him. "Come on, you didn't seriously think you'd get away with this James Bond bullshit, did you? This entire facility is practically one giant camera, and besides, we traced the error to your scanner last week. Smooth of you to try to delete the evidence, though, but really, you should've just 'fessed up. It would've made this a lot easier on all of us."

Higgins held up a shining hypodermic needle, pulled the plastic applicator from the syringe tip, and pricked it into Dave's neck, and soon he didn't have to worry about inventory codes or scanners or unemployment or anything else.

WHEN DAVE'S EYES opened again it was dark and his vision was blurred; from somewhere close he heard the idling of an engine, but when he tried to move, his limbs felt leaden and the tight ache at his wrists told him he'd been bound.

"Awake?" a voice behind him asked. Dave sat up, startled, but with the sedative wearing off the voice's owner was clear: Higgins.

There were footfalls in the dark, the crunch of gravel rather than the smoothness of steps on tile, and Dave realized he was outside. When the limousine's headlights flicked on, Dave recoiled from the sudden brightness, but after his eyes adjusted and his surroundings came into view, part of him wished they hadn't.

He was lying in an abandoned lot littered with the cast-off urban detritus of unwanted tires and rusted appliances. There was a smell in the night air, offensive and rankling, like roadkill on a hot day; beside him an oblong pit had been dug deep in the ground, the earth from the hole piled high on the opposite side, a shovel poking ominously from it.

Dave struggled to his knees. He still felt groggy, but in the limo's light he saw Higgins standing a few feet away, a balding, sober-faced older man in an impeccably expensive grey suit next to him.

"This is the employee who's caused all the trouble?" the man in the suit asked, studying Dave. Higgins nodded.

"Yes sir, Mr. Stephenson."

Stephenson said nothing, but Dave looked at Higgins in confusion. "What . . . What's going on? Where the hell are we?"

"It's like I told you, kid, you should've just come out with it when you screwed up. Now it's too damn late."

"Too late for *what?*" Dave asked, confusion sliding into fear.

Higgins sighed. "Corporate won't allow themselves to look like fools. After all, our clients designed this company to fit their purposes, and this incident reflects badly upon them and us."

Higgins was about to say more, but a noise from behind Dave drew his attention; at the far end of the lot three figures emerged from the shadows, and their shambling, shuffling footsteps sent a chill straight through to Dave's core.

The figures hesitated just shy of the light cast from the limo's high beams. Two of them were female, in long, flowing white dresses, veils obscuring their faces, while between them the third being was taller, more obviously male, and clad in a black suit.

The tall figure took a cautious step forward, and once in the light, any lingering doubts Dave had involving the existence of vampires were swiftly murdered, for the thing standing not more than ten feet from him had long ceased to be anything remotely human. Its head was hairless, skin withered and waxy; in some ways its features resembled a rat, with long, pointed ears and a tapered chin, but it was its mouth that drew Dave's horrified gaze the most. A hideous overbite of sharp, crooked, jagged teeth protruded over the lower lip to the point where its mouth couldn't close, and Dave couldn't help but stare as the cadaverous creature neared. It was truly a dead thing, a thing of the earth, of the grave; reeking, rotting, yet still moving.

The tall vampire bowed politely to Mr. Stephenson, who returned the gesture.

"It is unfortunate that we have to meet under these circumstances, Adomaitis," Stephenson told the creature. The vampire stood impassive and quiet at first, but when it spoke its heavily-accented voice was little more than a rasp.

"It is, Mr. Stephenson. But there is business to attend to," it pointed a gnarled finger at Dave. "What is this one's name?"

"David McKinney."

"He is the one responsible for our All-Father's true death?"

"He is," Stephenson said grimly. "Is this offering sufficient to avoid a lawsuit?"

The vampire's sunken, hollow eyes raked Dave over like a piece of butcher's meat before turning to its silent compatriots; both creatures nodded their veiled heads and Adomaitis looked again to Stephenson. "It is. If he is the guilty party, we concede this as a proper out-of-court settlement."

"We have evidence tracing the error to him and video surveillance footage of him attempting to cover-up his crime," Stephenson said. "We can send the information to your headquarters if you'd like."

Adomaitis waved a hand. "Unnecessary. We have trust in you and your company. The situation is rectified."

Stephenson nodded and turned away, going back to the limousine, not even glancing at Dave. Higgins slowly followed, but unlike the executive, he gave a mournful look over his shoulder that Dave seized upon, pleading with him: "Mr. Higgins! Please! You've got to tell them it was just a mistake . . . Just an honest mistake! I'm *sorry!*"

"No, kid. *I'm* sorry," Higgins said solemnly. "But I told you I wasn't going to risk my retirement for anything. Not even you. You're a good kid, but in the end, we all dig our own graves, don't we?"

He didn't say anything more, not even when Dave started blubbering like a baby. The supervisor simply sat impassively in the limousine next to Stephenson and closed the door. The car remained there, idling, when the vampires descended upon Dave like ravening wolves, tearing with tooth and claw, the night echoing with his shrill screams.

Dave was still alive when the creatures finished feasting, his breaths short and erratic and faint as they heaved him wantonly into the depths of the pit, and there was just enough life left in him to feel the first cold shovelful of soil land on his face before it went black and he too became one with the earth.

Land Girl

Laura VanArendonk Baugh

WHEN I WAS a little girl, we had a class assignment to draw a picture of ourselves playing. I drew myself in a pretty blue frock between fluffy sheep with improbably large eyes and several black and white birds standing upright around us like tiny soldiers.

"What are those?" asked Mrs. Greenheart.

"This is me, and I am playing on the peat with the sheep and the penguins," I explained with the earnestness of a child who understands that adults are often bad at pictures.

Mrs. Greenheart shook her head. "I'm afraid your imagination has run away with you again, Petra. You might play near sheep, but certainly not with any penguins."

Because I was a good girl, I put away the mistaken drawing and started another with only sheep.

"IT'S A MESS," Peg reported over her sandwich. She brushed the back of her hand over her temple as if to push her hair back into place, unnecessarily. Peg's hair never was out of place, a feat greater than any war report out of London. "The cows have already got into Gallagher's field for certain. We'll have to go and fetch them out."

Mrs. Walsh, frowning at the pitcher she held, half-nodded without looking at us. "Gallagher will be that angry when he finds them," she said curtly, as if it were our fault the cows were in the neighbour's field. "You'd best get to them before he notices."

I sighed and finished my tea, standing with the rest of my sandwich still in hand. I could take a hint. "Let's go, Peg."

I'd joined with the Women's Land Army because it felt like the right, patriotic thing to do, and because I was sick to death of living in the city, and because the recruitment poster—a gorgeous brunette looking proudly over an immaculate field, pitchfork in her dainty hand—looked so much more glamorous than my secretarial duties.

In fact, I had to learn to do things with cows which I had never imagined might need to be done with cows, from the predictable milking and mucking to the unexpected wrestling with an unborn calf to pull it into life. I stayed with an old farming couple called the Walshes who, like many, resented us Land Girls as poor replacements for their beloved sons and nephews and neighbours, but who treated us well enough, considering.

Peg and I were both Land Girls from the city but neither afraid of animals nor work like some of the urban recruits. She could castrate a pig faster than anyone.

She was the first to find a broken wall.

When she took me to it now, I saw only the pushed-down tumble of stones. The drystone wall on either side of the gap seemed well enough, but the break in the middle was large enough for a cow to pass through. And at least a dozen had, tempted across the unfamiliar gap by the call of Gallagher's sweet young crops. Peg and I had just managed to bunch them together toward the gap when we heard his gruff voice shouting across the field at us. "What are you girls doing with your cows in my flax?"

"Just checking for quality," Peg called back cheerfully. "Government wants us to be sure crops are attractive, and we wanted to see if they attracted cows. Now that we've seen they do, we're taking the cows back home."

Gallagher stalked across the tillage toward us, unamused by Peg's humour. "You get these cattle out of my field."

"We're sorry, Mr. Gallagher," I tried, "but something happened to the wall."

"Things don't just happen to walls," he huffed. "One of your cows pushed through it."

I shook my head. "I don't think so." That would be very unlike one of our placid dairy cows, tempting new crops or no.

He didn't much care for my protest, either. "You get your cows out of my crops or I'll have the Ministry on you."

If taken seriously, such a complaint could displace Peg and myself or bring the government down on the Walshes for incompetent farming in this time of crisis. It wasn't likely a single incident of wandering cows would count for much, though. "Mr. Gallagher, we're right now trying to fetch them back, as you can see."

"And keep them out!"

Peg and I turned our backs on him and set back to the cows, which had taken the opportunity of the dispute to choose fresh browse in his field.

MY EARLIEST MEMORY is of sitting in the warm sun, holding tightly to a large rock in each fist, my fingers barely long enough to keep the stony masses in my palms. The damp peat smells comfortably familiar, and I am happy with my bits of stone. Somewhere behind me, my aunt is arguing with my parents, words I did not comprehend at the time but now recall (or imagine) in bits: *should never have come* and *godforsaken land* and *you have no right*.

I went to live with my aunt after my parents died. I remember a ship, and people trying to distract me from the glaring fact that my parents were not on it with us. I remember starting school with Mrs. Greenheart and a lot of new children, more than I had ever seen before.

I remember missing the warm peat and the cool stone.

IT'S IMPORTANT TO keep the way along a drystone wall clear, lest a shrub push into it and dislodge stones. No shrub or tree had grown near the break in the wall, and the dislodged stones had fallen into the pasture, not the tilled field. "This was pushed over from Gallagher's side," I said.

Peg chose one of the larger stones and heaved it back into

place, turning the lichen side out. "I don't suppose the flax did it."

"I don't suppose he did it, either." I picked another stone and slid it alongside hers.

"I don't suppose we'll ever know, then." She set another stone.

We rebuilt the two outer walls of large stones, tied together with a flat, shared throughstone halfway up, and filled the centre with smaller pieces. It wasn't as neat as originally done, but neither of us were skilled wall-builders, and we were already losing chore time.

We made it home in time for evening milking.

THE OLDEST DRYSTONE walls in Great Britain are thousands of years old, set when men knapped flint for tools. The walls about our farms were not so venerable, but they were just as practical, marking fields and keeping livestock in pasture and out of crops. They did not work, however, when they tumbled down. Peg found another hole the next day, this time tumbled in toward Gallagher's field, letting the sheep into Gallagher's crops.

"Petra, come on!" she called, and we ran, anxious to retrieve the wayward sheep before he noticed. But it was our luck that he was working the hayfield that day, within easy sight of the offending ewes and our dashes about them.

He turned his new tractor—a bright and powerful thing—to idle and stalked across the field toward us, his face set with disapproval. I waved and turned to chase a startled ewe, leaving him behind. I knew what he would say, and it would make no difference in how quickly we cleared his hayfield of sheep.

Gallagher was not content to leave things as they were. A decisive banging on the door interrupted our supper that night, and Gallagher made long abuses of negligence toward Walsh, who shouted back that Gallagher couldn't be trusted to report a darts match between a man and a fencepost. Mrs. Walsh had to end the argument with a firm command, and Gallagher slammed the door on his way out.

The next day, the wall was down in two places.

I MET SIMON in the town market. He stood out firstly because he was a young man where young men, even with farming as a protected occupation, were conspicuously absent to us lonely Land Girls. He stood out secondly because he was a head shorter than anyone else in town and because the lower half of his left leg was missing, requiring a crutch to get about on the rough paving. I had a half-day to myself, and I felt I wanted to become friends with this newcomer.

We took our biscuits and sat down on a grassy slope outside of town, our backs to a drystone wall. My government-issue dungarees and green jersey would have felt cloddish and unpretty but for Simon's equally plain garb.

Simon had grown up on Gibraltar, he explained. "I evacuated last year with the others. They want only able-bodied men."

"I thought the refugees were housed in London?"

"But who wants to live in the great dirty city, all noise and crowds and artificial light? Not to mention Jerry dropping bombs on you every Tuesday and Thursday. I came out to find decent farm work."

"That's why I joined the Land Army," I agreed. "Though it's harder work than I imagined. Still, I hadn't much to speak for me at home, or many connections."

"Not much to speak for me, either," Simon said. "Not many want to hire a one-legged man for labour. And I haven't got good connections, either; Jewish families aren't high in the Rock social order."

I gave him a sidelong glance. "Did you purposely drop that into conversation, just to have it in the open?"

He looked down, his cheeks faintly red. "I suppose I did. It matters to people."

I shrugged. "I'm an orphan who can't quite remember where she's from, just that her aunt in Derbyshire called it a godforsaken land."

"God forsakes no land," Simon said, and he gave me a shy smile.

I offered him half of my remaining biscuit.

"What do you remember of it?" he asked, chewing. "Where you grew up?"

"I was just a little girl when I left," I said. "But what I remember was not so different from here, actually. We had peat, and sheep, and a few cows. And . . ." I stopped.

He was fiddling with the base of the wall. "And? Maybe you grew up here in Northern Ireland. Or even in Ireland, which your aunt thought godforsaken."

"I don't think it was Ireland," I said, "because—this is silly, but when I was a girl, I used to draw pictures of the sheep, but I would include other animals, too. Animals that don't belong in Northern Ireland, or even in Ireland." I noticed he held a palm-sized stone in each hand. "Hello! I used to do that."

"Hm?"

"Holding rocks. I remember that as a child, holding rocks as if they were dolls or toys. I just liked it. I did it until my aunt made me follow more ladylike pursuits."

He glanced from the rocks to me, as if self-conscious of them. "What does your aunt think of your Land Army work?"

"She's hung somewhere between disappointed in my muddy dungarees and proud of my patriotic efforts."

He handed me a stone, warm with the heat of his hand, and it fit perfectly in my palm.

THE BLITZ WAS ongoing in London—last December's firestorm had been quite the topic of conversation—and other sea ports and industrial cities, and there was some official concern that it would come to Northern Ireland, but no one thought it very likely. Belfast was thus utterly unprepared when, on Easter Tuesday, it arrived.

Over two hundred thousand people fled into the countryside, scattering across villages and farms and into Ireland. Reports came with them, how more than half the houses in the city had been damaged, how hospitals, churches, and schools were destroyed, how the government's complacence—no blackouts, no searchlights, few public shelters, few emergency plans—had left all unprepared for the disaster, and unidentified bodies were being pushed into mass graves.

"Do you think we're in danger?" Peg asked at supper, her hair still infuriatingly set after a day of weeding. "With all our food production?"

"No one is going to choose a farm over Belfast or Liverpool or Portsmouth," Mrs. Walsh declared. "We're not so important. No German would fly so far just to bomb sheep, and wool won't burn anyhow."

Gallagher, angry over another invasion of his crops and not content to let the Germans have all the local strife, filed a complaint. Walsh grumbled and pretended to shrug it off, but Peg and I could see he was more worried than he let on. The new Defence of the Realm Act allowed the Ministry to possess land which was being mismanaged to secure the maximum production of food, and repeated damage to badly-needed crops would carry some weight.

We walked the walls, checking for weak places, and found none. I even stayed up late one night to watch for wandering loose cows or vagrants, but with miles of wall, I couldn't keep an eye on everything, and anyway we had plenty to do during the daylight, and I couldn't afford to miss all my sleep.

Peg and I divided the chores, and she helped Walsh dig a new ditch while I set to wall repair yet again. Simon came to help me. He couldn't carry stones, not with his crutch, but he was a wizard at setting them again into the wall.

"Do you like caves?" he asked, fitting a throughstone into place as if it had been carved to fit.

"I don't know," I said, stacking collected stones within his easy reach. "I haven't been in any."

"No? We have lots of caves on Gibraltar. The rock is riddled with them. More than people know."

I laughed. "Really? Then how do you know about them?"

His eyes flicked toward me and then back to his work. "I've felt the rock."

A little giggle half-escaped me. Part of me wanted to laugh, because it was so plainly silly, and part of me felt bad for laughing at him. And some other part of me, a tiny inexplicable part of me, wanted to believe him.

"Maybe you can feel what's disturbing this rock," I said to cover my discomfort. "If these walls keep going down, Mr. Gallagher's complaint is going to cost Mr. Walsh his farm, aside from what it will do for Peg's and my Land Army records."

Simon gestured for me to stand beside him. "Put your hands here," he said, and I spread my fingers over the newly replaced stone. "Now close your eyes and tell me what you feel."

I laughed. "Stone."

"More closely."

"Warm stone, with bits of lichen."

"Listen to the stone."

I wasn't sure what he meant, so I stayed silent, and the warmth of the stone filled my hand. My right hand rested on the intact top of the wall which had not fallen, and it felt solid and comfortable. My left hand sat lower in the gap partly filled by Simon's repairs, and there was something faintly uneasy about it. Certainly it was just the uneven surface and my own frustration with the damages which gave the impression, but it seemed the stones were . . . unsettled.

"Do you feel it?" Simon asked.

I started, realizing I had been lost in the explicable sensation of the wall. "I feel stones," I said, but my voice lacked the cheery flippancy of the first time.

"They don't like being displaced," he said.

"What's displacing them?"

"They feel it's a betrayal," Simon said seriously.

This was more than I knew what to do with, so I withdrew my hands and smiled as if I understood the joke. I picked up another stone and placed it in the gap, and Simon helped me adjust it snugly into place.

MR. WALSH'S CROPS were dying. A whole field down the hill near Gallagher's wall was browning and looking peaky, just when it should have been greening up. We spread manure and dug a ditch to draw away the excess spring rain and watched hopefully, but the plants stayed sickly.

"They're dying just for spite," Mr. Walsh opined. "I wouldn't sell three years ago because I said it was good land, and now we need it more than ever, they're dying just to spite me."

I thought of Simon feeling through the wall and wondered for just an unguarded moment if one could feel the soil and know what troubled the plants.

We'd just come in for supper one night when Mrs. Walsh stood silent in the kitchen door, waiting with a bit of paper in her hand. She looked at us with hollow eyes. "The County Agricultural Committee has sent a letter," she said. "They're sending someone to look over and see if the farm's being run properly."

Peg and I had nothing comforting to say. If the farm were considered in neglect or incompetence, it could be seized and handed to another farmer—most likely Gallagher. We'd all done our best, but whatever was knocking the walls, restless cow or rural vagabond, had not stopped, and the sickly field showed like a badge of poor production.

"We'll have to show we can be graded B," Mr. Walsh said after a moment. "We can show a B grade, at least."

Peg and I exchanged a glance, doubtful but unwilling to dash hopes by speaking aloud.

"I SPENT MOST of my time in caves," Simon said. "Safer down there, not knocking about with the boys who didn't want a crippled Jew in their games."

"That's so sad," I said. We were sharing lunch in the field. I'd been hunting rats all the morning, but their burrows were well into a thorny hedge and I couldn't get to them. I would have to bring in a WLA rat-catching team.

"Not for me. I loved those caves. Broke my heart to leave them."

"I suppose you know all the famous ones, like the Ape's Den and St. Michael's Cave."

"I preferred to stay lower, in the caves under St. Michael's."

I pushed his arm. "Oh, go on, the caves are famous. Even I know there's no cave under St. Michael's."

He only grinned at me.

"You think I'm gullible," I complained with a belying smile. "If you're so good at caves, go take care of my rat problem."

"Kill that rat, it's doing Hitler's work," quoted Simon. "Sorry, I'm afraid even I'm a bit tall for those tunnels."

"A lot of use you are," I teased. I sobered. "And just when we need the help, before the War Ag officers come."

"You can help that," Simon said, pointing with his sandwich.

I followed his gaze to the brown field opposite us. "What, the dying crop? I don't think so."

He looked at me with immense brown eyes. "Put your hands in the earth and listen to it. Feel it."

"Simon, I like you, but you are—"

"Try it, Petra. Just try it."

I rolled my eyes and put my palms to the grass, warm with the spring sun. I closed my eyes. "I don't hear anything except the sheep across the way."

"You don't always listen with ears." Simon's hands came down over mine, strong fingers wrapping mine and plunging into the dirt like roots. "Even the prophets say the stones will cry out. Listen."

I kept silent and felt the warmth of his hands, the warmth of the dirt, the quiet joy of the spring grass in the sun, the basso reliability of the bedrock and the laughter of the boulders rising an eighth of an inch with each spring thaw, pushing their way to the sunny surface with patient inevitability, the contented peace of the nurturing soil, the bright pang of discord beneath the dying crops—

I jerked my hands away and turned to stare at Simon. "What was that?"

He beamed at me. "You felt it!"

"I felt—everything. The earth and everything on it, at least here."

"And what did you feel in the field?"

"There's something wrong in the soil." I swallowed. "But I don't know how I knew that. Or how you knew, or knew that I could know."

"I knew from almost the first we met," Simon said a little hesitantly. "We are not the same, but we are similar. And I had my family to teach me, but you did not."

"Teach you what? How to feel if there's something in the earth?"

"I can sense it in the same way that you can, or how an ordinary person can see ripples in water." Simon held my eyes. "But you can do more than sense it. You can mend it."

"What?"

"Coax the poison out of the soil."

What he said was madness, but everything he'd said was madness, only madness that I could feel myself while with him. I closed my eyes and flattened my hands to the dirt again.

There was indeed a poison in the soil. Now that I knew it was there, it was impossible to miss, a painful boil against my questing mind. It burned. *Lye.* How had lye come into the field? That was a question for later. First, I had to draw it out, an intent as natural with my hands in the earth as righting a spilled bucket on the kitchen floor.

Tiny pores and tunnels in the soil like capillaries opened to take in the caustic lye. They spread to the southeast, toward the edge of the field, and I thought of where the rat burrows were. I pushed and drew the poison to the burrows we could not reach, attacking from below, and left the lye to do our work.

Simon embraced me, jarring me from the half-trance of burrowing through the dirt. "Petra, you grand girl, you did it!"

I blinked and stared at him. "I—I think I did, but I don't know what."

"I watched it all. You did a fine job."

I had questions, enormous questions that were too large to ask. I started with one which felt slightly safer for its distance. "What are you, Simon?"

He swallowed, and I could see it was a leap of trust for him, too. "I'm a Jewish fellow from an old Gibraltar family," he said. He took a breath. "Whose mother married a half-kobold."

I should have laughed. I should have fallen back in the grass and roared with unladylike delight. But the earth had opened to me, and I could not laugh.

The next question was larger, more dangerous, more urgent. I took a breath. "What am I?"

"Don't you know?"

I shook my head. "Not at all."

He hesitated, clearly worried that I would doubt him, though why he should stick at this late point I couldn't guess. "Our mothers each had unconventional husbands," Simon said. "Yours took a giant."

I finally laughed despite myself. "Papa was tall, to be sure, but he wasn't that tall," I said. "Even in my child's memory he is an ordinary man."

"He was no ordinary man," Simon corrected me, "or you couldn't do what you just did. You've inherited your share of giant blood."

"And that makes me . . . ?"

He leaned close. "Very interesting," he said, and he kissed me gently.

The next day, against all my disbelief and half-hopes, the seedlings looked straighter and brighter, and the hedge was littered with dead rats.

THE COUNTY WAR Agricultural Executive Officer and his Tillage

Officer arrived late in the afternoon, as a storm was rolling in. They only just had time to look at the dairy cows before it grew dark. As the nearest inn was miles away and anyway filled to bursting with Belfast refugees, Peg and I shared a bed and Mrs. Walsh made them places to stay, to complete their inspection in the morning.

It was full dark when I woke as if an alarm had gone off. All the night was still, but an alarm was ringing in my head. *Heavy. Pressing. Machine.* I could feel the crawling weight across the surface a mile away.

The hill and drystone wall called me.

I pushed aside the thought of how ridiculous that was in my desperation to stop the damage. I slid out of bed without waking Peg—should I wake her? But what would I say? —and pulled on my dungarees against the chill. My gumboots were waiting near the door. The rain had cleared, and I ran down the lane by the light of the waxing moon, knowing the way well enough and unwilling to risk a torch and betray my observation.

I could hear the coughing roar of the tractor. I slowed, though it was unlikely anyone driving would see me in the misty dark when he had to watch for the tractor's path.

Betrayal, Simon had said. The stones had resented being torn down by a farmer.

The lingering damp made it nearly too dark to see despite the moon. Gallagher was dedicated to his mischief, to be working in such a night. But this was his chance to prove Walsh's mismanagement to the War Ags and get the fine land for himself.

I could see him now, setting the tractor to the wall and fixing an attachment—I was not familiar with the new machinery— over the top of the wall to pull it down after him. No mistake with the direction of the stones, not now when victory was so near.

I knelt in the lee of the stone wall and pressed my hands to it. *Stay strong.*

The wall groaned as the tractor's engine kicked louder. I held my breath.

The wall resisted, but it had never been made to defy great modern machines. The top stones gave way, spilling onto the ground, and his metal contraption scraped the throughstone.

Gallagher reset the tractor's device lower, ready to pull down the rest of the wall and make a clear cow-lane.

If strength could not defeat him, weakness could. I rooted my fingers into the soil. *Soft.*

It was unnatural. The soil on the gentle hill drained well, and it had no reason to slide apart. But I coaxed it to release bonds, to become fine and slippery, individual grains of dirt sliding across one another as if still lubricated by heavy rain. The tractor wheels began to slip on the surface, tearing the neat rows.

Good! Soft.

The ground burbled like warm soup, and the tractor sank into the tilled soil like marsh or quicksand beach, pausing briefly when the axles caught the surface and then continuing into the liquid morass that had been Gallagher's field. He worked gears and cursed over the straining engine and finally threw his hat, but the earth settled to itself again about the wheels and axles and the tractor could not move.

With my fingers still in the dirt, I grinned like a naughty child. The best part was the pale light creeping over the eastern horizon. It was time for the War Ags to examine our walls.

The War Ag men came to breakfast with stern faces. Mrs. Walsh served with a flurry of pathetic pandering and an obvious display of breakfast bounty, bacon and eggs for the men, and bread fried in bacon grease for Peg and me.

Gallagher arrived at our door while we were still eating. "You know," he started, his eyes darting from the door to the table to the clock on the wall, "I might have been a bit hasty in my complaint. It occurs to me we don't need to involve the Committee in this. I'm sorry to trouble these gentlemen, but I spoke in anger. You and I can talk over the issue of the walls, maybe in a few days when we've had time to cool our heads and words."

Walsh started to answer, but I jumped up first. "Oh, no, Mr. Gallagher, you were right to be concerned. There's no excuse for negligent endangerment of another man's livelihood at any time, but especially in this time of crisis, it's essential that we all work together as a harnessed team, for the good of Britannia. I'm sure these gentlemen could not in good conscience go home without confirming the efforts of all here."

"We are here, after all," said the taller Committee man, a little startled by my enthusiasm. "While I'm happy to see that neighbourly concord may be resumed, we must see what we came for, and the farms must be graded. Let's go out and walk the walls, to see how they're maintained."

"Let's start to the north, as it's so pleasant there in the early morning," I suggested, and Gallagher's face blanched.

So we put on our boots and walked down the damp lane to the most glorious sight of Gallagher's treachery and lies laid bare.

Walsh spat a series of curses and had to be held back from striking Gallagher by one of the Committee men. Gallagher slunk out of reach and offered a series of pitiful explanations about extra tilling and sliding into the wall, which no one entertained for a moment.

"But it's curious," the Tillage Officer observed, "how the ground came so soft even on the hill, where it seems it would have drained."

"The rain has been quite heavy," said the Executive Officer. "And those tractors are powerful machines, easy to get into trouble if one does not know how to use one properly."

Gallagher's face burned, but he could say nothing.

"But that doesn't say anything about the crops which have been doing poorly," said the Tillage Officer, "if indeed they are."

"Excuse me, sirs," I said, "but you'll recall I suggested coming this way? I've been picking up after Mr. Gallagher's wall breaks all this time. I also happen to know lye was put on the seedlings. He's using the County Agricultural Committee to take the land he's wanted for years."

I don't know how I would have proved the lye, but Mr. Gallagher's face upon hearing me was so full of shock, it was all but a confession. "I—you can't—there's nothing to show what you say! I did no such thing, there's lye in my barns like in any farmer's barns, and I have no reason to waste it on my neighbour's fields!"

The Tillage Officer frowned at the disordered protest. "I suppose it's possible to look up the records for county lye distribution and see if Mr. Gallagher might have taken more than seemed needful."

Gallagher set his jaw. "No one can say I didn't need more lye.

Everyone uses it. And if I did put lye on the field, why would it look so green now?"

The men turned to me, and I made myself smile. "You wouldn't expect me to leave it be? I neutralized the soil, of course." Not with acid, but effectively.

All eyes shifted back to Gallagher, who snarled at me.

Peg and I brought the team and hitched them to the front of the mired tractor, and as Peg coaxed the horses forward, I silently coaxed the earth to release its prize. The Committee men were so impressed by our quick work that they agreed we should learn to drive a War Ag tractor to use for Walsh's farm and others in the area.

"It would certainly be put to better use in their hands," the Tillage Officer said. He looked at Gallagher.

"I was trying to push the stones back from where I found them," Gallagher mumbled, and he looked as if he knew how ridiculous it sounded.

"I wonder," said the Executive Officer, his mouth turned down with disapproval, "given the extraordinary circumstances and the need for a national effort, if this might be considered sabotage of war production. Certainly this time and labour could have been put into Gallagher's own fields. Is this mismanagement?"

Gallagher's eyes opened wide, and he renewed his sputtered protests with more enthusiasm and less sense. The Executive Officer put a hand on his arm and gestured that they should walk up the road together, back to the house and the car.

Mr. and Mrs. Walsh declared a celebratory supper of one of the kept lambs. I snuck away and related all to Simon, who laughed with glee and beamed with pride at my earthworking. In a fit of confidence, I asked Mrs. Walsh if I could bring him to dinner, and in a fit of generosity, she agreed.

IT WAS NEAR dark, with the sun low and red in the sky, and we were drinking tea and lingering about the supper table, full with roast lamb and unwilling to break up the party just yet. Mr. Walsh was speculating on opening another field with the new tractor, and Peg was watching Simon and me with knowing eyes.

None of us were prepared for the door to burst open,

crashing against the wall, and three muddy men with pistols to rush into the room, pointing the guns at us. Peg gasped, I could make no sound, and Mr. Walsh made it only halfway to his feet before a pistol muzzle was at his face.

One of the men spoke, but I understood none of it, and in the shock I needed a moment to realize it was not English.

"Who are you?" demanded Mrs. Walsh, brave in the face of threat. "This is my house!"

The man snapped a response, probably not an answer, and this time I registered, *German.*

Peg gasped. "You're saboteurs. Invaders. Do you have a ship? Is there a landing?"

The man turned his gun on her, but another caught the barrel and pushed it up with a half-whispered scolding and a gesture toward the windows. The other answered with a wider gesture. I didn't need to understand the language to know how isolated we were; no one would hear shots or our calls for help.

I'd known enough RAF fellows to recognize a flier's uniform, even if it were Luftwaffe. "They came in a plane!" I gasped, keeping my eyes on the men and making my voice shake—which proved less difficult than I'd hoped.

Peg, quick as a whip, picked up my tactic of pretending protest to speak. "They must be separated or shot down," she wailed.

"Another run on Belfast," Simon supposed, and one of the men looked sharply at him. Simon realized his mistake, but it was too late.

The men gestured sharply with their pistols, and we filed obediently out the door, bunched together like fearful sheep. Simon's crutch slipped in the damp earth but he stayed close to me. We were guided to the edge of the pasture behind the house.

Mrs. Walsh's defiance had evaporated with their identification and silent tears rolled down her cheeks. Mr. Walsh held her, glaring disapproval at the men.

The three argued together for a moment and then pointed us to the corner where three stone walls came together. Peg held my arm tightly, and Simon hopped at my other side, struggling with his crutch.

"You're brutes and dogs, and I hope the pigs eat ye," growled

Mr. Walsh.

"Halte das Maul!" A German raised his pistol. Simon lunged forward to knock his arm aside as the shot rang out. Mr. Walsh grunted as his wife screamed, and he folded, clutching his shoulder. Blood darkened her fingers in the twilight as she reached for the wound.

The man snarled an epithet and kicked Simon's crutch from him, spilling him onto the ground before I could catch him.

Simon stared wide-eyed at the gun above him and whispered, *"Sh'ma Yisrael Adonai 'eloheinu Adonai 'echad."*

I don't know if the German recognized the words or not. He aimed his pistol.

"No!" I shouted, and I shoved the man away. The shot went into the ground, and someone screamed, and the man whipped the pistol back to strike me. I fell backward against the stone wall, my head striking the rock so that I should have been stunned.

Instead, I felt the strength of the stones pouring into me, everywhere my back and arms and head touched the drystone wall. Behind me, the joined walls ran out in three directions over the farm, linking with other walls, spreading over all the county farms and over all Northern Ireland and connecting to the bedrock that made up the whole great island, heedless of men's borders.

Like a pool at the centre of a dozen hundred streams, I drank the energy from the stone lines crossing the earth. Then I turned it on the invaders.

Far below the grassy field, the granite shifted and yawned, a giant waking to an unwelcome disturbance. The ground heaved and grass rippled like water around a dropped stone. The Luftwaffe men looked around and at each other, startled and confused, and then with a sound almost too low and grand to hear, the earth opened and devoured them.

They hardly had time to shout as they fell into the chasm, and then granite shifted back and closed upon them like a door.

Peg stared open-mouthed at the place where they had been, marked by marred grasses and a dimple of disturbed earth. Then she looked at me, with a suspicion that could not have been countenanced in anyone who had not been present for the swallowing.

Mr. Walsh, pragmatic as ever, saddled a horse and set off with his bound shoulder to warn the county of downed German pilots. Mrs. Walsh loaded a shotgun and kept it in the kitchen as she made tea for us. Simon held my hand tightly, wordlessly. Peg fingered her hair into place and asked no questions.

"MUST HAVE BEEN a Neolithic well or some like," suggested the Executive Officer. "I've never heard of one around here, but the historians are always saying we're full of ruins. Looks solid enough now, but you'll want to be careful of the sheep there."

"I never heard of such a thing, and my family's always been here," Mr. Walsh replied.

The officer gave a puzzled shrug. "Agriculture is what I know, not druid ruins or what have you. But there are some government men come down to look at it, and they might be able to give you some answers."

The government men, in suits inappropriate for the countryside, introduced themselves and asked Mr. and Mrs. Walsh a few simple questions. They had no questions for Peg, and I assumed they must think a couple of Land Girls wouldn't know anything about paleolithic wells.

But they came to me while I was feeding the pigs, alone in the yard. One still wore the aviator sunglasses he'd come in, even in the grey drizzle. "Miss Luxton, we'd like to speak to you about what happened."

"It was terrible," I said quickly. "I'm so glad it's over."

Simon had never said anything about keeping things to myself, but it didn't need to be said. Even accepting that a Jew from Gibraltar might be more conservative in sharing personal secrets than the average British citizen, it seemed the kind of knowledge that shouldn't be advertised. At best, I would be thought daft.

But the government men were not content with my anxious dismissal. "We believe you might tell us about the incident," said the man without sunglasses. "Something about how this might have happened."

I shook my head, making my eyes wide and innocent. "It was terrifying."

The man with the dark glasses sighed and withdrew a notebook, which he opened without removing his glasses and clearly without necessity. "Miss Petra Luxton, volunteer for the Land Army, daughter to Bres and Gretchen Gilling, born in the Falkland Islands but brought to England as a child of—"

"Wait," I interrupted. "Born in the Falklands?"

The man smiled patiently. "Your aunt was not keen for you to remember, but we have those records—and more."

The Falklands. With the word, memories shifted into place like tumblers behind a lock. "Our farm was at Seal Bay. It was eleven hours by horse to Port Stanley," I said, "and we used to gather sea cabbage to eat. And the penguins—I did not imagine the penguins."

He shook his head.

I pushed down my new excitement and gave him a firm gaze. "Can you tell me other things?"

He closed the notebook he had not consulted. "We are gathering a small cadre of very special citizens," he said, "who might be able to contribute to efforts in the war."

"I don't know . . . What kind of efforts?"

"More than merely assisting with farm production." He tipped his sunglasses down and looked at me with strange eyes, hazel with a near-orange tint and curiously narrow pupils. A little shiver ran through me.

"Miss Luxton, you are doubtless aware of our shipping difficulties in the Atlantic. There is a very secret experimental U-boat presently off the Iberian coast, unofficially welcomed by Franco and officially unnoticed by Salazar, and a great danger to our food convoys."

"And you think I could help with a U-boat? I'm a Land Girl."

The hazel-orange eyes blinked. "You are a Land Girl, indeed."

I swallowed. "I would like to bring my friend."

"Simon Tobhelem, lately of Gibraltar, missing from refugee quarters in London? Yes, I think we could speak with him as well."

I nodded, my heart in my throat. "Then please, tell me more of what you would like us to do."

*On the 25*ᵀᴴ *of November, 1941, a small tsunami was observed at Cornwall, the result of an undersea earthquake along the Gloria Fault, off the west coast of Portugal.*

The Stone Alphabet

Catherine MacLeod

APPETITE

A psychological disorder characterized by an appetite for stones.

Ugly description, Jackson thought. Lovely word, though. Lithophagia: delicious syllables.

He stood at Elaine's grave, looking for exactly the right stone. And there it was, small and smooth, under those godawful lilies.

He'd swallowed one from each of the girls' graves. Like having a drink in their memory, he thought. He did so enjoy the flavours, which always seemed, somehow, to match their owners' temperament—sour, fiery, salty, tart.

But he wasn't a glutton—he *could* control his appetite.

Nor was he unreasonable. If the stones caused him a little discomfort, well, considering what the girls went through before they died, that was only fair.

Elaine had been his favourite so far. He popped her stone in his mouth.

Sweet.

BONUS

Her cigarette smelled of sulphur, but he decided her long

legs made up for the second-hand smoke. He said, "So I get everything I want for 25 years, and then you collect my soul?"

"Yes."

"I sign in blood?"

"That was an early error in translation. I actually require an offering of pain. But that usually involves blood."

He imagined there'd be enough pain at collection time; he didn't care to give more now.

At least the quartz stylus was what he'd expected. He stabbed it in her thigh and signed. "Doesn't say the pain has to be mine."

She laughed horribly. "So few people ever amuse me." She changed the contract so that *25* read *30*, then initialled it. "Call it a signing bonus."

CELLAR

The sky is darker than I've ever seen it, and the thunder like the world screaming.

Elias unlocks the storm cellar door, and says, "Run, you'll be safe there."

Years ago, he came to my father with a set of blueprints, a heavy bag of gold, and a request for my hand. My father accepted all three.

Elias was known to have strange ways, he said. But, as wives do, I'd come to know him well enough.

I haven't. But as I go down, and down, and down, I know well enough he's been good to me, I love him for all his strangeness, and I hope he joins me soon.

Just as I know this staircase was never in the blueprints, and this house has no storm cellar.

DEJA-VU

Years ago, a hospital. She remembers a nurse, slight and pale, hovering. The sheen of a long, silver probe entering her stomach, cleaning a slow-healing incision, pulling out bloody ribbons of packing. She remembers being stiff with fear, a scream building in her throat.

The nurse saying, "Don't watch. If you don't see it, it can't hurt you. Keep your eyes closed."

Now, a spaceship. An alien, slight and pale, hovering. A long, silver finger probing her stomach, pulling out bloody ribbons.

Stiff with fear, a scream builds in her throat.

Don't watch, she thinks. *If you can't see it, it can't hurt you.*

Keep your eyes closed, keep your eyes closed, keep your eyes closed.

ESTHETICS

Talia's hands are gentle on her clients' faces, feathering mud over persistent frowns. She doesn't offer much information about her beauty treatments, and her clients, happy with their results, don't ask many questions.

But she does say the mud is from a local source and has healing properties. They seem to like that.

It's true enough. The grave where she collects the mud *is* local, and, while staking its inhabitant was unpleasant, it looked young and lovely right up to the end.

She suspects her clients will, too, as long as they keep coming in. And, addicted to beauty, they will.

She can afford to be gentle with them, she thinks, and keeps smoothing the mud over their faces, burying them one caress at a time.

FOUNDATION

"The foundation looks good," the owner says, scrambling down into the basement.

It does. I'm careful about getting just the right mix, and it pays: my walls don't crack or honeycomb, and good quality is good for business.

"We'll lower your house tomorrow," I say. I run my rasp along the top of the wall, levelling it. He follows, inspecting the job.

"Isn't construction a difficult career for a woman?"

"It's easier than it used to be."

"Really?"

"The ancient Romans buried their enemies in their foundations, so the anger would strengthen the walls. I expect that was time-consuming."

He thinks I'm joking. "You don't seem to mind getting your hands dirty."

I file a fingertip off the wall and crush it before he sees. "I like doing things the old-fashioned way," I say.

And I do. But mostly I just like sticking with what works.

GALATEA

Pygmalion, known better for his hatred of women than for his exquisite sculpture, carved the perfect woman from stone—and fell in love with her. He named her Galatea, this lifeless thing, the one woman guaranteed not to love him back.

The goddess Venus, when she finished laughing, showed mercy and made Galatea come to life under his hand.

She doesn't come alive at his touch anymore.

But Pygmalion isn't easily hurt, and he still has his chisel, maintained with care and honed to a good edge.

He carved her to perfection once, and can do it again.

HOME TRUTHS

Salt kills them, those things like clutching hands that claw up out of the ground.

But they don't stay dead.

The first time they came, they dragged my parents through the kitchen floor, and almost got my brother Ewan. I torched the house to stop them and then ran for help. Ewan broke me out of the padded cell. We shut up after that.

Sixty years we've salted the property, spring and fall, to stop them travelling. Time hasn't slowed *them* any. But this morning I poured salt over Ewan as they hauled him down screaming.

I got today's job done. Next time, who knows? I've heard salt attracts lightning. Maybe it'll strike and sterilize this place forever. Or not.

It's just them and me now, and I've got the whole winter to stock up on salt.

Come spring, we'll see.

INTARSIA

Sometimes, late at night, he thinks about his father, a jeweller with a strong work ethic and unnerving determination. A man fascinated by the art of creating a jewel from small pieces of different gemstones.

The son disliked the artificiality of the finished stone, but understood the lure of all those intricate pieces. Neither father nor son could ever resist a puzzle.

The father had hoped his son would follow in his footsteps. The son had fought because old habits can die hard.

But they *can* die.

Even now he can't honestly say he misses his father, but he thinks he's come to understand him.

Sometimes, late at night, Victor Frankenstein shudders to think his father might have been proud.

JET

I notice the jet mourning brooch at Mrs. Stanton's throat immediately: her late husband's silhouette carved in ivory, strands of his hair woven around it like filigree.

Widows so rarely wear them nowadays. Obviously an old-fashioned woman.

"Your references are excellent."

And our young ladies' academy needs another teacher. But her brooch draws my eye again, and, at second glance, the silhouette seems . . . off.

What was surely a well-groomed moustache could almost be mistaken for tusks. His ear looks pointed, almost horn-like. His hair seems too coarse to be human, but I can hardly take a closer look.

I confess to feeling uneasy.

But we're short-staffed, and—she'll do. She's quick at math and writes a fine hand, and it's a respectable woman who mourns her husband.

No matter what it was.

KRAKATOA

"The Earth is an egg," Cameron says, just to see his grandson take his earbuds out.

"If it was an egg, it'd be cracking by now," Corey huffs. "You reading that weird philosophy again?" He sticks his buds back in without waiting for an answer.

Cameron shrugs. If the kid had ever read *that weird philosophy,* he'd understand that the egg's *been* cracking for a long time. He'd know the wind is made of echoes, and you can hear the cracks, if you know what you're listening to.

You can hear Krakatoa sending a shockwave around the world seven times. Mount Toba exploding, destroying Atlantis.

Hiroshima, the Halifax Explosion, the crackle of five thousand active underwater volcanoes.

The Earth is an egg. And, as is so often the case, the winged thing inside wants out.

Any day now, Cameron thinks.

The kid probably won't even hear it coming.

LAPIDATION

Even now, Erri thinks, her husband only gets it half-right.

Out in the cornfield, buried up to her chest, she watches Haden gather a crowd and a pile of rocks. Lapidation. Stoning. A slow, painful death. A fitting punishment for adulterers and witches.

Half-right: she was never unfaithful.

Elia's here, too. The daughter Haden assumes isn't his. Made to see this, punished for being her mother's child.

"The sins are in the blood," Haden says. Half-right: *something's* in the blood. "Any last words?" he growls.

When this is over, he'll banish Elia. She has no other family and nowhere to go. "Give our daughter a dowry."

Haden laughs. It's terrible. "She can have the stones when we're done with them."

Erri laughs. It's worse, and doesn't stop until she's dead.

The crowd walks away, and Elia picks up the stones turned to diamonds by her mother's blood.

MOURNED

After the expected quiet moment, I drop my handful of dirt in Colin's grave. It's an old tradition, satisfying in a hurtful way. It reminds us that our bodies return to the earth. It involves me in the burial.

And it's meant to be a tender gesture, I guess.

I believe I always gave him the respect he was due, even though he didn't always return the favour. But the tenderness wore thin long ago.

He said once he didn't want his funeral in the church. That suited me fine. I promised I'd say the prayer and bury him myself.

Didn't say how long I'd be about it.

He's still moving some. The next handful will need bigger

stones.

I'm going to return him to the earth, no matter what.

But it might have been easier if I'd just cremated him and got it over with.

NEPHILIM

Cleo blamed the night on a lack of information.

She'd known that her wings grew another inch every year; that they glowed softly in the dark; that only an obsidian blade could cut them. She hadn't known that nothing would stop a determined thief.

She'd trusted the man who made her feel valuable. Loved him for calling her priceless. Then she'd seen the obsidian axe and realized he was talking about money.

She dragged him further into the old cemetery, her wings protruding from his back. He hadn't known how strong Nephilim—angel-human hybrids—really are, or how angry they can be. Or that severed wings dissolve at sunrise.

Cleo dropped him and looked around. Some of the statues guarding the graves had ragged stumps on their backs, too. Maybe she'd come back and visit them sometime.

She'd fit right in, she thought. Just another stone cold angel.

OUBLIETTE

A deep, windowless, stone dungeon, accessible only through the top. No ladder, no stairs. A prison for enemies of the state and queens who've grown too old to breed. An *oubliette,* my husband says, dragging me toward it. From *oublier—to forget.*

He's locked everyone out so no one will witness my imprisonment. He craves control to the point of carrying the one key that opens every lock in the castle. He decides who may stay and leave, and when.

Not this time.

I strike him with my fist and he backhands me in, the hatch locking as it slams.

I open my hand. I've stolen his key. We're both imprisoned now. The castle will be a fitting tomb for him.

But not for a while yet.

Oublier: he'll remember me for the rest of his life.

PATIENCE

Gargoyles are patient, in the way of all stone, and nothing if not forgiving. They know humans think they're merely ugly waterspouts, but gargoyles keep their peace.

Gargoyles were put on the roof to throw rainwater clear of the walls—but also to stand watch against evil spirits. They remember this, even if most humans don't. They guard the occupants of their buildings, and have for uncounted years. Gargoyles are nothing if not faithful.

All the rain flowing through them, pouring from their deformed mouths, erodes them slowly but surely. One day they'll blow away on the wind that precedes the storm.

The evil spirits, as patient as gargoyles, but much less forgiving, wait.

QUARRY

So romantic. Knowing I like silver, you lured me to this place of fog the colour of doves, of stones like old pearls and pewter.

A gravel pit, you call it. A *quarry*. How droll. And what a perfect place for our last dance.

I so enjoy the waltz of hunter and prey. And if you've taken a few wrong steps, well, what partner hasn't? The bullets that did nothing but ruin my dress, the holy water that did nothing at all, and the ash stake that didn't even come close. I know your heart was in the right place, even if you couldn't find mine.

But we both knew it would come to this, didn't we? Romance is all about the thrill of the chase, no?

And your dance skills have been improving.

Shall we?

REMEMBERING

Sometimes, rocks stacked up to look like men.

Or, boulders piled to serve as directional aids.

This one, constructed with a "window" through which you can see another inuksuk, and so form a sightline. They could line you up with the polar star and the mid-winter moon. Indicate the safest route home. Point to places of rest and refuge.

Always remind you of other travellers who've passed this way.

If you look through the windows in a certain light, they line up to a point just above the horizon, and at certain times of the moon, the wind through them has the low pitch of distant voices. Words you think you could understand if you could just get a little closer.

If you could only remember why they make you think of home.

And if only you remembered that travellers can follow navigational aids in both directions.

SISYPHUS

For the crime of talking too much, Sisyphus is sent to Hades, where every day until the end of the world he must roll a giant rock uphill. Every evening, when he reaches the top, it teeters promisingly, and then rolls back slowly to the foot of the mountain.

His punisher, the god Zeus, tells him, "But take comfort, for your task will forever be appreciated."

Sisyphus doubts it, but now knows better than to comment.

The rock rolls up the mountain, the rock rolls down the mountain.

The moon rises, the moon sets.

TELEPHONE SERVICE

Perry would be calling soon, complimenting her breathy voice, her slight Mediterranean accent, her softly hissing laugh. He was so easy.

And right on time. "Hello, Perry."

"Hello, Marina, how did you know it was me?"

"I always know when it's you."

He imagined himself a scholar, but didn't imagine she might have caller ID. Or that he could find a real companion instead of dallying with a phone sex operator.

"I want to meet you," he said. Again. "I know we'd be great together."

"Meeting me . . . wouldn't be good for you."

"You know I can find you." Probably, she thought sadly. A determined fool could cause all kinds of trouble. "At least tell me your real name."

"Medusa."

"Like the Gorgon?" He sounded pleased with himself for knowing that.

"Yes, Perry, just like that."

She'd really hoped it wouldn't come to this again.

USHABTI

I know the stone figurines in my office aren't *really* ushabti. They represent my first wives, not their servants in the afterlife. But I like the word.

Both have a matching stone storage jar. Noreen's is alabaster, to match her skin. Theresa's, calcite, a soft rose the colour of her lips.

I know that removing their brains through their nostrils with a hook isn't *really* the ancient Egyptian method of preserving their memories. But I like the procedure.

More than they did.

There comes a moment in every relationship when you think, "It doesn't get any better than this." That's the moment you want to hold on to.

I want to hold this one.

Leanne looks radiant tonight—the happiest I've ever seen her. Her ushabti and jar are jade, to match her eyes.

A good marriage is all about the memories.

VARIATION

Sean Riordan lives for auctions. A rich collector of oddities: rare fish, radioactive minerals, anything Garbo. Bad loser, worse winner, every smile a variation of *Gotcha*.

Charming when he wants to be, but charm wears thin, and I don't like clutter, no matter how expensive.

He phones a month after the breakup. He's leaving town, can we get together before he goes?

I'd rather not, but I want to return the things he left at my place.

His house is almost empty. "Ditching your worldly possessions?" I ask.

He passes me a scotch-rocks. "I've heard you should get rid of everything that doesn't bring you joy."

At least his mineral collection is still here. The gold carnolite is beautiful. But the green masuyite is gone. "You're selling your rocks, too?"

"No."

I swallow half my drink. It glows softly in the overhead light. Sean's doesn't.

He's wearing that smile.

WARM

Ouroboros, the giant serpent who surrounded the world, was banished to the moon. He remembers he was once feared, and mourns the loss of his power, but, being a snake, he mostly just misses his favourite warm stone.

He scrapes himself across the light rocks, feeling relief like pleasure as his too-tight skin splits and peels off. He watches it shimmer and twist like a borealis as lunar winds carry it away.

It circles the Earth now as the great snake once did, and little heat escapes its scales.

As once suspected, damage to the ozone layer *is* mythical.

The Earth will be ready for him when he returns.

X

Ava loved exotic travel—Katmandu, Marrakesh, moonrise over the Sphinx. She adored mystery. Loved a little danger.

Loved me more.

I could never bring myself to hold her back. I promised I'd always wait for her; she promised she'd always come back to me. Said she'd never get so lost she couldn't find her way home.

Ava loved being on the road.

This one, maybe not so much.

It's called a corpse road, a gravel track from the church to the cemetery. Sometimes, when they're close to houses and businesses, they're made to intersect so the dead will lose their sense of direction and not return.

I sit here most days, beside this road like an X marking the middle of nowhere. It's been a while.

But I promised.

And so did she.

YOU CAN ONLY BELIEVE

Grandma always said family stands with you. But my family's gone, and this stand is my last. I have Daddy's truck, Mama's rifle, food I looted from a store twenty miles down the mountain, and Grandma's *hag*, a smooth stone with a hole made by running water. She said a lot of stories about it are true, but you can only believe one.

It gives you the power to know when you're being lied to? Please. When the president said the contagion was contained, *everybody* knew he lied.

It protects you from sickness? I doubt it. From nightmares? Nope.

It wards off the dead? Nice thought, but I know they're lurching their way up here. I have more faith in the gun.

If you look through the hole, you'll see a clear path to the next life?

Huh.

I'll take it.

ZACHARY

At midnight, the small click of pebbles against my window: Zachary wishing me happy birthday. In fifty years he's never forgotten.

The day his family moved next door to mine, we sat on the porch roof eating birthday cake and talking *what I want to do when I grow up*. I wanted to move to a big city and live in a beautiful apartment. Zachary wanted us to be friends forever.

We blew out the candles together.

I left town after he died in a car crash. He was hitchhiking home from college. Coming back for my birthday.

He always does.

I smile when I think of him. Even now, in my penthouse apartment, with an uncut cake, and empty chairs for glittering acquaintances who had better things to do tonight.

The small click of pebbles against my window.

Winner Takes All

Mara Malins

IT ALL STARTED with the Night of the Dragon Cards.

Three cycles ago, I combined two of the world's strongest magical cards together in the table-top card arena and created a mythical character, the strength of which had never been seen before. Not in all the thousands of cycles of the card arena. Two extremely high-level dragons combined. *As fiery as fiery can be*, I remember thinking that night—with no idea of what was to come.

The beast was too strong. It should never have been created. Within minutes of the game starting, the dragon broke free from the table-top arena—tore through the protective forcefield and broke free into our world—and went on a rampage, roasting everything and anyone nearby, reducing the card room to ashes, and killing over two hundred people.

But that was just the beginning.

In hours, the dragon had destroyed the entire planet. Gavala, once a thriving trading world and hub of Confederacy activity, was reduced to flames and screams. Nothing was left untouched; no buildings remained, no humans un-burned, the forests were set alight, the seas were choked by ash. The once deliciously breathable air turned rancid, stinking of sulphur and charred flesh. The destruction was absolute.

Offworld, I'd heard the planet had been given a grim new nickname; the Unholy Smoke. Onworld, it was called nothing because everybody was dead.

Except me.

With a gas-mask and a couple of imported storage containers full of dehydrated food, I'd made the Unholy Smoke my home. I had no choice; the Confederacy had given everyone left alive—a pitiful handful compared to the millions who'd once lived here—safe passage off planet. Everyone except me. The sentence for my crimes was to live with the destruction I'd caused. There was nothing here but scorched skies and charred soil, but it was more than what I deserved after what I'd done.

I was okay with that. I wanted to be anywhere that dragon wasn't, and the last I'd heard, it had burned up four trading planets, the monk planet Flava, and was on its way to a mining planet at the edge of the Confederacy border.

But that news was at least a month old so, really, I had no idea where the fucking thing was. I just knew it wouldn't return to a planet that was already burned up. It had no power here. I was safe on this planet, I guess. And it wasn't so bad actually. The days all merged into one and there wasn't anything to do but breathe in ash and walk by burned out buildings . . . but I didn't have to face the wives of the husbands I'd accidentally killed. Or see the hatred those children had for the killer who'd taken away one or both of their parents.

So, I walked. For three cycles now, I walked from one coast to the other, carrying just enough food for the trip. Today, I was walking up what used to be a thriving high-street with shops on either side of the road. Ash, stirred up by a gentle breeze, was blowing lazily across the cracked earth like phantom tumbleweeds. To my left was the old card house, the start of all the horror. I walked hundreds of miles every week, but for some reason, I always ended up back here. Where it all began.

Sometimes I feel like I'm in a huge card arena myself, the scorched skies overhead keeping the damage to this planet in just like the invisible shield did. There was no escape for me.

Not like the dragon.

I leaned against the remains of a stone wall and took out my canteen of water and a protein bar. How long did I stay, eating and staring at that card house? I couldn't say. Time passes strangely here. Even the twin suns high in the sky were useless; just two dull globes of light behind the duvet of angry dust clouds still passing overhead. The clouds blocked out most of the light giving everything a strange dying purple colour. There were no days and no nights . . . just lots and lots of *time.*

"I thought I'd find you here," someone said from behind me.

I hadn't heard a voice in over three cycles. I pushed myself away from the wall so hard that my heavy boots tangled and sent me sprawling. My jaws clicked together, catching my tongue between them, and I cried out in pain. My canteen fell to the floor with a thump and water gurgled out.

From the floor, I stared up to see my old friend Poole looking down at me. Behind his gasmask, I could just about see the puckered scars of his burns running down one side of his ugly face, the angry reminders of that terrible night.

"Poole," I greeted, standing up and brushing myself down. I could taste blood in my mouth but, wearing a mask, spitting wasn't an option, so I swallowed it down. "What are you doing here?"

"Are you okay?" he asked, not offering a hand to help me. "That looked like it hurt."

"I'm fine. What are you doing here?"

"What do you think I'm doing back on a ruined, wasted planet; looking for you." He glanced around, saw the remnants of the old card house, and sighed. "You know, Tuttle always said you'd change the world. He said a pretty girl with your poise, your poker face, your determination, could blag anything, but that I'd better be careful around you."

"He said that?"

"Yeah. And I believed him." He paused, looking me up and down. I couldn't read his expression. "But even he didn't think that you'd change the world—*destroy* the world—for the sake of winning a wager."

"The ultimate wager," I said immediately. Even amidst the destruction I'd caused, I still wasn't able to downplay just how big that card game was. Downplay the desire to win. The *need.* I'd played against the second-best player on the planet, Flick, and I'd wagered everything.

And lost.

Had I? That hateful voice whispered in my mind. *I won the game. Flick was dead. I defeated him and remain unbeaten. I'm the ultimate card player. There is no one better than me.*

"The ultimate wager," Poole agreed, shaking his head slowly. "Was it worth it?"

I was silent for a long moment. "What do you want, Poole?"

"The Confederacy sent me."

I blinked. "What?"

"The Confederacy sent me," he repeated slowly, as if speaking to a child. His eyes were hard on mine, and I could read a little distrust there. It was obvious that the last three cycles had brought something out in my friend Poole that hadn't been there before. He'd always been a hanger-on, nervous and unsure, someone easily manipulated into following my plans. Now there was something stiff in his expression. Unforgiving. A strength I'd never seen before. And, I noted, there were no red stains at the corners of his mouth. He'd always had a nasty habit of chewing salamander berries, a habit he'd obviously kicked.

Yes, something had changed in him.

Poole took another step towards me. "Tuttle . . . he works with the Confederacy now."

"What? Your husband works for the enemy?"

"No, *you're* the enemy."

It was like a slap to the face. "Okay . . ." I said slowly.

"They know of my past relationship with you," he continued, looking down at his hands. "They know that we used to smuggle together and, well . . . they wanted me to come and speak to you."

I resumed my slow pace along the road, and as expected, Poole fell into step beside me. "What do they want to speak to me about?" I asked, already knowing the answer. "What do they want from me now? I haven't left the planet—though I could. I haven't done anything but obey them, even though it sticks in my throat, so what do they want from me?"

"What everyone wants. They want you to tame the beast, Samus. They want you to put right what you did. Only you have that power. If such a thing can be done, if that beast can be controlled by anyone, it's you."

My heart was hammering in my chest but I made myself appear calm. The idea of facing that dragon again . . . it brought a rash of goosebumps out along across my skin. I thought about it for a long moment, then I turned to him. "Why would I do it? I've been left here to die. Everyone got taken to safety except me—"

"—it was your punishment."

I stopped and turned to him. "To be left to die?" I shook my head. "Besides, we both saw that thing in action, Poole. We both saw how quickly it killed . . ." My throat made a clicking sound, and I swallowed hurriedly.

"I said you'd be like this. That you would need motivation. That you'd need payment." For the briefest moment, a flash of disgust rippled over his face, but it was gone before I really knew it was there. "The Confederacy met to discuss the legal ramifications of what happened that night."

I raised an eyebrow. This was a man who'd never had any kind of formal education, had rarely used words longer than three syllables. "Ramifications? Do you even know what that word means?"

He met my eyes square on. "Do you? Things have changed, Samus. Our way of life, it's gone. The Confederacy rules everything, and they're holding you responsible for everything that happened that night. Every death is on you. And not just those in the card house either. Oh no. On your slate is the tally of every death from every planet."

"What . . ." I gasped.

"They've declared you a murderer ten billion times over. There has never been a person in the history of the Confederacy who has committed more war crimes than you. The punishment for one death is execution."

"They can't execute me ten billion times," I said, trying to joke, but the words felt strained even to my ears.

"They can and you know it." He kicked at a stone, sending up a whirl of dust. "If you fix your mess, they'll leave you be. You can stay here on this planet. Live out your days unbothered. But if you don't . . ."

He let the words trail out, watching me. I let out a deep sigh. "If I don't, they'll kill me," I finished.

"Yes. Over and over again," he confirmed. Then a flash of the old Poole returned. "It's an all or nothing, my friend. That's how you like it, right? If this isn't a wager, then I don't know what is."

I fixed my eyes onto the charred skeleton of the card house, the memories of that night making me sweat. "The ultimate wager," I whispered, the old excitement flaring to life in my stomach. Then: "Deal."

THE DULL DAYLIGHT was slowly bleeding into darkness. It was a strange change, one that I still wasn't fully accustomed to. There was no such thing as day and night on this world anymore, just a slow sludgy movement from dark and angry to darker and angrier. Each night more and more tiny insects seemed to come out to zip about in the early evening, though I hadn't seen anything larger than a cockroach since the Night of the Dragon Cards.

I was sitting on a pile of charred debris, trying not to think of the ashy bodies that must surely be buried beneath me. They were everywhere on this dead world and I stumbled across them all the time. The only sound apart from the gentle breeze stirring ash into the air was the quiet footsteps of Poole as he approached. Without a word, he came and sat beside me, clasping his hands together and resting them on his knees.

We sat in silence for a long moment before he said, "This world, man, I can't get over the destruction." He swallowed. "I don't know what's worse; seeing something unrecognisable burned completely to a crisp and wondering what it was, or seeing something I definitely recognise only partially crisped. It's just so fucking . . ." He stopped, unable to continue.

I nodded. I knew exactly what he meant.

"Okay, so, what's the plan, chief?" Poole asked after another few minutes of silence. "How do we salvage this mess? How do we defeat the dragon?"

The answer was on my lips immediately. "Cards."

Poole turned to stare at me, his face twitching. "Excuse me?"

"Cards," I repeated. "It's the only way. The game created that beast, it can stop it too."

"You still have cards? How? The Confederacy banned the game after that night. They've confiscated all of the . . ." He stopped and stared at me. "You didn't hand yours in, did you?"

My shoulders slumped. "No, I couldn't . . ."

His face twisted with something I couldn't recognise. "Are

you fucking kidding me? *You're* the reason the game was banned. You're the reason I nearly fucking died, man! And now you're telling me that you want to play with cards again?"

"Yeah," I said, my voice faint and full of shame. "I just couldn't seem to get rid of them . . ."

"And now you think to clear the mess you made is to play cards again? Seriously, is this some kind of joke?"

"Look, I'm not even sure it can work. I lost most of my cards that night and I only have fire or earth cards left. There's certainly no way I can play fire—not against a double-fire dragon. That would be suicide. So, that leaves earth. It might work, Poole. There'd be no elemental benefit, but . . . it might work."

Poole shot to his feet, running his fingers through his limp, overgrown hair. "I can't even listen to this. My hands are actually shaking. Look!" He held out his trembling hands. "Cards got us into this mess. Billions of people have died. Six planets have been completely destroyed. All because of that fucking beast you created."

"Cards can get us out of the mess. I'm sure of it," I insisted. "But there'll be some . . . difficulties."

"You think?" he asked scathingly.

"First, there are no table-top arenas left," I continued, as if I couldn't hear his complaints. "And if I can't activate the card, then the whole plan is a non-starter anyway. We have to find a table on this planet." I looked up to the broken skies, the charred atmosphere that looked so much like a forcefield. "The battle has to be here."

He snorted. "Because there's nothing left here to burn?"

"Partly." I answered, startled to find my throat closing up. I forced myself on. "But also, because there's no one here left to kill."

"Except you and I."

"It's an all or nothing kind of bet," I reminded him. "You said it yourself. Does your husband know you're here?"

Poole sighed, then gave me a rueful smile. "Yeah. He says you can't cause any trouble now you don't have any cards. Little does he know, huh?"

"Tuttle was always too clever for his own good." I opened my canteen and took a deep swallow. "So, the question is: how do we get a working card table so we can activate the card?"

Poole took the canteen from my hand but didn't drink. "No, there's two questions: how do we get a working card table so we can activate the card *and* how do we get the dragon here?"

"Once we activate the card, the dragon will come to us."

Poole turned to me, surprised. "How do you know that?"

I shrugged. "Because that's what those beasts do. That's what they're created for; to destroy other mythical cards. It's one of the reasons the Confederacy banned the game. Did you not wonder why the dragon targeted those six planets? It skipped over at least ten on its journey."

"No."

"They were the planets with gaming quarters," I explained. "The beast might be out of the arena but it's still playing the game."

"I didn't realise. Makes things easier, I suppose." He paused. "What about the table?"

I stood up and dusted the seat of my pants. "Let's hunt around. The sooner we find a table, the sooner you can get back to your husband."

In my mind, I wanted to stay silent. I wanted to think nothing at all. But that mental voice that I just couldn't control added in a gleeful tone; *and the sooner we find a table, the sooner we get our wager on.*

"SON-OF-A-fucking-bitch," Poole cried, dropping the crumbling beam of wood he was lifting. He jammed his thumb in his mouth and sucked noisily. "Goddamn splinter the size of a needle. Look!"

He held out a grimy thumb, but I couldn't see anything apart from one small bead of blood. I wiped at my forehead, probably smearing the ash of a body across my skin. "Seriously? You're showing me a splinter?"

"It hurts."

I eyed the wooden beam. "Anything under there?"

"Nah, I don't think so."

We were in one of the lesser known card houses at the edge of town, one that had been burnt but not utterly destroyed like the one I'd played in. The room had collapsed inwards and only three walls were left standing. "There's got to be something in here," I said, staring around, despair starting to creep in. If there was no card table then the plan would fail, and then what could I do? The Confederacy would kill me. Over and over again, according to Poole. I could feel the hot ball of helpless panic building in my stomach. "There has to be something!" I said again, kicking a pile of debris with my boot.

As the thick dust swirled into the air, I saw a faint glimmer of blue. My entire body clenched and my mouth went dry at the sight of that familiar pulsing. Every night of gambling came back to me then and I was flooded with emotions. Shock? Hope? Despair?

Eagerness?

Yes, I could honestly say I felt all of those. Shock, that I'd found what I was looking for. Hope, that the plan might actually work. Despair that I would have to face that dragon again, after everything I'd seen it do.

And eagerness. To play the game once more.

To win.

I dropped to my knees and started to dig around in the soot, my fingers sinking into god knows what was in the pile. Seeing my excitement, Poole forgot about his splinter and came running over to help. Within a few minutes, we'd cleared the table of debris. Three of its legs had burned away, leaving only blackened stumps, and the edges of the table crumbled beneath my fingers . . . but that flash of blue surrounding the arena edges gave me hope.

"How has this even . . ." Poole whispered.

I was barely listening. I snapped off the remaining legs with a few swift kicks from my boots, and then I set the table flat on the floor. I glanced quickly at Poole before reaching forward and pressing a button inset to the wooden top. The button didn't depress smoothly and needed a little prodding, but we both cheered when the table locked in with that familiar high-pitched *seeeeeuuuuuutttt* noise I still heard in my nightmares.

A silvery shield snapped closed, encapsulating the table-top arena. Almost reverently, I touched it with my finger, hissing when it gave me an expected zap of electricity. "It works," I breathed.

"Then the plan might actually work," Poole said, still staring at the table with a barely hidden hunger. He might not *need* the game like I did, but there was definitely a love for it there.

I pulled my cards from my back pocket and started to rifle through them. I considered each card at least ten times, the heat in my blood growing by the second. I had six cards; three unplayable fire cards and three earth cards. A golem, a giant, and an earth dragon. Out of the three, the earth dragon was the strongest card but all the stats were around defence. It wasn't an attacking card. Strongest, yes, but unplayable against the beast I had created. It could hold out from a lot of attacking but eventually the dragon would tear it down.

So, that left either the golem or the giant; neither card particularly strong. I only ever played them when I needed the element aspect. They weren't strong enough to build up or play on their own merit. The plan was starting to feel more and more hopeless by the second. These cards could never win against the fire dragon.

"That's all we have?" Poole asked, looking over my shoulder. His breath had that familiar but revolting sourness to it that brought back years of boozing and carding together. For years it had driven me crazy. Right now, it was strangely comforting. It steadied my nerves.

I glanced back and saw the tell-tale red stains at the corners of his mouth. "You brought salamander berries with you?"

"I needed a little courage. Don't judge me. And don't tell Tuttle. He disapproves."

"So he should." I turned back to the cards. "What do you think?"

"Honestly? I don't think you stand a chance with those cards. You created the strongest mythical beast ever known during the Night of the Dragons. Your double-dragon is slowly wiping out planets, Samus, it's *that* strong . . . and you want to play a mid-level giant or golem against it?"

I felt a surge of despair. "I know, Poole, but I can't play fire cards, I have no ice or water, so these two are the only cards I can play."

With a deep sigh, Poole walked away from me, stopping when he came to the crumbled wall of the building. He was still for a long moment, clearly thinking, then he unslung his canteen from over his shoulder and drank. When he held it out to me, I accepted. Inside was a cool and spicy liquid that burned as it went down. "What do we do?" I asked, handing him back the canteen.

Poole scrubbed at his face, still thinking. He lowered his hands. I could read fear in his eyes. "Why do I let you get me into these messes?"

"What . . ."

He waved me silent. "Look, I need a promise from you, Samus."

"A promise? A promise for what?"

"That you will never *ever* reveal what I'm about to show you. If you ever tell anyone, I'll flat out lie and say you made the whole thing up."

"What . . ." I sucked in a breath. "You still have cards!"

"No, I have *one* card," he clarified. "I couldn't give it up. I gave up all the rest but this one . . ."

I went to take a step forward but it would have meant leaving the table, and something inside me didn't want to do that, so I stayed where I was. My entire body was rigid with excitement. "What have you got? What card is it?"

"One that cost a couple of pounds . . ."

"When have you ever had pounds?"

"I didn't say it cost *me* pounds. I nicked it, didn't I?"

"Who from?"

"How do you think Tuttle and I met? We were on a job together."

"You . . ." I closed my mouth. I was scarcely breathing. I wouldn't—couldn't—be distracted from that card. "What is it?"

"It's a card that triples the elemental attack on a card."

"A strengthening card?" I let out a low whistle.

"Yeah. With the cards you have, and *this* one," he shook it, "this plan might actually work."

"It *has* to work," I said back, reaching out behind me for the comforting sturdiness of the table.

WE HAULED THE card table outside and rested it on a boulder. It rocked a little but we steadied it with a few bricks that we found scattered around. Poole was panting from the effort. He stood off to one side, one hand on his hip and the other wrapped tightly around his canteen. He was eyeing the table warily, like a man who'd been savaged by a dog and was now unwilling to trust any animal.

After what I'd done, I should have felt the same. But where Poole kept his distance from the table, only touching it when absolutely necessary, I kept my hand on it. I caressed it like a possessive lover.

"When do you want to start?" asked Poole, screwing on the cap to his canteen. He wiped at his mouth with the back of his hand.

"No time like the present," I replied, trying to hide my eagerness.

Poole heard some of it because he shot me a hard look, but he didn't acknowledge it. "What card are you going to play—the golem or the giant?"

I studied both cards for a long time. "The giant," I decided.

"Because it's stronger?"

"No, it's just a feeling." I answered honestly. The cards were split pretty evenly but I just *knew* the giant was the card to play.

Poole stared at me. "You're betting our lives on a feeling?"

I didn't answer. Instead, I threw the card down onto the table-top then I held my hand out to Poole. He was quiet for the longest moment yet, then he sighed and plucked his only card out of his pocket and held it out to me. "We're gonna die, aren't we?"

For the second time, I didn't answer. I tossed his card down on top of mine and then pressed the button to activate the table. The high pitched *seeeeeuuuuuutttt* noise echoed out across this silent world. The last time I'd played two cards, they'd snapped together in the air like magnets before hitting the table. This time, the cards kind of oozed towards each other, melting like two pats of butter in a hot pan.

Besides me, Poole moaned. "It's happening again . . ."

The hairs at the back of my neck stood on end, and my breath behind the mask was coming quick and uneven. I watched as the cards start to crumble and smoke. The worst thing was the *smell*. The shield held most of it in, but I could still smell the acrid earthy stink, one that was redolent of decay and deterioration, so different to the sulphuric stench of this world. The table-top started to vibrate and roll as if the midst of an earthquake. There was a loud explosion and then a deep crack appeared, splitting the table-top arena almost in two.

Poole's eyes widened and he turned to me. "What the *fuck* is going on, Samus?"

I couldn't tear my own eyes from where the table was shaking so violently that I genuinely thought it might explode into a thousand pieces. Two huge hands reached out of the crack and plunged into the wood of the table, gauging great scars into it. Then the hands heaved and forearms appeared, then elbows, then huge monstrous biceps, then . . .

A giant.

It climbed from the crack easily, slowly, and stood upright, one muscled leg either side of the crack. Its smooth skin was the colour of dust and moss, and it had long twisted hair hanging down its mountainous back. What looked like a small forest of young saplings were growing from its shoulders. The giant grew upwards like a tree, slow and steady, and within a few minutes the top of his boulder-like head was touching the shield. He had to kneel to avoid being zapped.

"Will the shield hold it in?" Poole asked, his face pale and damp with sweat. He rubbed anxiously at his lips.

"Probably." I took a deep breath and forced myself to say the next words. "But we need it to break free. It can't fight the dragon from inside the arena. It needs to be out here."

"We can't do that . . ." If possible, Poole's face went paler.

The giant glanced slowly towards the sky. He turned his head this way and then the other, listening to the music of the evening that only he could hear. Then he rolled his head back on his shoulders and let out a deep, cavernous roar. Even behind the shield it was loud enough to hurt my ears.

A few miles away, there were the sounds of a huge explosion. No, that's not quite right. It was like an explosive snap, like something had suddenly appeared. A vicious wind picked up around us, ruffling my hair into my eyes. Dust swirled faster and faster as the wind grew. Then we heard the sounds of flapping, like a sheet in the wind. Or a large bird. Or . . .

Or a dragon.

"Oh, god . . ." Poole whimpered. He took an unsteady step away from the arena. "Oh, god, it's here . . ."

My eyes fell to where the giant was still roaring into the shield. Feeling an overwhelming surge of *déjà vu,* I started to bang on the shield, feeling that tingling zap of electricity run through my fingers. "Here! Up here!"

The giant stopped roaring and watched me, his face passive but interested, as I brought my hands down on the shield over and over again. After a few moments, the giant got slowly to his feet, one knee unbending and then the other. He was so big now that he had to bend from the waist. With one upwards glance, he curled his fingers into huge fists and started to bang on the shield with his insurmountable strength. It looks less than a minute before he'd punched a hole and was climbing through. He hit the floor with such a force that both Poole and I staggered.

I saw something move out of the corner of my eye and terror seized me. The dragon was like a shadow against the ruined sky. A glorious and jewel-like shadow. It had grown in the cycles since I'd last seen it and was now at least fifty feet wide. Its fiery scales winked in the dull light of the sky.

Free from the restrictions of the gaming table, the giant continued to grow. It now stood taller than both me and Poole, then taller than the remaining walls of the burned down card building, then taller than the old oak trees that used to stand on the street corner.

Neither me nor Poole hung around. I gripped him by the shoulder and pushed him into a stumbling run towards the building where we found the card table. There wasn't much safety to be found in a burned-out building that only had three walls left, but it was definitely better than nothing. We crouched behind a crumbling wall and waited.

The vicious wind whipped at our clothes and hair. The skin on my cheeks stung from the dust whirling in the air. I watched with watery eyes as the dragon flew closer and closer. The giant didn't move, didn't even react to the threat. He just stood calm, the sprouting saplings bending in the wind. The dragon spotted its target and, still airborne, let out a deafening screech. It tilted its wings back until its entire body smoothed into a "V" shape and then it dove towards the giant, still screeching.

Slowly—so slowly—the giant brought his fists up to chest level, his stone-like biceps bulging. Beside me, Poole was shouting, pointing up to the sky.

"What?" I screamed. But the screeching was so loud that I couldn't even hear my own voice.

He pointed again, his expression urgent and terrified, and the message clicked; if the two beasts collided, then we were in the way. We would be crushed. I grabbed him by the upper arm and wrenched him to his feet. We half-sprinted, half-stumbled to safety, but every second my eyes weren't on that giant, my terror grew.

We were almost at a safe distance when the two beasts smashed together. The force of the impact was like an old-world bomb, and we were knocked from our feet and sent sprawling into the ashes. A plume of flame shot passed us, missing by inches. The heat was so intense that I could barely breathe. We clutched at each other like frightened children.

But then the heat was gone as quickly as it had come. The giant had reached up and stopped the flames with his hand. The dragon blinked once then reared up onto its back legs. From our flat position on the floor, we watched as the beasts attacked. The giant was standing his ground, huge and unmoveable like a mountain. Two enormous fists flew out and connected with the jaw of the dragon with startling speed. It hopped backwards, letting out a surprised snort of flames, its small oil-drop eyes suddenly wary.

The giant didn't hesitate. He took two lumbering steps forward and threw out his fists again, barely reacting when a great fireball hit him square on the chest. The fireball rolled off his bulky body, not even singeing his marble skin, and flew off into the distance. I let out a terrified bark of laughter, knowing that the fireball would have hit us dead-on if not for the giant standing in the way.

The giant pounded on the dragon's neck, each blow landing with a meaty thump. I thought he was winning, but the dragon whipped him effortlessly away with his tail, sending him flying into the air. The giant smashed into an old card house, ripping through the half-standing walls with a tremendous crash.

"This isn't going to work! We've got to get out of here!" Poole screamed into my ear as another ball of fire shot by. The giant wasn't there to stop it this time and I made the mistake of breathing in just as the wall behind us exploded in flames. The heat was intense, so intense that my breath caught in my throat and I couldn't release it to take another. My lungs were burning up! Panicked, I started to fumble at the straps of my mask, but

Poole wrenched my fingers away with a shake of his head.

"You'll die. You can't breathe this air." He staggered to his feet, and I saw with horror that the scraggly hair at the back of his head was alight. He must have felt the burn at the same time because he slapped at it, crying out. "We have to get out of here. The fire . . ."

"I can't . . ." I croaked.

Where could I go that the Confederacy wouldn't find me?

They will kill me, over and over again.

But at least here the dragon can only kill me once.

Then that other voice spoke, whispering a truth I didn't want to hear.

You can't go because the wager isn't over yet. The winner isn't decided.

The game is still on.

Overhead, the dragon circled and breathed fire down onto the giant.

The giant barely noticed, absorbing the flames like they were sunlight. The only thing moving was his eyes as they followed the beast dancing in the air around it. They went on like this for a few minutes, in a holding pattern. Suddenly, the giant threw its head back, let out an ear-splitting roar and dropped to his knees, plunging his fists into the ground. The earth thundered around us, and I could feel deep rolling vibrations beneath my body which grew more and more violent as the seconds passed. Smoking cracks appeared, just like the one the giant had climbed out of. One opened up close to us, and I could smell that earth stink rising out of it.

"Fuck this!" Poole screamed. His clothes were smoking, and his eyes were dancing wildly. "Come with me, Samus, or die here . . ."

"I can't . . ."

"You have to!"

"I can't!" I yelled. "The game isn't over yet!"

Poole gave me one last agonised look—one that was full of an expression that I couldn't decipher—then he legged it, crouching as low as he could to avoid detection. Less than a minute later, his ship was in the sky and soaring away, leaving me on this terrible planet alone.

I lifted my head to look over to where the giant and dragon

were still battling. Neither looked damaged and neither looked tired. Even so, I knew something terrible was going to happen. A deep sense of foreboding filled me. Struggling to breathe as I was, I climbed unsteadily to my feet. I couldn't breathe. I could barely see. I was so hot that I was burning up . . .

But I needed to watch the game.

The giant was still on its knees, one huge arm embedded in the ground, and the dragon was no longer flying. It rested one wing on the floor like a crutch, its terrible claws scrabbling at the ground. It was watching the giant warily. Then, as if some signal had passed between them, they moved. Synchronised, the dragon started to inhale, its nostrils wide and quivering, its head twisted over its shoulder just as the giant wound its fist back, his muscles as hard as rock.

But instead of punching the dragon, the giant forced its hands downwards, ripping up the earth. The ground, so dusty and sandy before, suddenly became viscous. It *flowed* up his arm, around him and into him. I could see it running beneath his stony skin. He was absorbing the planet by the tonne, accepting the dust into himself as if it was returning home.

And the giant grew bigger.

His muscles got harder, more lethal-looking.

The saplings on his back became stronger, thicker, bushier, and more . . . *alive.*

Soon he was towering over the dragon.

I scrambled to my feet and started to back away. The atmosphere was crackling like a pre-storm. The dragon opened its jaws, let out an ear-piercing screech and then the flames came. What he'd breathed before was nothing to this. This intense heat, this scorching agony, surpassed even the Night of the Dragon Cards.

I could feel my skin blistering and my blood heating in my veins. Every hair seemed to curl up and crisp. I wanted to cry out but the pain, the heat . . . it was all too much.

Is that how all those people felt as they burned up?

But even now, as I felt like I was being burned alive, I still couldn't tear eyes from the game. My last dying thought would be . . . did I win?

With a roar, the giant bent at the waist and forced his hands down the dragon's throat, stopping the flames in their path. The heat immediately dulled and I could breathe again. He kept surging forward, his fist sliding further and further down the dragon's throat and deeper into the core of its belly. He was like an earthy river, flowing into the beast to smother the flames at the source.

The dragon lurched, its claws drumming and scrabbling around for purchase in the earth. Smoke and steam started to pour from its eyes. It let out one last screech of agony and then it burst into flames. The fire travelled across its body, setting every scale alight with a strange white-blue flame. I watched, on the brink of unconsciousness, as the dragon sank to its knees, its head hitting the ground with a tremendous crash.

Even then the giant didn't stop flowing into the dragon. Soon there was nothing left but two smouldering piles of dirt.

And at the very top was one little sapling, rocking gently in the warm breeze.

Kiln Fired

Steve Toase

TOPSOIL IN A pile on the left of the table, clay in the middle, and river silt to the right. Sophie picks up a handful of the last and squeezes. Stagnant water drips into the table cloth. Her skin smells of waterfalls and drowning. She presses the dirt into the woven willow branches. Slides in a small clay ball pierced with thorns. Continues building.

WALKING TO THE factory Sophie stayed close to the walls as if the brick clay would protect her. In the distance smoke plumes rose up from kilns already firing plates and cups made by the night shift. The air smelt of soil and scorching. She inhaled and the scent calmed her.

Through the gate the Barton sisters clumped around the path to the painting hut. There was no way past them. Iron fencing cut off choices. Funnelled the workers in only one direction. Their words of spite hung in the air and tainted the scent of clay. Spoiled each breath. Sophie ignored them, staring straight ahead as she marched past.

Her workstation was at the end of the row, farthest from the little natural light coming through high level windows. A single angle-poise lamp made up the shortfall. She draped her coat over her chair, ignoring the slight discomfort of her hood pressing into the small of her back. Better that than to find it slashed once more.

The first plate was already on the stand. She reached for the gilding brush. This time the sisters hadn't cut the bristles, instead they'd creased them. Bending and crushing them, so any attempt to run the gold paint around the plate's rim would be an error. A docking from her pay-packet. She raised her hand and waited for the supervisor to notice.

"Yes?"

Sophie held up the ruined brush, one hand around her wrist. Still she shook.

"Third one this week."

She nodded, because how could she say anything?

"It will come out of your wages."

She nodded once more. Wages already lower as she was fifteen plates behind the rest of the shift. Across the table Janine Barton smirked, even as the gold-heavy bristles of her brush swept around the porcelain and moved onto the next.

A HANDFUL OF topsoil next, with all the rotted crop and blackened barley left in place. Patches of fertiliser bags and rust flakes. This is harder to work into the willow. Harder to keep from crumbling than the silt. Using water from the sink she dampens her hands and presses hard. Forms muscle strands along the willow. Cords of soil. She glances at the loop of wood at the top. The poppet does not have a face yet, but she knows what expression it will wear when it does.

HISTORY IS WRITTEN in the blood of picked scabs, and Sophie had a long history with the Barton sisters. Nursery and school, they'd marked her growing older in punches and punishments. Always far from anyone in authority.

From the factory door Sophie watched them stand together outside, cigarettes in their hands held low. There was no way out apart from walking past them toward the main gate.

The burning ash went right through her sleeve, though she managed to pull away before it scorched her arm. Her coat was ruined nonetheless. A bullet wound of a burn filling the air with the reek of melted nylon.

"Careful," Fay Barton, the eldest said, turning the yellow filter around in her fingers. "You've ruined my smoke now."

Carole and Janine both laughed and turned their backs on Sophie. They didn't need to do anything else. Just keep pushing. Keep chipping away. Keep wearing her down until they drove her out of the painting huts too, like they had driven her out of two schools and the streets where she'd grown up.

Even as Sophie grabbed Fay's hair, tearing clumps of scalp loose, she knew she would not win the fight. They were on her in moments, welts opening up and down her face as their nails raked her cheeks. Then the older women on the shift dragged them apart and it was over. Sophie shoved her hands into her pockets before covering her face. The scars would heal white. She could live with that. It was the scars that left no mark that hurt the most.

COLLECTING ALL THREE soils together, Sophie binds them with white lily petals. Compresses the dirt against the table until the flowers crease and crack. Once she has the vague form she wedges it into the wicker hoop. Next she builds up the ball with clay until the head is shaped.

THE FOREMAN'S OFFICE overlooked the working floor. The smell of paint more intense near the roof of the factory where the fumes rose and settled. No wonder he spent so little time in here, Sophie thought.

The door opened, window glass shifting slightly as he let Fay, Carole, and Janine in first, then slammed it shut behind her.

"Miss Fothergill. I'm extremely disappointed in this behaviour. You've always been such a good conscientious worker. Now we seem to have problem after problem."

He paused, adjusting his coat as he sat down in the chair, re-arranging papers on his desk as if he needed to keep his hands busy.

"I'm especially concerned that the focus of your poor behaviour has been the Barton sisters. I know you've been here much longer, but just because you're established doesn't mean you can bully newcomers."

Sophie had never heard Fay cry before.

"It's not our fault that our Dad got ill and had to retire and we had to find new jobs. It's been so hard on the family. We're just trying to fit in. Make the best of it."

Sophie watched the foreman stand and put his arm around Fay. The two younger sisters stayed in the background and kept silent. Sophie felt her cheeks burning. Whether through anger or injury she wasn't sure.

"You're suspended without pay for one week, Sophie. Come back with a better attitude."

Sophie nodded. In her pocket her fingers twisted through the follicles of hair.

BITS OF SKIN were still attached to the strands. She pulls them out of the old night cream pot and holds them up in the air. Laying them on the table, she plaits them until they make a single braid. Clay crumbs stain the scalp. It does not matter. She presses the hair into the wet clay of the figure. Picks up another handful of clay. Layers it until the hair is no longer visible.

THE ASHTRAY ON the table between Sophie and her aunt Margaret was piled with cold cigarette filters by the time she'd finished talking. When Sophie went silent Margaret walked across to the sideboard, grabbed the bottle of sherry, and poured two glasses.

"You're not going to win are you?"

"In a fight? No. There's three of them, and they're sneaky. Do everything on the quiet."

"Drink your sherry," her aunt said, sipping her own. Sophie picked up the glass and swilled the fortified wine around then took a mouthful.

"Then if they're going to be sneaky, you have to be sneakier. Sharper. Work in the shadows. I may have a solution."

The book was early 20th century, pages stained with dirt and some accident that had sodden the paper in the past. Across the front was written one word; Lutumancy.

"Clay magic," her aunt said, noticing Sophie's confused expression at the unfamiliar word on the cover. "Latin."

Some of the entries were about processes she knew happened on an industrial scale down at the factories where generations of her family worked. Others were smaller. Precise.

"The whole area's built on clay magic," Aunt Margaret said.

"The transformation of dirt to beauty. Soil to porcelain. As with any magic there is a flip side, a hidden side where the maggots clean the bones of the dead. Where the fire of the kiln burns away instead of creates."

Her aunt opened the sideboard. Moved her bingo pens and puzzle books. Showed Sophie the artefacts she'd made over her sixty long years working in the factories. Sophie did not ask where the bodies were.

For three days of the suspension it rained, for another two Sophie left town to visit friends in Manchester. On the Wednesday at the heart of the week she found herself on the edge of town by the overgrown claypits, where furrows and river met. From her rucksack she took three plastic bags. Into the first she shovelled river silt, fine and foetid. Heavy with stagnant water. Into the second, topsoil. The third the clay underneath. Even the birds stealing seeds from the dirt did not pay her attention. The rucksack pivoted her back with the extra weight. She walked back to the bus stop and waited in the cold to head back into town.

SHE DOES NOT need to be able to read the words to write them on the curling piece of paper. Some were less letters than angular symbols. Sophie copies each one perfectly, wrapping the thin strip around a pin and forcing it into the poppet's spine.

HER BREAK CAME late that first Monday back. A fifteen minute interruption in painting delicacies of gold around the plates. She had just enough time to get to the kiln and back. Slide the figure into the firing batch. The cost, a pint of beer already delivered the night before. Everything was done for the price of a beer. Even dark magic.

The figure of dirt and death was still crude, the fingers not separated or feet shaped well. It did not matter. She watched the supervisor slide it onto the rack well away from the fine porcelain. Close the door and turn up the heat.

"Come back in five hours."

She was back on time, sat at her station and painting. Her eye caught Fay's across the room. Watched her smile as she mimed putting out a cigarette, probably on Sophie's arm. Sophie put her head down and stared at the tip of the brush curling gold around the rim of another plate, and another and another.

SHE HAD NEVER been near the kiln when it was opened before. The hit of heat scorched her skin, and filled the air with the reek of burning hair. She stepped back and nearly knocked over a stack of plates waiting to be boxed.

"This is yours, I think," the kiln foreman said, holding out a soot blackened lump of clay. It was intact and recognisable, though not evenly fired. She wasn't sure what the result would have been if the poppet had exploded in the kiln. Destroyed itself before the words had burnt away in the heat.

Someone pressed a hammer into her hand.

"Do it out of sight in the yard."

She nodded and cradled the figure as she left into the sunlight.

THE FACE DID not need to be life like, or even precise. Truth be told it did not need to be there at all. Hair and clay were enough, but Sophie itches to decorate the figure. Sitting down at the kitchen table, she spreads out the paints and brushes and slowly decorates the head, swirling on eyes and a downturned mouth. Painting a cigarette between the undecorated fingers.

AN OLD ICE-cream tub emptied of sewing supplies cradles the poppet when she travels into work. A bed of kitchen roll cushions the fragile clay against breaks. She does not know if it will work. She does know she is running out of choices.

THEY CORNERED HER against the wall, neck gripped against the corrugated iron.

"Been sneaking out, have you?" Fay said, her nails digging into the tight skin around Sophie's throat, the torn edges drawing half moons of blood.

"Going to be hard to keep that apartment when you have no job."

With each word she dragged Sophie's head forward and smashed it back against the scorching metal. Sophie's arm was up before she could stop herself.

The pieces of scalp that spattered across Sophie's face were soft and warm. When she brought the hammer up a second time the, claw got stuck in Fay's skull and she pulled it loose. A large fragment of bone folded out still attached to the skin, and Fay fell to the ground. Sophie couldn't hear the two other sisters screaming. She glanced down. On the floor the poppet lay shattered, blackened scalp and hair caught in kiln hardened clay. Real fragments of scalp mixed in with the clay doll's. The other two sisters were facing away from her. She lifted the hammer once more.

Goblin Harvest

Suzanne J. Willis

AFTER THE EARTH had turned brown and the elders' memories of rain had turned to myth, the goblins crawled from underground. It wasn't clear, at first, that an unknown race was migrating from the darkness beneath the dust; they were just glimpses of shadows slipping between brittle trees or odd slitherings across the sand under bloody sunsets. Sometimes there were strange whisperings in the night, and the elders said they sounded a little like the wind that used to sweep across the plains.

Everything had been still for so long before the whispers and the shadows.

One morning the boy, Dart, awoke to a cracked-bell call ringing across the Taie settlement. It shook the crumbling minarets, the broken-down buildings, and mixed the silt back with the water in its purifiers. It was a new unknown, and everyone walked, with trepidation, into the streets. Later, they learnt that it had happened in settlements across the land.

Insubstantial no more, the goblins stood in their hundreds. They were man-shaped but no human ever looked like this. As though hewn from the earth itself. Those closest were formed from the rocks that lined the seashore, the planes of their bodies eroded into shape by the ocean. Others walked through the dust towards the settlers on tree-root legs, their bodies of rough bark and arms spindled, leafless branches. What Dart had first taken to be morning shadows slid along the walls and patched roofs with a scuttling sound, slipping from sight as he turned to get a better look.

The goblins vastly outnumbered them, and weapons would have been no use anyway. Dart's mother pushed him behind her, protecting him with her body. Another woman began to cry softly.

One of them stepped forward—it was eight foot and monstrous—water slowly dripping from the stalactites on its ears, chin, shoulders, down its limestone skin, and pooling at its feet.

"The land is ours. Our governance will be fair. Anyone who chooses not to submit can leave, peacefully, and move to the Interior."

Only a fool would head into the desert. The journey itself would leave them as bones. No-one moved. And as quietly and quickly as that, the goblins became the earth's caretakers, and the people began life on their ruined planet anew.

THE GOBLINS PAIRED up settlement children with their own young—forcing friendships between the children of two different species, forging ties between them.

Dart was paired with Sorrell, although he couldn't understand why: a dusty, unruly, tow-headed boy with a daughter of the ruling clan—the Gaeia. She was as close to a priestess or princess as the goblins got.

Sorrell was like something from another time, a dream. Head to toe she was cloaked in verdant moss, something incredibly rare in their parched land. Tiny white flowers grew from her on the full moon. She smelled like water and aniseed and earth. Raw fire opals grew at her throat and encircled her wrists.

On the day Dart met her in the yard of the old wooden meeting hall, he was terrified. No-one had explained what was happening or thought to soothe the fears of a frightened child. Sorrell's face was impassive, unreadable. Then he noticed it— the tiny flower growing from her left hand was trembling. She was scared, too.

Dart smiled in relief and Sorrell took him to her land, a vast, grassy paddock, basalt-pocked and surrounded by ancient cliffs.

She led him through the long grass until they reached a strange object that didn't seem to fit at all. It was made of carved, polished wood and sat, still and regal, under the endless blue sky.

She asked Dart what it was and he laughed at the absurdity of it, once it dawned on him.

"It's a piano," he said, before realising she would have no idea what that meant. "It makes music." He pressed one of the keys, then another, and another. "Well, when they're played right they do."

"They're all over my land," she'd told him. "And they keep appearing. Almost as if they find their own way here."

And, with a mystery to share, Dart and Sorrell became friends.

TO THIS DAY, she is my closest and most trusted friend.

DART STOOD AT the edge of the airfield, waiting for the rest of his squadron to return. He had counted eight others so far. Two more to go. His skin prickled slightly as he sniffed the air. As the best weathermaker of the Taie settlement, Dart was deadly accurate. He knew that the rain would be here soon, for today's cloud-run had gone well. Until the end.

The Weathermaker Wars between the Taie and Cathla settlements were escalating. In the twenty-odd years since the goblins took over, the Cathla had become their sworn enemy. Without fighting, their weathermakers would steal the clouds and take the water for themselves. Finite resources meant an endless struggle to survive.

His dark eyes searched the skies for the telltale flash of silver and copper against the black clouds, heavy with iodised precipitant. They should be coming in from the north, he knew. There would be no sound to herald them, for the aircraft—many-winged, with cogs and peripheral, coppery projections—were powered by goblin-breath, drawn up from underground by great turbines that lined the field. It made for silent, stealthy aircraft.

Dart wasn't sure why the Cathla pilots didn't use the same fuel, but their craft thundered through the sky with murderous fury. He shivered at the memory of the sound pounding through him. The enemy had been fiercer than usual today, had seemed to come from *nowhere* as his squadron bombed the clouds with the last of the silver iodide. He had never known them to be so bellicose. So desperate.

With the Cathla in pursuit, Dart had banked sharply then flown up towards the sun, knowing that his silvery craft would be lost in its glare. Shots volleyed below him and smoke thickened the air.

Dart flew low and crossed east, west, north in an attempt to evade any Cathla tracking him. But one hundred klicks north-east of the settlement, he saw something green and shimmering on the dusty plains below that puzzled him. Symbols were carved around its border; he didn't understand them but they had a familiarity about them that made Dart uneasy and were guarded by giant limestone goblins. It worried him worse than the Cathla ever had.

Now, as the first fat raindrops spat down from the clouds that rolled towards the settlement's meagre crops, he knew the last two gunners weren't coming back. There simply wasn't enough fuel after so long. Dropping his head, he whispered a word of goodbye. Gunner lives may be cheap to the goblins, but not to *him*.

The aircraft lining the field gleamed in the last of the light. Where the raindrops hit, spindly fingers of steam rose from them, reaching skywards.

Dart turned and put his hand on the fuselage, running his fingers along it as he walked. Reaching the tail, something delicate and cobwebby caught his eye. He reached up and brushed it lightly, his skin freezing under its sweeping touch.

A thready piece of cloud had snagged on the tail; cold, grey, ephemeral. Opening his leather coat, Dart pulled an empty glass vial from the rows that lined it, and scooped the cloud snippet into it, then replaced the stopper. In tiny handwriting he recorded the date on the label, then "Miet" and "Belle": the names of the friends he had lost that day to the skies.

THAT NIGHT, DART slipped away from the town, with its taverns and back alleys and squalor, to meet Sorrell. He still felt raw from the long, long day. He knew that he had seen something on the cloud-run that was supposed to be a secret. His fingers fluttered as they did when he was uneasy, counting in fours as his thumb touched each one, then starting again, as he walked away from the bustle of the settlement.

The rain beat down—*my rain*, Dart thought—in neat drops. He calculated that it would stop by the time he reached Sorrell.

It eased steadily and starlight broke through the clouds as he climbed through the narrow, rocky passage and made his way across the paddock. He passed a square, dark wooden box with curved legs nestled in the dry branches of a fallen gum. Its top half was still vaguely L-shaped, although the weather had stolen all the colour and sharp lines from its teeth.

Everywhere, under trees, half-hidden in the grasses, and at the cave entrances were pianos in various states of ruination. He thought about the day he had discovered the secret of the pianos. It had happened one afternoon, when he was only thirteen, lying flat on his belly and dozing while he waited for Sorrell. A rustle in the grass woke him: a huge piano trundled across the land, not twenty feet away. For a strange moment, Dart thought that he and Sorrell were right. They *did* make their own way here.

Then he saw the oily blackness underneath it, with its telltale shadow movements. Chitter-goblin—best known for informing on errant humans to the Gaeia.

But Dart was young and bold, and crawled over to it as it pushed the instrument against a tunnel opening. It turned to face him as he slithered forward, staring at him with beady eyes.

Dart smiled and pointed to the piano. "Why?" he asked.

The chitter-goblin blinked. "We reap your harvest," it rasped.

"I don't understand," Dart replied.

"Beautiful things should be with us. We reap your harvest of the past," it said, stroking the ivory keys. The chitter-goblin shimmered, mirage-like, in the afternoon heat. Then it was gone.

He had never told Sorrell about that afternoon so many years ago.

"What's an old weathermaker like you doing out tonight, Dart?"

Her voice broke him out of his reverie. He looked around and found her propped against a hunk of basalt, smiling at him in the orange light of the rising moon.

"Sorrell." He felt lighter, less alone, here with her.

She touched a mossy fingertip to his cheek as he sat beside her. "What is it?"

He shook his head. "Do you think there will ever be a time when we don't kill one another for clouds and a splash of water?"

She put her hand over his. "This is survival. If someone tries to take what's yours and without it you'll wither and die, what else can you do?"

He nodded, but didn't reply. After what he had seen today, doubt nibbled at him.

"Have you brought me something, Dart?" It was an old habit between them, since he was a boy.

He opened his jacket. Lining it on both sides were a series of pockets and hooks, flaps and tiny belts and buckles. Glass vials and cork-stoppered bottles were strapped securely in place. It was his memory collection—copper cogs and cloud traces from the war; dried leaves of sage and rosemary from his first lover's window-box; fragile fish scales from the forbidden coast; goblin-breath, stolen from the decommissioned turbine on the settlement's southside.

He rummaged about for a moment, pretending to have forgotten where he'd put her gift, until Sorrell grew impatient and pulled his ear.

"Ow! Okay, close your eyes." He laid the jar gently in her open palm.

"Oh, Dart, it's beautiful!" She tipped the bright blue wisp into her hand and stroked it. "What is it? I've never seen anything like it! Where did you get it?"

"It's a feather," he said. "We were on a recon, in the small balloon. It's so quiet up there, peaceful." He knew how much Sorrell, as an earth-bound creature, loved to hear about the open skies. "It was early morning, the sun just rising, and there was nothing else around. And the feather swirled past on an updraft. I reached out and got it for you."

The feather shifted a little in her hand as Dart pulled a rumpled piece of paper from his pocket, pointing out the picture of a blue-wren. "It's from a bird, just like this one. I've never seen one, but they must have been around a long time ago."

Sorrell looked excited. "It must mean that there's one around here now, don't you think? That has to be good. If creatures are coming back there must be water—" she stopped suddenly, suspiciously. *What was she keeping from him?*

He shook his head, telling himself he was being foolish. "I'm sure it's good, too. Now, I want to know what you've been doing to keep out of mischief."

She gazed around her, as though searching for the right words. "It's time for me to form clan bonds—to become part of the Gaeia. I'm betrothed." She held out her right hand. Sorrell's palm was branded, a deep burn in her soft, mossy skin.

Dart felt cold with horror, wanting to speak but feeling as though he was choking on the words. He knew, now, what the symbols he had seen meant. "There's something your people are hiding from us. They've built—I'm not sure, I think it's a reservoir. And I think they're directing most of the rain to it rather than the crops. It's not right, Sorrell, it didn't seem right at all. It was huge and on each corner of the dam, carved into the earth, is that same symbol you've got on your hand. I—"

"Stop it, you're hurting me!"

He hadn't realised he was gripping her wrist tightly. Letting it go, he stood and began to pace. "You're in this, too. What is it? What aren't you telling me?" Dart's fingers fluttered frantically—one, two three, four, one, two, three . . .

"I don't know what you mean, but this is my duty, my birthright. I can't imagine that the clan fathers would be doing anything against the settlement."

Dart frantically scratched something in the dust and motioned for Sorrell to look. "This is the symbol for our settlement, the Taie. And this is for the Cathla. That brand is those two symbols bound together. Don't you see? This is a union between the two settlements, but we were taught to hate the Cathla!" Dart thought about all the flashes of copper and silver craft plummeting silently to the ground under torrents of Cathla bullets. He and his squadron went out afterwards to retrieve the bodies, only to find that the Cathla had always gotten there first and cut the throats of any survivors. The earth was stained crimson with their blood.

Sorrell was looking at Dart as though he was a stranger. It unnerved him and he counted in agitation.

"We're *dying*, and your people are creating secret alliances!" *We kill one another for rain, and we are taught who to hate.*

The fear buries itself deep inside us because we don't understand the things that scare us. It makes us feel righteous. But while I have been taught to hate, my love and my desires are my own.

Dart's desire was for a life that wasn't ruled by war or scrabbling out an existence. He didn't hate the goblins, who shared their ways with the settlers. Like the goblin-breath that was mined from under the earth, built up over millennia like the fabled peat. They used it to fuel the planes and then released it into the clouds, after the silver iodide, with secret words to send them where they needed them. And being part of that made Dart feel like a god. *Like I could soar through the clouds on burnished wings, shifting seasons and saving my people from privation.*

Back on the ground, though, as the casualties were counted, Dart didn't want to be a god. So he took comfort in his friendship with Sorrell, who would never know the skies or the terrible exhilaration of its battles. That was his peaceful place.

"I . . . I know." She held his hands in hers, the pair of them dark shadows against the bone pale grasses.

They sat quietly for a moment, the moon just a ghostly sliver on the horizon. Only the starlight and the luminous dust of the moon-moths flitting through the trees lit the night.

"Don't you see, though? You *are* right," she blurted out. "There is an alliance between the two settlements—but it's not new, it's been like that always. My betrothal to the daughter of the Cathla is part of a union of centuries." She looked around uneasily and lowered her voice. "If they find out you know this, that I've told you . . . but I can't tell you how awful I feel for you . . ."

Dart was too shocked to think clearly. "But the war. I mean, people are dying and—" Anger surged through him and he shouted. "Why haven't you told me this before?"

"I never knew until today! It's only because of the betrothal rights that they've told me. And keep your voice down." She sighed, a sound like wind through the plain grasses. "You're my truest friend, Dart. Do you believe that if I knew this all along, I would have let you fly all those missions?"

He stared at the ground, shredding grass tips with his fingers. Something slithered in the darkness behind them and the far-away sounds of the settlement's taverns echoed across the night.

"I trust you. But we trusted in all of you. So why a war? Why this life for us?" Dart knew that, as earth-bound creatures, the goblins needed the weathermakers to direct the rain. But it had to be more than that. More than something so *practical.*

Sorrell lay back, staring up at the cold blue stars. Dart lay beside her, resting his head on her chest and wishing that he could hear a heartbeat inside it. Wishing, perhaps, that she was human.

She stroked his hair as she whispered to him. "We lived under the earth for millennia, we are of all her elements. This new age, our living on the surface, is only a little younger than you are. Our young come from the rock, the soil, the water, the trees. The earth labours for us and we nourish her in return. The Gaeia tell us that our race will live forever, but that yours . . ."

Dart shivered but didn't pull away. He knew the ugliness of history, but still.

"We have survived this long," he replied.

"But just as we are of the earth, you humans are *of war*. And while you fight one another, you don't rebel against us. The very nature of your people is not to strive for peace—you need a cause to believe in, enemies to revile, heroes to worship. The war exists because *humans* exist."

"You speak as though it's me who thinks like that. You know that's not so." He pushed away the memories of that god-like feeling and the thought that maybe Sorrell was right. "I can't live like this forever."

She held him close. "I know. But the land is ours, and there's nothing here for you but the life we write for you. I want more for you than that, but what can you do?"

He sat up and pulled her with him. "The first of the weathermakers—all gone now, dead or disappeared—told stories of another land, out in the open oceans. It wasn't ruined in the same way that the rest of the lands were. Exiles made their home there, but the ocean around it is fierce and cruel, it can't be reached by boat. Only by plane. Only weathermakers. And there's no—"

"None of us there," Sorrell finished for him.

It had only ever been an embryonic dream. But with every

person lost in battle, every paltry crop he saw grow from the hard earth, it grew stronger. It seemed to him, now, that it may be the only alternative.

"Come with me."

Sorrell shook her head. "You know I can't do that. I'm bound to the earth here—good or bad, it was gifted to me by the Gaeia. It's mine to guard and will bear my young. Even if I survived the flight, I wouldn't survive a different place. I'm not like you, Dart."

Shaking his head, he stood and began to walk through the paddock. Tall grass, pale gold and the green of dried sage spread out, edged by the caves and cliffs that hid the land. Gum trees and black-stumped, green topped bushes grew in clumps and red desert peas were scattered everywhere. It made him think of a dreamscape: there was so little colour among the sand, beige, brown of settlement life. He walked among the ruined pianos that dotted the land. Many had lost their lids and covers, exposing the hammers and strings like a dead man's ribs. In the salt bush one was merely a key-board and rotting wood case, the rest gone back to the earth. Some looked like drunks who have stumbled in the grass, unable to find their way home.

Stopping at one on which Sorrell tied her feather, he wondered if the ghosts of their music had snaked underground and soaked into the earth. The pianos, with their crumbling, sinking beauty suddenly felt hopeful to Dart. Understanding flooded through him—*"we reap your harvest."* Humans had harvested trees to make the pianos, in order to create music and awaken pleasure. In turn, the instruments were taken by the goblins and set in the open air, to be stripped back to their beginnings and washed back into the earth again, a completion of a cycle.

He plunked a bass note, held it down. It sounded like the distant drone of a Cathla engine, reverberating after he'd lifted his hand from the keyboard. He thought about the stolen goblin-breath he had in his vials. Would it be fuel enough to make it?

"I need to think about how to leave. It won't be for a while, and I might need your help."

Sorrell smiled at him and nodded. "I'd rather know that you're alive and safe, even if it's far away from here." She ran her hands across the piano's hammers.

"Don't you want more for yourself?"

"Things are as they should be, for me. Mostly. But there is one thing, though, that I've always wanted." She leaned forward and whispered it to Dart.

"Really?" he laughed and held out an empty glass vial. "Speak your wish into here. I'll keep it safe." He stoppered it when she was done and watched the tiny light and dark shadows flashing inside it. As he left, he promised to return once he knew what he was going to do.

Unseen by either of them, the oily shadow of a chitter-goblin slid through the trees. It pooled for a moment at the rotting base of an old upright, and then sunk beneath the earth.

THE NEXT MORNING they came for Dart, the goblins who looked and smelled like wet soil. He wouldn't let himself think about who had betrayed him or why. He knew (didn't he?) it couldn't be Sorrell, though. Never Sorrell. His fingers fluttered—one, two, three, four, one . . .

They took him to the divisional leader, who met Dart on the airfield among the gleaming planes and wisps of smoke rising from the vents of secret underground chambers. They looked like ghosts wafting between gravestones.

It was the same limestone and stalactite goblin who had spoken to the settlement on that first day, a lifetime ago. He was brief.

Special mission—storm clouds over the Tyness Seas—imperative for the Taie to win. "Succeed and you'll be a hero."

Dart knew the stories of weathermakers who were sent on special missions, so he knew, even before he got into his plane, that there wouldn't be enough fuel to return home. The fuel gauge was broken, so he was even robbed of the dignity of knowing when it would run out. The Tyness, though, could lead him to the land of weathermaker legends, but he wasn't nearly ready. Then again, he didn't have much of a choice.

He thought about fighting them, but they had the advantage in number, strength, and power. And Dart didn't want to die on the ground like a cur.

They may very well have shaped who I am, he thought, *but I am a weathermaker, and if I am to die, it will be far above the red and brown land to which the goblins are forever-bound, in the wide blue skies of which I am king.*

DART FELT LIKE he was flying through an enormous blue bubble, the sky searingly bright and the sea below sparked to life like a great, rippling creature. The two gunners, in their smaller craft, flew behind him, although they felt like warders instead of companions.

There, ahead—it took his breath away. The storm was unlike any he had ever seen—swollen, blue-black clouds, boiling and rolling across the sky. It funnelled water up from the ocean in a great spout. Lightning flashed and burned inside it, and Dart could hear the low rumble of thunder. In spite of everything, exhilaration leapt inside him. Now *this* was a storm.

As he got closer a few drops spattered his goggles and the wind lifted his hair.

Over the thunder was a low drone, barely audible. He looked around. Coming in from two o'clock—Cathla gunners. With the storm almost upon them, he turned to see his own gunners peel off and turn back, leaving him alone and wondering what lies they'd been told to convince them to do so.

The Cathla came in fast and low, the first spurt of bullets just missed his aircraft's nose. Dart didn't bother with evasive manoeuvres, which would have been useless in the open against two of them. Knowing it was his only chance against the less able Cathla, he turned his craft of copper and silver and secrets, and flew directly into the storm.

The Cathla were close on his tail as turbulence battered his plane and black clouds swirled around him like the remnants of old dreams. The noise of the storm roared and the thunder shook him, but Dart *felt* where the lightning would strike before he saw it. He swung his aircraft to the right then banked sharp left as it sharded through the air and caught one of the gunners following in his wake. The fuselage sparked a bright, almost-white blue and the engine screamed then shut out. The plane was tossed about, inconsequential to the storm. It spun, nose downward, out of sight, swallowed up as if it never existed.

The remaining gunner was craftier, not wasting his bullets or fuel on heroics. Instead he followed Dart at a distance, barely visible through the mist and driving rain. Dart's plane still shook and bounced, the wheel vibrating in his hands. If he had been any less a pilot, the storm would have bested Dart. With its tricksy, greenish light and thick cloud, it robbed him of any sense of direction, almost of up or down. But his craft responded to his weathermaking thaumaturgy.

Buffeted by the wind, stung by the rain, he whispered into the storm like a lover in the hours before dawn, flying in ever tighter circles downwards, downwards through the tempest. A flash of the Cathla's craft showed the left wing tipping downwards and the nose tilting. Dart knew that the gunner's sense of gravity was lost to him and he was hurtling through the air much faster than he imagined.

A sudden crack of gunfire burst out, almost grazing Dart's upper wings as he pulled up sharply, accelerating into the maw of the storm. He laughed aloud as, looking over his shoulder, he saw the gunner spiral away and crash into the white-capped waves, having realised too late that he had been lured into a death spiral and a briny grave.

Dart flew upwards, towards the daylight shining through the clouds in a funereal halo. They thinned, then he broke through to the eye of the storm, silent and still as death.

The great walls of cloud surrounded him, lit within by lightning. Misty tendrils whipped up and away in tiny funnels. At that moment, graced by violent beauty, he knew he was no god.

He pulled out the vial that contained Sorrell's wish and uncorked it, held it high. Rapturous, he listened as her words flew out. "I wish that a storm would come to my graveyard of ruined pianos. Fierce enough to lash the trees and drench the earth, gentle enough not to destroy. A storm for me, just for the joy of it."

Goblin words carried on goblin breath have their own magic. Her words swam around him on updrafts and currents, growing faint then fading as the storm snatched them away. He sent her a storm for her own joy and, at last, his weathermaking was not about war.

Having traversed the eye, the plane listed as Dart flew through the cloud's upper reaches and into the clear sky above.

WRAPPED UNDER A rock, Sorrell couldn't quite place the low

rumbling or the smell of something fresh and cool and entirely unfamiliar. She unfolded herself and slipped into the open.

The storm marched over Sorrell's land, and she closed her eyes as the wind whipped around her, lay flat on her back as the lightning and thunder shook the ground. Turning onto her stomach, the rain soaked through her; the smell of moss and earthy, hidden things filled her. The rain first formed rivulets then small creeks in the drier depressions, and the grass bowed in waves against the grey sky.

The earth danced with the elements.

Under the storm, another sound came from across her land, discordant notes in haphazard tunes. The music of ruined pianos; songs like memory made into sound.

She walked: here the wind rattled the exposed hammers of one, its faded keys dancing in a staccato frenzy. Then she ran her hands across an old grand, half-buried in the earth at an angle, streams of rain rolling across the keys. Further on, a plunking, tumbling, crash of notes came from a fading upright instrument that was one of the more recent additions. Lifting the lid, Sorrell found a family of pearly glass lizards running and jumping across the strings.

Sitting with her back against its fading wood, Sorrell watched and thought of Dart, who had surely sent her this most precious of things. *I will remember every moment, every drop, every note*, she thought. *And when next Dart comes in the dark of night, I will thank him and tell him of my storm.*

DART FLEW WEST across the Tyness Seas for more than an hour. The empty vial in his hand had contained the last of the breath stolen from the decommissioned mine. As it now worked its way through the engine of his craft, he hoped it would be enough. He had made his choice.

Feather-blue sky wrapped itself around him and inked the glittering ocean below. If the legends were more than hopeful words, the new land lay just over the horizon.

The edge of the world curved between past and future as he flew towards it.

The Poacher and the Priestess

Blake Jessop

LORD TAKEDA'S HORSEMEN gallop along the road toward her hiding place with the speed and destructive certainty of an earthquake. Their huge black horses match black-lacquered armour, and the sun glints from broad, winged kabuto helmets.

The priestess tumbles into the ditch, and her red silk hakama soaks in water with the eagerness of a man dying of thirst. She scrabbles desperately, trying to grab onto crackling reeds. Safe for a moment from being sucked under the mud and drowned, she unslings a bundle from around her neck. Her mud-slick fingers lose their purchase, and the statue within comes tumbling out to splash beside her.

The figurine is a smooth, perfect representation of a catfish carved in porous grey stone, big enough that she needs both hands to carry it. As soon as it touches the mud it starts to tremble.

The next thing she loses her grip on is her ceremonial staff. She tries to grab it again and ends up indecently contorted, one hand gripping the haft like a lifeline and the other groping for the figurine. She stamps one delicate foot on the statue to keep it still, and emits a small, distressed squeak when she sees that the mud has sucked the sandal off her foot. She balances like a toad, exhales sharply, and prays that Takeda's men will ride straight by.

The samurai call to each other, and rein their horses to a halt.

As the hooves of the cavalry clatter to a stop above her, a low voice hisses from the rushes beside the priestess.

"Find your own muddy hole, this one's mine."

It's all she can do not to scream. A pair of dark eyes glare at her from further down the ditch. The man looks like a poacher; he's filthy and has a bow lying beside him in the mud.

"No," he hisses as she draws breath, "be quiet."

Her eyes narrow, but she holds her tongue.

The pungent smell of horses wafts its way down to them, and there's a muffled thump as one of the samurai dismounts. There is sudden stillness in the absence of galloping horses, but the statue still rattles wetly under the priestess's foot. She presses down on it and holds her breath. The man with the dark eyes winces as the footsteps stop at the edge of the road.

They cower, absolutely motionless, until there's a sudden sharp smell and a tinkle of liquid. The samurai on the road starts whistling.

A look of such exquisite misery crosses the priestess's face that the poacher has to stifle a laugh. Someone chides the dismounted man, and the cavalry mount up and trot away.

Once the Takeda horsemen are a smudge of dust on the horizon, the poacher helps the priestess gather her things, and in a few minutes they're shaking mud from their clothes onto the road. The priestess's pleated ceremonial skirt has turned from red to brown. She thumps the staff's butt on the ground and crusted mud drops to the accompaniment of jangling rings on the crosspiece. At least the icon on the top has a cloth cover. The poacher doesn't feel the worse for wear after his stay in the ditch. His worn yukata doesn't look much different than it did before.

The priestess carefully re-wraps the catfish statue in its cloth sling and winds it back over her shoulder.

"Nice fish," he says in a gruff voice, like he hasn't spoken to anyone in a long time.

The priestess nods gravely. When she speaks, her voice is deeper and more resonant than he expects.

"It is a statue of Namazu, the god of earthquakes who was subdued by Takemikazuchi-no-Okami. I am returning it to a shrine in Hitachi."

"That's a long way," the poacher says, glancing back down the road at the dust. It's the same way the horsemen went. "I know these lands pretty well. There's a stream back from the road a ways west, and I might hunt us a rabbit."

She puts a hand to her stomach and looks at him uncertainly. Taking his measure.

"I'm a poacher, I don't care why you were hiding from the Lord Takeda's men."

"I don't know if I can trust you," she says.

"Well, can you make up your mind off the road while I hunt some dinner?"

Something pulls at the corners of the priestess's mouth. Maybe a smile, maybe not.

"Is it far? I lost one of my sandals in the mud."

"I'll weave you another, sister. Come on."

THE POACHER AND the priestess travel, and their trust blossoms the way cherry trees do, unbidden and bright.

The priestess is very earnest about her task and refuses to let the poacher so much as touch the statue. For his part the poacher seems content to drift with the wind, unshaven, unkempt, and unconcerned. The quiver half-full of arrows at his waist clatters gently as they walk and gives their steps a comfortable rhythm.

"I'm surprised you take that statue so seriously," he says as they walk.

"It's valuable."

"It looks like plain building stone," the poacher says, reaching a hand inside his robe and idly scratching his chest.

"That's not why it's worth so much," the priestess says, pausing to switch her staff from one hand to the other and re-sling the bundle on her other shoulder. She carries it the way a woman carries an infant, swaddled against her chest and supported with one hand.

"I'll ask if you make me ask," the poacher says; "what does?"

"The catfish god is the source of all earthquakes in Japan. If Takemikazuchi doesn't step on it, it wriggles and the ground shakes. As you can see, no one is stepping on it, so I have to bring it back where someone will."

The poacher stops in the road and leans on his bow, which is almost as tall as he is. She turns back to look at him.

"What, don't you have any belief?" she asks, indignantly.

He scratches, shakes his head, and shrugs.

Just as he does, the priestess seems to quiver. She claps a hand to her burden and looks around wildly.

"Oh, no," she says, "not now."

"That's not funny," the poacher says, "I wasn't born yesterday."

"Namazu is the god of instability and conflict. That's what an earthquake is. He causes war, conflict, and pain. He makes the world shake!"

The priestess gives up trying to hold the statue and spills it out onto the ground. It lands in a vibrating puff of dust. There, it begins to wriggle and the earth around them shakes. The poacher staggers and falls, dumbstruck, and the priestess stamps one foot down hard on the Namazu. Leans on it with all her weight. Carrying it seems to have made her strong.

"That's impossible," he says.

"That's not the problem," the priestess hisses through her teeth, "the problem is that it causes strife. Look around us. Something is wrong!"

"No, nothing is wrong," the bandit who emerges from the woods by the road says, "just give us everything you have."

The men who try to take the priestess, the statue, and the poacher's life are men cut from a fraying cloth. Men left behind in a country at war, on roads marched more often by armies than constables.

They are armed with the detritus of war. Their tattoos are faded reflections of the gods of war. The poacher knows they will not spare him, or her. Gaunt men, desperate men, men with nothing. There are five of them and one horse, tethered and half-hidden in the trees. The poacher should have smelled it. As the priestess leans desperately on the quivering statue, he nocks an arrow and draws the bow. Aims it at the man in charge.

"You'll only get one of us," the big bandit says, pointing at the poacher with a worn katana. "You'll—"

The arrow flies without warning, the way a hawk dives for a pigeon. It passes through the bandit's throat without a sound and buries itself in a tree twenty feet behind him. He drops the sword and clutches his neck. The poacher scoops up the battered katana.

The priestess watches the poacher swing the sword. He fights the bandits off with more desperation than skill, but there's dignity in his movements. He fights without shame. Like it's something he takes pride in.

From the corner of his eye, the poacher sees the bandit outrider drop from his horse and charge toward the priestess with a long knife. The priestess ducks as he charges and sweeps the holy stave in a clean, low arc that tangles his feet and sends him sprawling. In a frantic maelstrom of dust, the poacher cuts the bandits down. A lone survivor scrambles back toward the horse and flees at a gallop.

"Are you all right?" the priestess asks with surprising calm.

For an answer, the poacher scoops up his bow and nocks a second arrow. She watches him do it, and it's as stark a contrast to his work with the sword as brass is to gold. He draws the bow deliberately, long and smooth, all the way back to his ear. Angles his whole torso up into the wind. His feet are as still and stable as roots driven into the earth. The rider is a distant blur now, half-hidden in rising dist. With a sharp sound like tearing silk the poacher lets the arrow fly. He shades his eyes, and then looks over at the priestess.

"Thank you," she says. She takes her foot off the Namazu, and the earth stays still. The poacher wonders if he imagined it shaking.

"Bastards," he says, "masterless scum."

"Desperate men," the priestess says sadly. "I'm surprised you wasted that last arrow. You have an angry heart."

The poacher grunts, runs a hand through his sweat-soaked hair, and starts collecting their meagre possessions. The priestess refastens the Namazu in its sling.

THEY FIND THE horse an hour later. The wind has turned chill, rustling the trees by the road and combing the long grass.

The priestess claps a hand to her midsection, and this time the poacher pays attention.

"More of them?"

"I don't think so, it's not very strong. Wait, though: touch the statue. I need you to believe in this."

Reluctantly, the poacher approaches her. Her nostrils flare for an instant, and for the first time in what feels like years, the poacher wonders how he smells. The priestess isn't exactly beautiful, and it's hard to tell what she looks like under the big skirt and heavy Haori jacket, but her eyes have the clear, focused authority of a hawk's. He reaches out slowly, and she takes his hand and touches it to the bundle.

The Namazu figurine vibrates gently through the folds of cloth. A weak pulse.

"This statue is valuable," the priestess says. Wordlessly, the poacher pulls away.

"I think that's what it likes," he says, and points at the horse, which is ruminatively cropping grass in the field by the road. The bandit is slumped in the saddle with the poacher's arrow protruding from the centre of his back.

The priestess's face, so open and earnest a moment ago, closes. The poacher expected her to be disturbed by the sight of the dead man. She looks at him evenly.

"That's a very good shot, even for a poacher."

"I practice on birds and rabbits," he says diffidently.

"Do they usually gallop away at that speed?" the priestess asks innocently.

"I am a poacher," he says, "trying to survive an age of war."

"And I am a priestess," she replies, "trying to return an icon to its rightful place."

Clouds gather on the horizon and threaten rain.

"I HAVE A little money," the priestess says, almost yelling to make herself heard above slanting autumn rain, "we can buy lodging."

"Why bother? Your precious statue is a fish. It's probably very happy."

The poacher knows towns are dangerous, but is almost too cold to care. Cavalry from any of the warring clans might stop in the village for food and fodder. They are still in Takeda lands, and that clan hangs poachers.

"No one will know us," the priestess says, "and we'll take sick if we stay in the cold. We need shelter."

They descend to the village with the light vanishing and

sheets of rain making the ground slick.

The inn is an island of warmth and light. Almost empty, but the landlord is friendly and his wife serves them dumplings in a hot and fragrant broth. The priestess emits a tiny sneeze, and the elderly proprietress fusses over her and removes her somewhere for a bath. The poacher and the landlord talk quietly about the war. Lord Takeda is weak, and the mighty Oda Nobunaga will soon sweep him aside. The archers of the north are in disarray, and the great ships of the Hojo navy patrol the southern coast.

They retire to a room; small, thin-walled, and laid in the barest fashion with tatami mats and simple blankets. The poacher and the priestess bask in the warmth. The priestess looks radiant, washed, and content. It's the poacher who feels drab and uncomfortable alone with a woman at a country inn.

"We should have ordered sake," he says.

As if on cue, there's a polite knock at the sliding door, and a young woman enters with a bottle and an array of cups. She puts a finger to her mouth.

"I'm sorry to intrude," she says, "but I have to wait for my parents to go to bed before I could bring you the sake. We get so few visitors from far away. You're a hunter! And I had no idea shrine maidens were so beautiful. Do you drink?"

The serving girl lays out the cups, and the poacher teases her as she unstoppers the wine. He threatens to drink straight out of the bottle, and the mischievous serving girl giggles.

"What shrine maidens are not is rich," the priestess says tactfully.

"Then let's make this a little ceremony," the serving girl says, "to new friends. You have no idea how boring this village is. My name is Hana."

The priestess smiles, but gently chides Hana as she pours.

"If we're drinking a toast, you must arrange the cups from smallest to largest. Here. Now remember, three sips each, from three cups. There's nothing luckier than that. Oh excuse me!"

The priestess sneezes and knocks some cups over. The two women fuss with the cups and pour again. Their fingers dance like water bugs on the surface of a pond.

"You and I first, Hana."

"Hey, what about me?" the poacher says.

"You can wait your turn."

The priestess makes a little bow and drinks. Hana does, too.

"Your turn now," the serving girl chirps, and leans suggestively toward the poacher. He reaches for a cup, and the priestess stays his hand.

"That's enough, I think, unless you want whoever hired her to find you dead to the world."

Silence fills the room.

"What do you mean?" Hana says.

"I switched the cups," the priestess says; "whatever this does, I hope it isn't too bad, Kunoichi."

"Hey, that's not nice," Hana says, "tell her I'm not—"

The girl hesitates, then leans forward on her palms, breathing heavily. The poacher looks at the priestess in shock.

"What did you do?"

"I told you, I switched the cups. The important question is what did she do—and even that is immaterial. For who is much more interesting. Will you tell me that, Hana?"

The serving girl slumps over and lies still.

"Kunoichi?" the poacher breathes. "This girl is an assassin?"

"She must be very good. The Namazu hardly quivered. Put a blanket over her."

The girl breathes shallowly. Her skin is pale, and only with her features relaxed in something like sleep does the poacher see how deeply, fatally beautiful she is. He can't imagine failing to notice a girl like that, or how she hid herself from him. He casts his mind back.

"She wasn't here when we arrived," he says, "and she poured sake like a courtier."

"I could have found her out if she brewed tea or cut flowers, too," the priestess says, and there is something like arrogance in her voice.

The poacher touches the ninja's face. Her skin is cool, but she is still breathing, faintly.

"That's a bit worldly, for a simple shrine maiden," he says, "I suppose there's some way for her to warn her masters. We have to leave."

The priestess nods.

THEY FLEE INTO the rain, and the poacher is as adept in flight as the priestess was in ceremony.

He finds them shelter in an abandoned fishing hut by a roaring stream. They're both soaked to the skin. The poacher makes a small fire and they curl around it, steam rising from their damp clothes. Their sleep is as fragile and hollow as the bones of a sparrow.

Sometime in the night the Namazu figurine rattles, and the priestess isn't sure if she puts a hand over it in a dream or on the edge of the waking world. The figurine stills, for once, and she goes back to sleep.

She wakes to find the poacher's hand thrown over hers. She squeezes the figurine, as if she could change it, as if she could change anything, and his fingers are rough and calloused over hers. The priestess makes no effort to move the poacher's hand, just watches her breath mist into the morning air between them.

She shivers, and the motion wakes him. They meet each other's eyes with the Namazu in the gulf between them. Hers are rested and calm, and a little sad. His tired and angry, and a little sad. She runs a finger over the calluses at the joints of his string fingers.

The poacher entwines his hand with hers, and finds her calluses different; at the base of each finger where the wooden haft of the stave abrades her skin.

"Tell me who taught you to shoot a bow," the priestess says.

OVER A BREAKFAST as bare as winter trees, the poacher tells her. It doesn't take long.

"I am ronin, yes. Masterless scum. I only ever found one man I was willing to die for, and when he died I ran. I served Uesugi Kenshin and left my clan when he was assassinated. There isn't much else. His sons have been at war for three years. I'd rather hunt rabbits."

Her brow knits. He likes it that way; she's more beautiful when she's serious, so he ploughs on.

"What about you? You aren't a shrine maiden at all. Where did you learn to drink sake?"

"Certainly not a maiden, anyway," she says with a sudden smile, and he can't tell if she's trying to make him blush. He does blush, and she laughs at him. The poacher could leave it at that. It would feel wonderful; it's been a long time since anyone has held power over him. He could leave it at that. He doesn't.

"I don't imagine you'll tell me who you are or why you're taking this statue west. The only thing to the west of here is Omi province. Lord Oda's lands. If I had to guess I'd say you're using me to help you get to Azumi castle, but I don't care. You don't answer questions, but answer just this one: did you lie to me?"

"Of course I lied to you." She looks at the horizon as if she was looking at a grave, and the poacher knows his arrow has struck home.

"So you're not really carrying messages from the gods."

"No," she says, leaning on her staff. The cloth covering on its tip flaps gently in the breeze. The little rings clink.

"Are you sure?" the poacher asks. The priestess feels the faintest shake in the Namazu. The sunrise blurs with tears.

"Do you feel like the world is made of lies? Cry about it if you want, but there is only one thing you can do to change it. Forget Lord Oda and take the Namazu to the shrine. Change your lie to the truth. Lord Oda is ruthless. He will use any weapon to take control of Japan, and everything under heaven is a weapon. He has enough; don't give him this one. If we take the Namazu to the Kashima shrine, then you weren't lying to me at all. The lords and their samurai will decide the fate of the world, not a tyrant who is trying to make himself a god."

It is the longest she has ever heard him speak. At some point in the speech he has put his hands on her shoulders. She leans her cheek against one.

"It feels strange to be educated in duty and rightness by a poacher," she says. "Would you come with me, if I did?"

The poacher breaks into a smile that shows her what he must have looked like when he still had something to believe in.

"I always had a bit of a thing for shrine maidens," he says.

THE PRIESTESS AND the poacher turn south, away from the westerly road to Azuchi castle. They walk through wide fields of grass and late flowers, toward the sea and the Kashima plateau. They take the generosity of strangers, mindful of the priestess's worn vestments and the rattle of the rings on her staff, and the poacher hunts for them when the late afternoon chill drives the rabbits back to their warrens.

They walk as though through a still life, the only figures

moving through a painting of a more peaceful time. This is the edge of Takeda lands, and Lord Oda's power is weak here. The journey is made of steps as light and quiet as thrushes brushing the earth with their wings. It almost feels like the mere choice to bring the god of earthquakes home has set them free.

It hasn't.

The poacher is constantly assessing ground. Wondering whether it will hold his arrows without ruining the tips, listening to it to feel marching feet or galloping hooves. Old soldier's habits. Most imagine the air as the domain of archers, but really it's the ground. Once you let an arrow loose, it flies on its own. The earth continues to speak.

"Do you feel that?" the poacher says; "Horses."

"There are no horses, Takeda is probably keeping his men north to deal with Lord Oda. Besides, the Namazu is still."

"Forget the statue. I'm an archer, I spent my whole life avoiding cavalry. They're coming."

And come they do, as suddenly as a thunderbolt from a tree line at the edge of a great field. The Namazu lies still against the priestess's midriff.

"We have to run!" the poacher cries.

"There's no point in running," the priestess replies. "I know who it is."

THE ODA HEAVY cavalry are magnificent. Their armour is glossy and beautifully appointed. Their weapons are ancient and perfectly maintained. When they rise in their stirrups and bow to the priestess, the poacher suddenly understands why the statue didn't rattle. This isn't an ambush.

"My lady Hiroko," the leader says, curbing his horse. "The long nightmare is over. I have survived, you have survived, and you have Lord Oda's treasure. The future is glory."

The priestess recognizes the voice, muffled behind the warrior's menpo. The mask has a sharp nose and glossy red teeth.

"The future is war, husband."

"Not for us. You can come home. Lord Oda is waiting for you."

"My mother isn't. Your daughter isn't. Hatano killed them when your Lord took his castles."

The poacher should have guessed, should have felt it in the earth or smelt it on the wind. The shape of this betrayal is something he can hardly comprehend, but its weight is as obvious as the sky weighing on the earth. The priestess almost screams, "It was your daughter who was supposed to be a Maki for the gods, not me!"

"Return with me. I order it. Lord Oda orders it. Give me that statue and all is forgiven. This is what war is. There are no rules. You and I have both survived. Isn't that enough reason to come home?"

The priestess unslings the Namazu figurine and puts it gently on the ground at her feet.

"It's not that," the priestess says, "it's that I can't stand you offering me forgiveness. As though I have done something wrong."

She looks back at the poacher.

"Will you hold it down, this time?"

As if in a dream, the poacher joins her. He stands his quiver by the Namazu and leans on it with his leading foot.

"This is death," he says.

"For a shrine maiden," the priestess says, and pulls the cloth covering from the top of her staff. The poacher finally understands what she is.

The staff is not a Shinto standard, it is a naginata, a glaive tipped with a curving blade that has the sheen and sharpness of coral. She is not a wife or a nun or a spy. She is *onna-bugeisha*, a noblewoman, a samurai, and the poacher realizes she plans to fight ten mounted men on her own. His throat goes dry.

She kneels, the naginata tucked under her arm so that the weapon stretches far to her right. The blade is as still as the branch of a great oak. The grass blows in waves, and the stalks that touch the naginata's edge fall away in a sprinkle of stems. With the formal gesture of challenge complete, she rises. She gently kicks out of the bamboo sandals, and her feet touch the earth.

"If you want the Namazu," she says, "come and get it."

The horsemen charge, with the priestess's husband at their head. The poacher draws his bow and prepares to die. With a hundred Ashigaru and their spears, they could survive, but without them the samurai cavalry will mow them down as easily as a pack of hounds running down a pair of rabbits. The Namazu quakes under his foot, and he has to lean on it with all his strength to keep it still. If he doesn't, the earth will shake itself apart. He can feel it.

The priestess swings the naginata in a huge arc, too early, and her husband laughs behind his mask. For a moment, he thinks he's won. The blow hits his horse in the mouth, and the beast rears up with a heart-breaking scream. Rider and mount crash to the earth in front of her and the rest of the squadron has to veer around them. They slow to bring their swords to bear, and the Priestess slices and whirls her way through them like a scythe mowing wheat. Horses and men fall away from her as if she was cutting the earth itself from under their feet.

The poacher aims his arrow. It's hard to see in the whirling maelstrom of grass and men and dust and horses, but he looks for the flash of her blade and sees a horse rise like a monster to blot out the sun. He lets fly, draws and lets fly, and counts his success in screams.

Horses and men lie around the priestess like parchment swept off a table, covered in red ink. The poacher pats his yukata, and finds himself untouched.

From the field of bodies, only one rises again. Bloody, staggering, the priestess' husband is the last. He lunges at her suddenly, and his katana finds her ribs. She hisses with rage and beats him to his knees with great sweeps of the naginata's haft.

"Just tell me," she cries at him, "was it you who suggested sacrificing the hostages to ensure Hatano's annihilation?"

"No, Lord Oda made that request."

The priestess screams. It's even worse. All her husband did was follow an order. He struggles to draw the shorter of his swords, and the naginata scythes down. The Namazu quakes under the poacher's foot, then stills.

"You should never have let me train with this blade," the priestess tells her husband's head, sways, and collapses in the grass.

SHE AWAKES IN the dusk to find the poacher has bound her wounds. The air buzzes with flies. The one living horse is her husband's, and its mouth is a ruin that she can't bear to look at.

The poacher sees her eyes flutter.

"I've been thinking about it," he says, "and I did hear a story about Lord Oda offering hostages to guarantee a surrender, then sacking the castle once the defenders laid down their arms."

"I wasn't there. Hatano had many castles. When word came he was dead, his retainers came to kill me. Clean the naginata; I can barely move my arm."

"What?"

"It's different from killing with a bow. Rust starts quickly." She winces and touches the cloth binding her ribs; her slender fingertips come away red. "Am I going to die here?"

"No," the Poacher says, "but getting on that horse isn't going to be any fun at all."

THE POACHER HELPS her into the saddle and mounts behind her, holding her in place, and they start up the path to the Kashima plateau. He guides the horse with his knees; there's no place to put a bit.

To keep the priestess awake the poacher talks. The clop of the horses' hooves makes a faint percussive rhythm with the rattling of the arrows left in his quiver.

"I think I know why you like me so much," he says, and the priestess makes an inquisitive noise. She's curled up against him, holding her bandaged ribs, riding almost side-saddle to keep one delicate foot contorted to touch the figurine. She's lost her sandals again.

"I don't think the Namazu shakes the ground to hurt us. I don't think it calls us to war. I think the catfish only thrashes when we cause him pain. He shakes for war and love and poverty. He needs a master to step on him to keep these things from shaking the islands to pieces. In short, the Namazu is like me; just trying to get along without suffering too much."

The priestess almost laughs.

"What an excellent job you've done," she says.

THEY RIDE ALL night, and the priestess's side bleeds only a little. The horse, on the other hand, leaves a pitiful trail of blood to soak into the earth. Just as they reach the crest, the beast finally lies down and refuses to get up. The poacher helps the priestess up, and she doesn't utter so much as a squeak of pain when she stands straight.

"Of all the things I've done," the priestess says, "only this weighs on my heart. I feel nothing for Lord Oda's men. I think of my husband and feel emptiness as deep as a cut in the earth. But I can feel the suffering of this horse in my soul. I can't stand it."

As the sun rises, the priestess kneels by the horse and waits. She cries when it shudders and takes its last breath. The poacher gazes up the hill, then down into the valley below.

"I can see the tip of the shrine's pagoda," he says, "but look down there."

Far below them in the plains are knots of men on horses. They can be distinguished by the colour of their banners.

"Yellow for Lord Oda," the poacher says, "and black for Takeda. I'm not sure who flies purple banners."

"Hojo Ujimasa," the priestess says, "he's a tiresome old man. I suppose word has spread. They're all coming after us."

"They want the Namazu. Lord Oda made a mistake when he settled for that castle. What he should have taken—"

"Was this wretched statue."

"I was going to say *you,* but I suppose this earth shaking god figurine would run a distant second."

The priestess smiles, and the Namazu rattles. The poacher helps her put it down, and they each put a foot on it to keep it still. It wants to shake the earth. War is calling.

"We have to do something, or they will come here," the priestess says. "It will never end."

The poacher reaches inside his yukata and scratches his chest.

"That's a little uncompromising, even for you. Are you sure?"

"I finally feel the desire," she answers, "for a chasm between old and new."

In unison the poacher and the priestess take their feet off the Namazu. The statue gives a little shake, and then a low, sustained rumble. She takes his hand, and the mountain itself starts to tremble. Birds fly in terrified spirals from the trees. The earthquake spreads from the catfish like ripples in a pond, each growing and rebounding off the last.

Far below in the plain, the earth splits. The air is crushed by a rumble so deep, so infinite, that it sounds like the plain is trying to crack itself open, tear free of Japan and make a new country, a new continent, a new world.

Horses and men panic. Great cracks and sink holes open in the earth and swallow them whole. A chasm opens up before them and cuts the plateau in two. The road down disappears, replaced with a sheer cliff.

The Namazu's rumble slows, and the priestess puts a gentle foot on it. When it stops, she wraps it up, and the two of them carry it to the shrine.

THE POOL IS shallow, and just below the surface, at the centre, is a flat rock. High above it is the ornate structure of the temple, and poles around its edges sport zigzags of paper covered in prayers.

"That's it?" the poacher says. "It's tiny. How can Takemikazuchi hold him down against that?"

"Be helpful or be silent," the priestess says, and together they drop the Namazu figurine into the limpid water. The statue sends ripples across the surface, and for an instant the catfish is real, sleek and dark, thrashing under the surface. It flips its tail and disappears into the silt at the bottom of the pool.

Everything is still. The priestess sighs.

"Did your husband say your name was Hiroko?"

She nods.

"Mine is Yoshikane," the poacher says, and taking her hand, they turn their backs on the cataclysm and enter the shrine.

Mike's Massive Penis

Buzz Dixon

"WHAT THE HELL is that?"

"What does it look like?"

"A massive penis!"

Mike nodded. "Yup. Looks like that to me, too."

"What's it doing here?"

"I found it."

"'Found it'?!"

"Yeah. At the beach."

"But why bring it *here*?"

Mike shrugged. "Seemed like a good idea at the time."

And when you think about it, that's the answer to every "why" question.

Mike kissed his wife Suzy on her forehead. He smelled of fish and cold sweat and knew she wouldn't want him to hug her yet.

"But in our *driveway*? What will people say?"

Mike looked out the window. Neighbours already lined up to look at his massive penis. "It *is* a conversation starter," he said.

Suzy gestured vaguely, unable to articulate the thousands of questions bubbling inside her.

So Mike told her in excruciating detail about driving down to the beach to do some surf fishing, finding the massive penis washed ashore, and then all the myriad steps involved in loading it onto a rented trailer.

When he finished, Suzy had more questions that she couldn't figure out how to ask, so he went to shower and change while she tried to formulate them.

Mike had just finished buttoning his shirt when the police knocked.

"Excuse me, sir, but is this your massive penis?"

"Well, it's not *my* massive penis, if you catch my drift," Mike said with a wink, hoping to establish a bond of camaraderie with the officers but failing miserably.

"Yes, sir," said the older officer. It was clearly not her massive penis, either. "But do you *own* the penis? Or more precisely, do you own the driveway upon which said penis now rests?"

"Well, the *bank* owns the driveway . . . " Mike said then, seeing his joke falling flat, coughed and added, "Yes. Yes, I do."

"Thank you, sir. And you are aware of, and claim possession of, said massive penis?"

Mike coughed and nodded again.

"You are aware we have laws against public nudity, are you not?"

"Now wait a minute," Suzy said. "I may not enjoy Mike's massive penis, but you can't arrest him for it."

"You think we can't?"

"Laws against public nudity only apply to human beings," Suzy said.

Mike brightened. "That's right! Otherwise you'd have to arrest every dog and squirrel in the neighbourhood."

"Half of them," said the younger officer. Mike, Suzy, and the older officer looked at him.

"Half," he repeated. "The other half are female."

"Aha!" Mike said. "Sexual discrimination!"

"No," said the older officer. "Bitches and sows are covered with fur. You can't see their genitalia."

"'Sows'?" Mike asked. "When did we drag pigs into this?"

"Sows are the name for female squirrels," said the older officer. "Look it up.

"But that's not the point. The point is you have a massive human-looking penis in your driveway."

" . . . could be a whale's penis," said Mike.

"No, it's not," Mr. Knopsfred, their neighbour, shouted. He stood on his side of the hedge separating his driveway from Mike and Suzy's, close enough to eavesdrop on their conversation with the police. He held up his iPad for the others to see. "I Googled it. That looks nothing at all like a whale's penis."

The older officer nodded. "It looks exactly like a human penis, sir."

Mike almost said, "How would you know?" but fortunately common sense and self-preservation double-teamed his tongue and clamped his jaw shut.

"But it's not a *real* penis," Suzy said. "It's . . . it's a work of art, just like the statue down in the park or our neighbour's birdbath across the street, the one with Cupid peeing in the water."

The older officer turned to the younger officer. "Check it out," she said.

"The birdbath?"

"No, the massive penis."

"*Me?*"

"You. Now."

The younger officer looked less than enthused but stepped over to examine the massive penis more closely.

"Well, I'll be dipped in doggie-doo," said Mr. Knopsfred, checking Google again. "She's right! Female squirrels *are* called 'sows'! Hey, know what they call male squirrels?"

"'Boars'," said the older officer, stepping on his punchline.

The younger officer came back, gingerly holding his baton by its strap.

"Looks real to me," he said. "I poked it a couple of times, seemed spongy." To Suzy he said: "Got any bleach, ma'am?"

"I'll get some and a bucket," she said.

"It doesn't have to be metal or stone to be art," said Mike. "It could be silicon."

"Or it could be real," said the older officer. "In which case, I need to call forensics and have them determine if this might be evidence of a crime—*hey!* You kids! Get off that thing right now!"

Several neighbourhood kids slid down the side and

scampered back across the street.

The older officer glared at Mike. "See what I mean? It's an attractive nuisance."

"Not *that* attractive," muttered Suzy, handing a bucket full of bleach to the male officer, who swished his baton in it vigorously.

"Do you have a tarp?" the female officer asked. "I'm going to ask you to cover it up until forensics can get here." The " . . . or else" was silent.

Mike cleared his throat. "We have a drop cloth . . . "

"That should do," said the woman, then glancing at the massive penis, added: "How many square feet does it cover?"

Before Mike could answer, they heard a distant **thud-thud-thud** like giant feet approaching.

And they were giant feet, attached to giant legs, belonging to a giant who appeared to be missing one vital part.

"Hey, you found it! Great," the giant said. He reached down, picked up the now-not-so-massive-compared-to-his-hand penis, and reattached it with a sound that fell midway between "Squish!" and "Boing!"

"Thanks," the giant said. "I thought I lost it. Well, be seeing you." He tossed them a salute and headed back towards the distant sea.

"Wait!" Mike said.

The giant turned to look at him. "Shouldn't I get a reward?" Mike asked, voice faltering at the giant's frown. "A finder's fee, at least . . . ?"

"How about I don't crap on your front lawn?" the giant asked. "Fair enough?"

Mike looked at Suzy, who nodded vigorously. "Yeah," he said weakly. "Yeah, that'll do."

The giant nodded and turned back to the sea, disappearing from view and earshot in a matter of minutes.

The female officer said, "You know, I think the best thing for all parties concerned is just to pretend this never happened."

"Agreed," said Suzy. "Coffee, anyone?"

Where Green Things Grew

David L. Craddock

-1-

HIKOLA'S EYES WERE cloudy, had been cloudy for centuries. But she saw.

One gnarled hand reached out and touched the oak. Her fingers were bent, but her touch was light and sure. She knew this tree as well as she knew her own body. The trunk was bent and twisted, like her. Her fingers trailed up and found two holes, one set beside the other like eyes. Her hand roamed south, and one yellowed nail drew a loop around a third hole, the largest and widest.

This, the lone tree at the centre of the Fallowgrounds, had stood for two hundred eighty-four springs. It would stand for many more. Its naked branches stretched like flailing hands. Its bark was rotten and reeked of decay; the stink of it was almost enough to overwhelm the stench of the ash that blanketed the Fallowgrounds like snow. Hikola breathed through her mouth. Her wheezing was the only sound in a place that had once rang with celebration and feasting.

Hikola let her hand fall from the tree. Then she stood for a while and remembered.

Behind her, weight shifted from bare foot to bare foot. Her

nephew, Jaranim, made a sound of disgust as ashes crumbled beneath his weight but offered no other complaint. He was a patient boy. *No, a man, now,* she corrected herself. Seventy-four springs grown. Well, she was three hundred. To her, he was still a sapling.

Jaranim shifted again.

"Something weighs on your mind," Hikola said without turning to face him. His heart rate accelerated. Although they stood on a thick carpet of ash, she could sense him. The layer of things best forgotten—though she never would—was a patina of dead skin, hardly thick enough to block her connection with the Mother.

"We have made this journey every spring since I can remember," Jaranim said.

She did not turn.

"It pains me to be here, Aunt. My lungs cry out for fresh air. Yours do as well."

She waited. The blank canvas of her eyes dimmed as clouds suffocated the sun.

"Mother never told me why she wanted to return to the earth here, at this place." He made a face she could not see, yet she saw. "I do not understand."

She waited.

"One tree grows," he continued. "Is she—"

"It does not grow," she snapped.

Silence. Her sense of him through the earth faded and sharpened, faded and sharpened. Confusion. Hikola silently admonished herself. She was a druidess, and too old for such agitation.

"We do not grow when we return to the earth," she said, soft as a leaf against the cheek. "Flesh to wood, blood to root."

"To sway in the breeze, and forever be," Jaranim finished.

Hikola let the silence stretch for a time. "What do you know of your mother?"

"Yamalyn Kalliphaeia d'Oakia was a renowned druidess."

"Indeed. Fully committed to the Mother and Her will."

Jaranim's mouth tightened. "But she was cold for one charged with growth and warmth." He swallowed. "I am sorry, Aunt. I should not speak ill of the dead."

"Do not be sorry. You are half correct. Your mother was not

cold. She was . . ." *Broken. As hollow as a dead trunk.*

Perhaps the truth should be passed on. If that was to be, it must be on this day.

"Would you like to know her?" Hikola asked.

Silence again. Her sense of him grew and shrank, coloured and paled. Seventy-four springs' worth of consideration. Ash crunched as he came to stand beside her. She felt him reach for the tree. She caught his hand, lowered it to his side. At last the vibrations of his anger and impatience grew still. She released her grip.

"Let me know her." His words were a whisper, but pleading. "Please, Aunt. I would know everything. Who she was. How she lived. How she . . ." He swallowed hard.

Tears leaked from the crow's feet around her eyes—the first tears she had shed in centuries. She sighed, and the years piled atop her shoulders like stones grew heavier.

"Very well."

-2-

"OUR GROVE STOOD near where we stand now. It was small, a population of one hundred and twenty. Everyone participated in the Planting and in the Harvest. We needed every hand.

"I was sixteen when I became a custodian. The priests detected my ability at birth, and my mother named me well: Hikola Apricoris l'Aster. *The fertile heart,* in the druidic tongue. All green things begin as seeds planted in our hearts, Jaranim. During the Planting, the men tilled the ground. Then the custodians blessed the soil. You do not know the blessing, not really, because you are a man. You hear the words, but to hear them is not to know them. You see the miracles they bring, but to climb a tree is not to be a tree.

"I said the words—Flesh to wood, blood to root; to sway in the breeze, and forever be—and Her honey dripped from my lips and into my cupped hands. With those hands I kneaded the soil until it became as dough for bread. Then, life. Where I worshipped, trees sprouted. Roots unspooled and took hold as branches stretched up and up to touch the sky and praise Her. Leaves budded and bloomed. From saplings to towering monuments in seconds—firs, oaks, cedars, spruces, beech, elms, hickories and hemlocks and aspens and birches, all of every conceivable shape and colour. Whatever she willed.

"You have seen it, Jaranim, but to see the years pass in the blink of an eye is not to hold that life in your hands, to shape it. It was glorious.

"Your mother was thirteen. You may not believe it, but her name meant *giver of care*. Yamalyn and I were two of six custodians that springtime. She was younger, but more gifted than I. I never begrudged her that talent. We were all of the earth and air and sun. Our hands were soft that first Planting as they cupped fresh soil and whispered the prayer. By the end of the first day, our hands were muddy and calloused.

"But the work was good. That first day, we planted hundreds of trees and crops. Over what remained of that Planting season, we covered leagues. Each night the custodians sang to the trees and the crops and the flowers and the plants. Every fall, the Harvest came, and we tasted the fruits of our labours. The food was so plentiful. We indulged like nobles in the south. There was corn, tomatoes, sweet peppers, squash, collard greens, carrots, apples, bananas, peaches so sweet and ripe their juices dribbled down our chins as our teeth pierced skin.

"The Mother was pleased—with Yamalyn most of all, I think. Her trees were the biggest, her crops the healthiest and tastiest. 'The Mother plants seeds in my heart,' Yamalyn said when the elders asked her secret. 'And from there, I plant the love She bequeaths me.' Her words mystified the elders, but they knew she was not hiding her methods out of pride. She was supremely gifted. Her methods could not be taught. Where Yamalyn touched, green things grew, and flourished.

"I was comely, tall and willowy, with long dark hair done in braids and adorned with burnished leaves that never lost their fire, even in spring. Men admired me from afar, especially Melor, one spring older than me. I knew that according to tradition, I would soon cultivate another type of life, one without the benefit of instantaneous maturity and health. The prospect terrified me, but I had my sister, your mother.

"Yamalyn was not a beautiful girl. She was short, with eyes of different colours, a hooked nose and a bent back. She wanted to be like me, walk in my footsteps. I told her I did not want a follower. I wanted a companion, and a sister. We worked side by side, ate side by side, slept side by side. I doted on her, taught her what I could. Not that she had much to learn.

"Then, death came."

-3-

"The invaders raped and pillaged, leaving few alive to spread tales of their horrors, but roots and dirt carry word as well as tongues and parchment. We could feel the earth dying from the north and spreading southward like a pestilence.

"We custodians put our ears to the ground, and what we felt brought us to tears. The invaders. That's what men called them, before they died screaming. Their screams pierced the earth as deeply as they pierced our souls. Trees that had lived thousands of years were razed to the ground, claimed by fire. We learned their names: Kenovians. Barbarians who had sailed across the sea and caught the nobles in the north, with their soft hands and feet, unawares. They aimed to kill and to conquer. Snow slowed them, but our father knew it would not stop them.

"Yamalyn's and my status as custodians afforded our family one of the largest trees in the grove. It measured one man-mile around, and the interior was palatial: Smooth walls, chairs, and beds fashioned so that they extended from the tree, a harmonious extension of Her life, rather than severed from it. Every night, our father would hold meetings. Warding magic prevented Yamalyn and me from listening through the tree, so we sneaked down from where we were supposed to be sleeping in the canopy and eavesdropped while the men talked. Their voices were low and deep. Frightened.

"During the day, the saplings held meetings of our own.

"'Who will protect the grove?' Comali asked. She was my age, and my earth sister bonded by soil and the Mother's honey. Like me, she was beautiful. The boys had noticed her two summers earlier, and their eyes grew larger every Planting.

"'The men,' Yamalyn said confidently.

"Melor, then eighteen springs, scoffed. 'We are farmers.'

"'We are druids,' I replied.

"'Our hands are our pitchforks,' he said. 'We wear robes, not armour.'

"Uneasiness planted itself inside me. Melor was right. We

141

were not fighters."

-4-

"THE MEN DEVELOPED a network. With the Harvest finished, nearly all of them left our grove and made camp in trees extending to the north. They were messengers who spoke through the roots of their tree as they heard things, saw things.

"'They're coming,' my father said one evening after supper. Two months had passed. We were gathered in the centre of the trunk. We no longer bedded down in the canopies. I missed the warmth of sunlight on my skin but was too afraid to venture outside for long.

"Mother went pale. 'How long?'

"'Weeks. Days, maybe.'

"'What will we do?' she asked.

"'Let the breeze carry us where She wills,' Father said."

-5-

"THE NEXT MORNING, Melor stood at the base of our tree and rapped his knuckles on it. I emerged and glared at him. Trees were not doors. When one druid needed another, we reached out through the roots.

"My father came to stand before me. Yamalyn, Mother, and I crowded behind him.

"'They come faster,' Melor said. His hands shook like autumn leaves, but his voice was steady. My heart swelled with love for him. He was so courageous.

"'Do we leave now?' Father asked.

"Melor shook his head. 'We will resist.'

"Mother covered her mouth with a hand. Father went rigid. 'We are not fighters, Melor.'

Melor's face turned the colour of autumn. The word of an elder druid was law in the grove, but he stood his ground. "'No, we are not. But if we do not fight back, we will die.' His eyes flitted to Yamalyn, then rested on me. 'Or worse.'

Father closed his eyes while my mother scolded Melor for his impetuousness. She insisted we flee. The Mother would protect us. At last, Father gently took her by the shoulders. 'You and the

142

girls will stay. I will fight.'

"'No!' Yamalyn and I cried.

"'Let us run,' my mother said. She was on the verge on panic. 'We will all go together. We will grow a new forest. The Mother, She—'

"'The trees carry word,' Melor said harshly. 'They come ever onward. There is nowhere to run that they will not raze. They are as fire through dead wood.'

"'Is that why you've come?' Mother said shrilly to Melor. 'To take him away from us?'

"Melor shook his head. 'I am here to ask for help. We are not the southerners. We do not conscript. You know this.'

"I was so terrified by the idea of my father leaving us to take up steel that I failed to notice Yamalyn leaving my side to step forward.

"'I will help,' she said.

"Everyone looked at her. 'You'll what?' my father said. He was dumbfounded. We all were.

"'I can help,' she repeated. 'I can pass messages, or grow food to feed our people. I will embed myself with the fighters, and—'

"'Out of the question,' Father said. 'I will go.'

"Over my mother's tears and our protestations, he changed from his robe into a tunic and pants and went to a bare expanse of trunk. He rapped his knuckles on it, and a panel slid away. He reached in and withdrew a spear.

"Mother eyed it as if it were a snake. 'You have steel?'

"Father placed the butt of the spear on the floor. The tip of its blade reached just over his thick head of hair. 'I have always had steel, though I hoped I would never need it.'

"'But . . . but . . . ' It was all my mother could manage.

"Father put one arm around her. The arm not holding the spear. Even so, Mother shied away from it. Sunlight flashed against the blade. Every time, I was reminded of an animal baring teeth.

"Our farewell felt like the passing of a day. One moment our father was hugging us, our tears soaking the shoulder of clothes we had never seen him wear. The next, he was kissing our mother goodbye.

"Melor took me aside. He opened and closed his mouth several times, but no words would come. At last he withdrew a ring woven from grass and twigs. 'Wait for me?' he asked.

"I let him slip the ring on my finger and kissed him goodbye."

-6-

"TWO NIGHTS LATER, Yamalyn and I felt them die. We had finally fallen asleep when pain took us. A fist of steel and stone squeezed our hearts, and pain as bright and hot as fire feasted on our skin. We thrashed in our beds, and from further into the tree I heard my mother wailing.

"Then the sensations were gone, but the truth sat as heavily as iron. Our father was dead. Melor was dead. Their bodies were ash. *Sacrilege*, I remember thinking as I stared at my ring.

"Their deaths were all the warning we had."

-7-

"THEY EXPLODED FROM the trees in a rush, men clad in steel atop horses encased in armour.

"Half the grove was razed. Some of the men were executed. Those kept alive were put in chains. Their rations were nominal. Druids who had been big and powerful withered like malnourished trees. Ribs stood out against their skin. Their faces were gaunt, bruised, and bloodied. The invaders put them in chains—I could feel the steel burning their skin—and set them to work chopping down trees and shaping them into palisades and walkways and walls. Not all trees fell. Kenovians liked the seclusion and thought our grove the perfect staging area for a large-scale invasion of the cities to the south.

"The men were abused, yes. But things were worse for the women. The Kenovians were big men. Hair covered their chests like moss. Their hands were the size of stumps. Their heads were shaved bald. Their eyes were the colour of cold steel. Their needs were the same as every man's. Every night, icy fear set in as the sky darkened. Soldiers pulled mothers from where they huddled with their children and took them right there. Others pulled them into the forest. They went far enough in that our ears could not hear, but our bodies were connected to the earth. We wept and sent waves of compassion and sisterhood through the roots and dirt until they were brought back, sobbing and bruised.

"After the first night, my mother told me to make myself homely. I was covered in dirt and soot. I did not bathe. I bent my back as I carried serving trays and performed other menial tasks. Yamalyn watched me and did the same.

"Comali and her family were not so resourceful. The first time her mother was taken, her father resisted. Three soldiers beat him and dragged him to the feet of a man as tall and powerfully built as an oak. This, I learned later, was Emperor Jogoth. He sat in a throne of steel. He did not speak. Comali's father was on his knees, his hands tied behind his back, but he glared into the eyes of the big man. The emperor rose slowly. Then he took Comali's father's head in between his hands and began to squeeze.

"I closed my eyes. We all did. All of us except Comali and her mother. Her mother was taken into the trees after and did not return. For weeks, Comali stared straight ahead. Every time Yamalyn our I tried to talk to her, she stared through us. Past us.

"Resistance broke out occasionally. Men refused to let their women be taken, or the women refused to let themselves or their daughters or their sisters or their nieces or their earth kin be taken. Occasionally, somcone attempted escape. Everyone who tried, failed. Heads were dipped in tar and skewered on stakes around thc encampment. Sunken eyes and mouldy flesh told the story. Try, and die."

-8-

"THERE WAS NO Planting, no Harvest. The soldiers were eating through our stores, but they had brought spoils from their victories. Yamalyn served with the rest of us, eyes downcast, face and hands and clothes dirty, blessedly ugly.

"One night, a soldier staggered out of the gathering and into our tree, bursting in while we ate our meagre rations. His sour breath washed over us, and as he stood there, inspecting my mother, sister, and me like we were meat, he reeled on his feet, clearly drunk. He grabbed me and pulled me toward him. I stumbled forward, forcing him to drag me. Not out of

145

resistance, I am ashamed to admit. Out of blind fear. My legs would not move. Breath froze in my throat. I did not know what to do.

"Yamalyn stepped forward. Her eyes were wide, her mouth open in fear, but the soldier must have mistaken it for open desire because he paused, his eyes sliding from me to Yamalyn. My sister swallowed. Then she stepped forward and rested one hand on his arm. Her eyes held his. Drool leaked from his lips, which were cracked and bleeding, like sap.

"Perhaps he saw something in Yamalyn that Mother and I had missed. Perhaps he decided he was too drunk to bother subduing a beautiful woman, and went for easier but less comely prey. Whatever the reason, he shoved me to the floor and snatched Yamalyn's wrist.

"Mother and I screamed, but the man did not care. I reached for Yamalyn. She gently pushed my hand away, and in her eyes, red and puffy, I saw steel.

"'Do not resist. I will be back.'"

-9-

"THE NEXT HOUR was the second worst of my life.

"My mother and I clung to one another, listening to the earth. And heard nothing. I was overcome with shame and horror. Yamalyn was my younger sister. I was supposed to protect her. Instead, she had sacrificed a sacred part of herself for me.

"Suddenly, a sensation: death, followed immediately by life.

"'What is it?' I asked my mother. But she was inconsolable. If she felt the growth, she gave no sign.

"One hour later, Yamalyn returned alone and unbloodied. Sobbing, Mother ran her hands over her face. 'Did they touch you, my giver of care?' she said, her voice hitching.

"Yamalyn shook her head. Mother clutched her to her bosom and rocked her. Later, just before the sun began its ascent, Mother drifted into a troubled sleep. At last Yamalyn threw her arms around me. I hugged her back, and we sat like that for a time.

"It took several moments to find my voice. 'Where is he?'

"'Who?'

"'The soldier. The one who . . .'

"She pulled away. Her eyes were wet and puffy. 'Dead.'

"I rocked back. 'How?'

"She hesitated. 'Will you walk with me in the morning?'

"'Yamalyn—'

"'Will you?'

"I ran my dry, engorged tongue over dry, bruised lips. 'Yes.'"

-10-

"AT DAWN, YAMALYN took my hand and we crept into the forest. We passed rows and rows of trees until we came to a clearing. The grass was trampled and muddy. It would have been the next spot for a Planting, if our lives had turned out differently.

"'This is where I was taken,' she said."

"A shudder ran through me. 'Where is the body?' I assumed she had murdered the soldier and buried him in a grave dug with her own hands, or perhaps stuffed the corpse in a tree. I should have remembered how smart she was.

"She pointed. I followed her finger. An oak stood at the far end of the clearing. Its trunk was twisted and gnarled. Its branches were bare and skeletal. There were three holes that reminded me of a pair of eyes and a mouth twisted in suffering. It had not been there before. The bark was rotting before my eyes, and it stank of death.

"I opened my mouth to demand an explanation. Then I remembered the sensation: death, followed swiftly by life. Slowly, I approached it and touched it. Screams rang through my mind. I winced, but did not pull my hand away. The screaming went on and on and on. It would continue forever, always at the apex of torment.

"When I turned, Yamalyn was shaking. I held her and whispered words of comfort. My words were strange to my ears, but I could not discern why. Not then.

"We crept back into the camp before the soldiers awoke. We lay next to each other, and we plotted.

"No—I plotted. She listened."

-11-

"COMALI WAS NOT eating. She was not speaking. She was not fighting. Yamalyn and I brought her into our fold to save her life, or to end it. We stressed that point: no one could know. If we were caught, if anyone even suspected, we would be killed.

"Something changed in Comali's eyes as she listened to our plan. 'When do we start?'

"'Tonight,' I said."

-12-

"ONE OF THE soldiers came by the tree with rations. I greeted him with a smile and a clean face and change of clothes. He smiled back. I talked lightly, touched his arm. The desire in his gaze burned away suspicion. I stepped close when I spoke so he could feel my breath against his cheeks, his lips, his ears. He trembled with passion. Of course he did. I was beautiful again.

"He wanted me then and there, but he knew he could not have me. His lips loosened. The emperor set hard rules, the man explained. Work by day. Play at night. I sent the soldier away, but hinted strongly that he should come back to me at nightfall.

"He returned immediately after dark. Mother did not try to stop me. Mother was unwell. I left Yamalyn to tend to her. Waves of fear coursed from Yamalyn to me, but I was not afraid. I was eager. My younger sister had protected me. Now I would protect her.

"I led my soldier by the hand to the clearing, listening to the hoarseness of his words as we walked. In the middle of the clearing, I turned to him, and he wasted no time. I expected as much. He'd been frothing all day. He tore my robe trying to remove it. His lips were on my chest, my shoulders, my neck, my ears. When he kissed me, I nearly vomited. His breath was rancid. His few teeth were yellow, and many were pitted or filed off, or both. But I played along. My hands looped around his neck, and I pressed my body against his. He let out a moan and stuck his tongue down my throat.

"I let my saliva flow into his mouth and whispered our prayer. 'Flesh to wood, blood to root.'

"He paused, momentarily confused, but he must have

assumed I was whispering sweet nothings and went back to his groping.

"'To sway in the breeze, and forever be.'

"I stepped back out of his grasp as his moan turned into a scream. The sound lasted a heartbeat. Less. Bones snapped as his arms curled around and around him. His upper torso twisted and cracked. Blood gushed from his body like water squeezed from a rag. His skin hardened and browned. His eyes and mouth widened and sunk into his trunk. His legs stabbed deep into the earth, where I knew his toes were splitting apart into roots.

"His head was the last to turn. I stepped forward and caressed his cheek. Bark swept over him, coarse, the trunk twisted and fully grown, but rotting, a reflection of the man it had been.

"When it was over, I placed my hand on him. In my mind, he screamed and screamed."

-13-

"OVER THE NEXT month, the camp grew. And shrank.

"One by one, soldiers came to us. To me, to Comali, to Yamalyn. One by one, they vanished. No one noticed. I learned from my men, my prey, that there were always deserters in an army the size of the Kenovians'. If one was to run, one ran hard, and always during the night, when the camp broke down into revelry and debauchery. Emperor Jogoth was a hard man. If one stopped running, one would inevitably die, and find one's head planted on a stake.

"These desertions went unnoticed because Emperor Jogoth's party was growing. More soldiers came through the trees or marched along their burnt and scarred path. More trees were cut down. More buildings erected.

"All the while, Comali, Yamalyn, and I did our work. We wore jewellery given as gifts during the day, with whispered promises of repayments at night. When I was offered a gold ring set with a ruby the size of a knuckle, I shed Melor's ring, which had wilted, without thinking twice about it.

"We served men, picking out targets as they feasted while our people wasted away. Outwardly, we were all smiles. Our eyes sparkled. We bit our lower lips. We laughed. We touched. We suggested. Below our beautiful, painted exteriors, tempers simmered.

"At night, we led men to the clearing. They expected to take us. We took them.

"When we thought no one was looking, the girls and I exchanged secrets. Tricks of the trade. Comali was the most damaged of us. Broken, held together by sheer force of will and a burning that could only be quenched by vengeance and blood, she refused to let seductions progress farther than kissing.

"'No man will have me,' she said fiercely. She got a faraway look on her face when she said these words and scrubbed at her eyes before tears could fall.

"Yamalyn was careful. One man a night was perfect. Two was acceptable, but a risk. Three was unheard of. The clearing became less clear. It was a graveyard of life, trees frozen in endless torment. Most were mine.

"A change had come over me. I still cannot believe I missed it. But it was gradual, Jaranim. Spring sliding into summer. I should have paid closer attention. Perhaps I would have, had I not been struggling to protect my sister. That's what I told myself. I was protecting her.

"To say I was bold would be to call summer storms light rains. Where Comali and Yamalyn pulled men one at a time, I worked myself up to small groups eager to play with me together. Yamalyn came upon me once. I had guided five to the clearing. Three were still alive when your mother found us. I had learned how to grow them slowly, you see. The bottom half of their bodies had become wooden. The upper halves were twisted, broken, covered in gore. Through a foam of blood, their lips moved soundlessly. I could read them. *Kill me.*

"I did. After a time. We were far from the camp, which was loud and boisterous, and the trees screened the sounds of their dying.

"'What are you doing?' Yamalyn hissed the time she discovered me at my work.

"I glanced at her, then turned to my next prey. Two down. Three to go. 'I like it.'

"Yamalyn's sleep was troubled that night, even though she slept on a mattress of straw with a thick blanket given by a suitor. I listened to her inner turmoil as I lay still. Killing was not only morally wrong. It was antithetical to our people. We were druids, and our women were Her custodians. Our gift of life was being seeded in men to rend, break, and kill.

"'We kill only to protect ourselves and our people,' she insisted to me the next morning.

"I had said the same once. 'They deserve it,' I replied then.

"'Yes,' she agreed, drawing the word out. 'But what of our souls, Sister?'

"I had no answer."

-14-

"Something died inside Mother when our father was killed. She saw what Yamalyn and I were doing, believed she knew what was happening to us night after night. Moreover, she saw that we appeared unaffected by it. Even eager for it. Yamalyn's zeal was an act. Mine was not.

"Mother fell deeper into a black hole of despair. Yamalyn wanted to confess to her, but I forbade it.

"'She'll make us stop. Or she'll try to stop us and end up dead. Is that what you want?' I said.

"When Mother did not emerge from her tree one morning, I stepped in to find her body. The emperor's attendants were kind enough to let us Grow her in a space behind our tree. *Flesh to wood, blood to root.*

"I held Yamalyn as she wept. I stared into the distance, my face dry."

-15-

"I did not want to kill all the soldiers. I was no fool. I was working up to something. To someone.

"I watched the emperor, making sure he saw me walking as I made my way through the camp. The emperor saw but said nothing. Did nothing. He sat on his throne and observed. His head never turned. His chest seemed to barely rise and fall. Only his eyes moved, seeming to follow every person as traffic flowed through his town.

"I seethed. No man had resisted my charms. His indifference

151

was the gravest insult. Yamalyn cautioned against what she knew I wanted. I listened to her, until one night two moons later. 'We have to leave,' I said. 'Tonight.'

"I had slipped into our cabin, built from ancient trees that druid hands had been forced to cut down. It was more spacious than most prisoners', and full of food and our gifts. At my words, I felt hope surge within Yamalyn. More than once, she had mentioned escape to Comali and me. Every time, Comali and I had refused. No one cared if one soldier or seven out of hundreds disappeared. The women were another matter. Each night we were counted. If we ran, we would be hunted down and killed.

"'Let's go now,' she said, taking my hand. 'We'll find Comali and the other women and we'll just go.'

"I shook my head. 'If we want to bring them, we'll have to think. To organise. It can happen after.'

"'After what?' she asked.

"'After I've taken him.'

"She did not need to ask who. By then, I had a plan."

-16-

"DURING DINNER, HOLDING a torch aloft, I strolled up to Emperor Jogoth's throne and rested a hand on his leg. The camp fell quiet. Men sitting at long tables crudely fashioned from fallen trees watched. Jogoth held me with his eyes. I did not look away as I slid my hand up to his thigh.

"He rose. Stepped down from his throne and to the ground. Took me by the hand and pulled me away. A wave of raucous cheers followed him. He betrayed nothing.

"Comali and Yamalyn had been threading their way from table to table when Jogoth and I left his throne. I felt them follow. They stayed far behind us, not needing to see the distant bobbing flame of my torch to shadow me. They halted outside the clearing. The graveyard. Jogoth and I stood in the centre, among the trees. The men. They were silent. They were screaming.

"I held his gaze as Jogoth undressed me slowly. He let his eyes roam. 'You are unmarked. How is it you can survive so long, be used by so many of my men, and bear no bruises?'

152

"'The men treat me well,' I replied, my tone low and sultry.

"Emperor Jogoth cocked his head, turning my words over. 'Perhaps it is as you say. Yet the talk concerning your talents is all supposition. No man among me has claimed to have had you. Only to want you.'

"'They want me again. And again. And again.'

"He traced one long, painted fingernail down the side of my face, around the curve of my chin. It paused, held there like the point of a dagger.

"'They talk as you move among them,' Jogoth said. 'But never after. Why?'

"There was a quick pinch, then a droplet of blood welled and ran down my throat. Without turning his head, Jogoth inspected the clearing-that-was-no-longer-clear. 'You brought me to this place. You knew your path.'

"'It is private.' My voice rasped.

"'Do you know what I think?'

"I knew. We all did.

"Comali and Yamalyn felt my fear. They leaped out of hiding and raced toward me. They were too late in some ways, just in time in others. I darted out of Jogoth's reach, dropping my torch in my haste. Yamalyn was not so lucky. Jogoth spun on her and his fists and feet blurred as blows rained down. Everything happened so fast, yet time seemed to slow as I watched my sister crumple. I didn't notice the flames right away. Fire from my torch had tasted dry grass and judged it good. Flames raced over the ground, tasted the trees, found them good as well, and spread. The heat was incredible.

"Jogoth was big and strong, but we were fuelled by terror and rage. Comali hooked her hands and slashed at his eyes. With one hand he caught one of hers and twisted. Her scream shattered the silence. I came straight at him. I listened to the earth, heard his weight shift as one leg rose to kick outward at me. I wove smoothly to the side, grabbed the back of his head with one hand, and pulled him in for a kiss. My tongue found his, and he swallowed my saliva, and I prayed and pulled Comali free of his grip.

"As I broke away, he raked my eyes with his nails. They pierced my sight. The pain was like fire and irons. I screamed— in pain, and in what Jogoth believed to be gibberish. The last thing I saw of this world was a sight I had witnessed too many times to count. Jogoth did not scream. He did not so much as grunt. His body shook as if it were fighting the changes overtaking it. He stood no chance, but a man does not rise to emperor of Kenovia without putting up a fight.

"I fell to the ground, my eyes throbbing, my hands pawing, groping for Yamalyn, the world a confusing blur of red and black. Her hand found mine. Flames raged and the earth cried out around us. Yamalyn's breathing was irregular. Her injuries were severe. She tried to speak. 'Ssh,' I said, over and over."

-17-

"YAMALYN'S BODY HEALED, but a change had come over her as well. It was my fault, I think. In many ways, our hearts were one. Mine had turned stony. No love grew there, and so Yamalyn grew distant as well. We could no longer grow. Perhaps the Mother punished us. We gave death, so she took away our gift of life. Years later, when we had regrouped with what remained of our people, we married druids out of duty. My womb was as fallow as my heart, but Yamalyn gave her husband a son. You, Jaranim.

"She did not know you. She did not want to know you, or anyone. She had fallen into the same pit that had swallowed our mother. When her time came, she asked me to bring her back here. I visit her every spring, to remember."

-18-

HIKOLA LOOKED IN Jaranim's direction. She knew he stood there. She waited.

Jaranim was silent, considering. "To return to the earth. That was her request."

Hikola nodded. Again, she sensed her nephew reaching toward the tree. Again, she gently caught his arm. "Let it rest."

Jaranim nodded slowly, then trudged away to wait for her to finish.

Hikola faced the tree again. Her time was coming. The Mother called to her. This would be her last visit. The fire from the torch she had dropped so many springs ago had taken the

154

other soldiers, the other trees. She had felt all of them die, while her people, aware of what was coming before men of steel and leather and blood and death, had escaped in the confusion.

Without their emperor, Jogoth's army had fallen. His nation was captured, the Kenovian peasants set free. There was another casualty: The fire had claimed all that had remained of the clearing and her grove. Only ash remained, and this lone tree, protected from the fire by the word she had spoken. A blessing. No storm, no pestilence, no fire, no tool of man could remove it. It would endure forever.

She had lied to Jaranim. Yamalyn had been buried leagues from here. Hikola returned every year for one reason.

One bent, quivering hand reached out and touched the tree. She stood like that for a while, listening and smiling.

In her mind, Jogoth screamed and screamed and screamed.

Troll Seal

Rose Strickman

THE HOUSE WAS older than Janet remembered.

Shady and secretive beneath the spreading branches of the oak trees blazing with autumn colour, it seemed rooted in the earth. The wind sighed through the branches, a peaceful sound, and sent leaves skittering across the flagstone path. The grind of the highway was muffled and distant.

Janet made sure the key the lawyer had given her was safely in her pocket before grabbing her purse and slamming the car door behind her. Stopping only to get her bag and violin case from the trunk, she headed toward the front door, framed by vines crawling toward the sloping roof.

The path cut through a lush garden. Autumn flowers bloomed, and the lawn grew thick and verdant. Here and there, ceramic statuary poked from the foliage: strange gargoyles, earth-coloured. A dragon. A squat goblin. Abstract shapes that seemed to suggest mushrooms and toadstools.

Janet negotiated the lock, holding her purse awkwardly to her side, and opened the door to a rush of slightly stale air; no one had lived in this house for three months now, since Aunt Vera died. She stood in the doorway, blinking against the dimness.

She'd only been to this house once before, as a small child. What she saw now confirmed her dim memories: a cosy entryway, with hooks for coats and cubbies for shoes. There was even an old plaid coat hanging from a hook. Janet sighed as she hung up her purse and put away her shoes; the lawyer hadn't been kidding about her inheriting *the house and everything it contains*. Clearly, she would have to sort through all of Vera's things herself.

This was confirmed as she toured the rest of the cottage. The kitchen cabinets opened onto disorganized hodgepodges of equipment and utensils; Janet sniffed at the chaos. She'd have to clear *that* up, no question. The living room was in a similar state, with brightly coloured cushions thrown around and books lying on the coffee table. There was a music stand in the corner, but any hope that Vera had played was dashed when she saw it held nothing but a mass of dusty playbills and newspapers. She placed her violin case nearby anyway.

She opened the door to the bedroom a little tentatively, absurdly nervous: this was where Vera had died. Thank God, someone had stripped the bed. The bare mattress stood out in stark contrast to the rest of the room, which was in disarray, with books and clothes lying in heaps.

Janet delicately removed a lacy negligee from a sculpture. It was another ceramic statue, a pot-bellied gargoyle. Vera had been a real artist, Janet thought: she'd captured the creature's bright eyes and the sharpness of its long teeth perfectly.

"Well, I hope you're a friendly monster," she told the gargoyle, patting it on the head. She rotated around, sighing. "Got to clean this place up."

She began organizing the chaos, heaping all the clothes together in one pile, stacking the books in another, and shoving loose pens into a jam jar on the desk. As she did so, she uncovered more sculptures, similar to the first: each made of clay, about a foot high, depicting a different gargoyle or monster. There were long limbs, claws, horns, and sharp teeth, but also roly-poly bellies and friendly smiles. Four sculptures, each positioned in one of the four corners of the room.

"Well, you must be glad to be getting a dust," Janet said to the last one, wiping it with a pair of shorts. "I wonder if there are any more of you . . . ?"

She set off, back into the house, searching. Indeed there were more: foot-high ceramic sculptures, all of them earth- and clay-coloured, tucked discreetly—almost secretively—into corners and behind furniture. Each depicted a unique creature, obviously dreamed up from Vera's active imagination. There were bat wings, crocodile tails, shark teeth, and insect eyes, all lurking in the shadows. Nevertheless, each had a surprisingly benign expression.

"I wonder why she made so many?" Janet wondered aloud. She glanced at the side door to the converted porch, and, after a moment's hesitation, stepped through to Vera's old studio.

Vera McMahon had been a ceramics artist of some renown and her studio reflected that. There was a potter's wheel, a great oven, racks for drying sculptures, and tools lined up on the workbench. But the oven was cold, the loaves of clay gone dry; no one had worked here since Vera's sudden death three months ago.

Janet stood in the doorway, a leaden weight of depression falling on her. She'd enjoyed exploring, but the sight of the studio—so alien, so utterly useless to her—brought home the fact that she couldn't stay here. And if she couldn't stay, she'd have to go back, back to the city, back to the memories—

Janet closed her eyes tight. *Stop. Don't think that.* She took three deep breaths before opening them again. She had the autumn, anyway. She had the house to clean up, the estate to organize. She'd set up an office here and, perhaps, after three months, memory's razor edge would be blunted and she'd be ready to go home.

Smiling grimly—the fact that she looked *forward* to settling a deceased relative's estate proved that things were definitely bad—she turned and headed back to the kitchen.

There was a small, white-painted door she hadn't noticed before. Opening it, she found a flight of unfinished stairs leading down. She switched on the light and headed into the basement.

It was surprisingly bare down here, with none of the usual detritus of basements: no cardboard boxes, no dusty old furniture shoved out of the way, not even a laundry. Just more of the sculptures: four gargoyles positioned around the oddest discovery yet.

Janet blinked down at the vast, round ceramic tile, set in the floor like a plug. At least four feet across, it depicted, in intricate, upraised detail, a monster.

Not a friendly, fat-bellied monster like the gargoyles, but a true beast. Its hulk and proportions suggested great height; its apish arms bulged with muscles. Its flesh was half furred, half scaled; claws adorned its hands and feet, and malicious eyes blazed above a mouth crowded with fangs.

Janet shivered, irrationally glad that the monster was depicted as being behind bars, inside a cage. The imprisoned beast was surrounded by three concentric circles of flowers and vines, each a different species. The fourth, outermost circle depicted a continuous, unbroken chain.

"Okay, creepy . . ." This seemed so different from the rest of Vera's artworks. Far more malevolent. And—now that she looked around—it seemed to her that the gargoyles here in the basement were a bit more ferocious than those upstairs: none of them had any friendly smiles. Each stood crouched, ready to spring if the monster escaped . . .

Janet shook her head with a little laugh. If the monster escaped! It was just a ceramic tile. She was letting the creepy basement get to her. It was time to go back upstairs, finish unpacking.

It was a relief to return to the sunny kitchen and close the door behind her. Janet moved around, unpacking, but did not quite avoid looking at the basement door.

On Janet's third morning in the house, Stephen arrived.

It was such a glorious day that Janet took her laptop outside, to sit on the front porch while the world brightened around her. This was the way to work, she thought contentedly: laptop on her knee, tea at her side. The sun burned off the last phantasmal mists of night, and the dew sparkled on the flowers. She would really have to see about taking care of this garden—it seemed such a shame to let it go to waste . . .

As though her thoughts conjured it, a pickup truck rumbled up to stop by the front gate. Janet tensed as the door opened and a man got out.

"Hello there!" He waved cheerfully from the gate. "You must be Vera's niece. Mind if I come in?"

"Um, hi." Janet moved her laptop onto the table and stood up. "I'm Janet McMahon. Who are . . . ?"

"I'm Stephen Young. I was Vera's gardener—took care of it after she passed, too." His smile faded. "I—I didn't think before I came today, though. Should I come back later . . . ?"

"No, no, that's fine," Janet said, although part of her did wish to send him away from her peaceful solitude. "Go ahead."

She stood back nervously as Stephen saluted jauntily and went to the shed, getting out garden tools with the ease of long familiarity. "I'm sorry," she said at last, "I—I kind of thought Aunt Vera did her own gardening."

"Vera?" Stephen laughed. "No, no, she never did. She was an artist, not a gardener. But she liked a nice garden. She used to sit right in that chair, watching." He nodded at her vacated seat.

"I was working," Janet offered. "I'm an accountant."

"Oh? Do you enjoy that?"

Janet had to laugh. "It's got its good points. I . . . used to compose music too, but just as a hobby. How 'bout you? Do you do other people's gardens?"

"Yeah. I'm sort of an odd jobs man: roof repair here, house painting there. I get by."

Janet sat down again. "How well did you know my aunt?"

"About as well as anyone did." He shrugged. "She was pretty private. But I knew her going on thirty years—ever since she moved in. She was nice. Bit odd sometimes, but nice."

"Odd?"

"Well, you know: artist. She had the whole creative genius thing going on. You should've seen some of the stuff she came up with." He chuckled.

"I have. The house is full of gargoyles."

"Oh, yeah—Vera called those the guardians." Stephen began rooting around the rosebushes, looking for weeds. "Said they were there to keep the house safe. She sold a lot of them, too."

Janet thought of the four gargoyles in the basement, all facing the huge tile. "Did she ever show you the basement?"

Was it just her, or did Stephen pause just slightly? "Why do you ask?"

"Well, there was something a bit weird down there . . ." Briefly, she described the tile.

Stephen listened and, when she was finished, said, "Huh!"

"What do you mean?"

"I saw that tile once." Stephen returned to weeding, a bit more vigorously than before. "Must've been about a year after she moved in. I was in the house for some reason, and she had it in her studio. A big ceramic plaque with a monster in a cage. Vera said it was a . . ." He broke off.

"What?"

"She said it was a troll seal. Something meant to keep a troll imprisoned underground." Stephen looked up with an apologetic smile. "Like I said, your aunt could be a bit odd."

Janet thought of the monster, caged in ceramic. The *troll*. "Odd. Right."

THAT NIGHT, JANET dreamed.

She dreamed she was back with Neal, and a bittersweet joy soaked the dream. She had Neal *back*—they were laughing and happy together, but even dreaming, she knew her happiness would end when she woke alone—

And then she did.

She lay in the utter dark of the rural night. A dry sob rose up her throat. She was in her dead aunt's house and Neal was gone forever.

She couldn't stay in bed. An urge she couldn't quite identify drove her to her feet and through the house.

The living room, illuminated by the lamp's golden glow, was still a mess, but it was an organized mess now: one of neatly labelled boxes and bags, full of things Janet was either going to keep, sell, or donate. She opened her violin case and removed the instrument and bow.

It felt good to hold her violin again. After Neal's death, she'd spent hours playing: long, melancholy tunes that filled her apartment like sobs and sighs. But she hadn't been able to compose anything. Every time she'd tried setting her pencil to the music paper, the pain had spiked, driving back any inspiration.

But now the night was a sea of solitude around her island of light, and the urge was rising again.

She went to fetch paper and pencil. Adjusting the music stand, she wrote out a few notes of the tune taking shape in her head. Experimentally, she played them. No—something slower, a more minor key. Yes. That was it.

Her pencil scratched out the revised chord.

"HELLO, MS. JANET!" Stephen peered at her through the morning sunlight. "You sleep okay?"

"Fine." Janet fought down a yawn. She'd composed for hours, the tune practically writing itself, and only staggered back to bed as the sun came up. Now she was bleary and heavy-eyed. Still, she felt more cheerful than she had in a long time, in an exhausted way. She was composing music again. Progress.

"You should head into town." Stephen loaded compost into his wheelbarrow. "Can't be good for you, locked up in that house all the time."

"I've only been here a few days."

"Yeah, but you don't want to become a recluse. We're having the farmer's market tomorrow—you should come!"

"Oh, yeah? Will you be there?"

"Probably. Just as a shopper, though." He dug his shovel into the compost heap. "I used to be a vendor," he said reflectively. "Years ago. I had my own plot of land. I grew organic berries."

"Why'd you stop?" Janet leaned against the porch rail.

"Something went wrong with my land." Stephen shrugged. "All my bushes died, one by one. The soil went strange—sort of chalky and nasty. I called in the experts, but they couldn't explain it. Then your aunt came around."

Janet blinked. "My aunt?"

"Vera had some sculptures she said I should bury in my land. Weird little golem things. She said—" He broke off.

"What?" He didn't reply. "Come on, what?"

"You've got to remember," he mumbled, "your aunt was a very unusual person. Intelligent and nice, but . . . Anyway, she said a *gremlin* was burrowing around under my property. Ruining the soil. That was bad enough, she said, but then it attracted worse things."

Janet thought of the basement. "Like trolls?"

"Yeah, maybe." Stephen dug in with more vigour. "Well, I told her it was nonsense. But soon after that, I woke up in the middle of the night. Something was screaming. It was my dog, Christy. Something had torn her to pieces."

Janet felt a dark shiver. "That's awful."

"Yeah. Must've been a bear or something. Anyway, that was the last straw. I got rid of my plot—got stiffed for it, too—and haven't tried farming since."

"Sorry to hear that." Janet paused. "Did you ever find out what really happened?"

Stephen shook his head. "Never did. The land recovered, though, with no one farming it." He laughed. "Maybe the gremlin went away!"

"Yeah." Janet's laughter felt false and flat. "Maybe."

JANET HAD ACCOUNTANCY work to do that day, and then she had to meet with the lawyer before dropping off donations, so she had no time to compose more music. The tune was running through her head, though, and she woke early the next day to take up her violin. She wrote notes, tried them out, and replaced them. Slowly, the tune grew.

It was a relief to get out of bed and work on the composition. She'd had a fitful sleep. She kept swimming up from dreams of whispering voices, rising from underground. She couldn't make out what the voices were saying, but they sounded malevolent. Janet pushed the nightmares aside. They were just dreams. She wrote another note, in minor key. This was turning into a slow, sad song, almost a dirge.

By the time she finished the day's composition, the sun was high and hot and dreams of dark voices seemed foolish. She remembered Stephen mentioning the farmer's market. Well, why not?

The little town on the river buzzed with activity; she had a hard time finding a parking place. She had to traverse most of the town to get to the market, but it was worth it: a riot of colour and happy activity. She shopped the stalls and ate at one of the food trucks, tucked underneath a tree. She left the market only to purchase blank music paper at a nearby art supply store. By the time Janet got back to the car, darkness was beginning to gather in the sky, filling the spaces under the trees and between the buildings.

Janet drove home through the twilight, pausing only when her headlights swept over a deer, crossing the road. Janet slowed and stopped; she and the doe stared at one another a moment before the animal slipped gracefully into the brush.

Still marvelling over the encounter, Janet arrived back at the house, groping her way to the front door and switching on the light in the entryway. It had been quite a day, she thought, hanging up her purse and hauling the bags into the kitchen. Still, she didn't feel *so* tired . . . perhaps there was time for more composition. She'd already had dinner in town, after all.

She started to head for the living room.

Don't.

She paused. What had that been? That soft, scratchy . . . voice?

Don't finish the spell.

The hairs on her neck stood up. "Who's there?"

Only silence answered her. Overhead, the kitchen light shone prosaically. Even the gargoyle in the corner looked almost ordinary.

Janet frowned at it. What was it doing here in the kitchen? She could have sworn that gargoyle—a cross between a bat and an alligator—had been in the hallway before.

She bent down to pick it up—and hesitated, pulled back by a sudden, irrational reluctance. What if she felt skin and scales instead of clay? What if it *moved*—?

She growled at herself. "Don't be an idiot." She picked up the gargoyle, and it felt like regular glazed ceramic, its hollow body giving a little scraping ring as she lifted it.

She placed it by the bench in the entryway. It looked so familiar there—so right—that she was almost convinced it had been there before. But then how had it gotten into the kitchen . . . ?

She pinched her eyes shut. "God," she grumbled. "Got to get to bed." She was going as mad as her aunt . . .

She headed to the bedroom, resolutely not checking to make sure the gargoyle hadn't moved.

THE NEXT DAY was grey, cloudy, and cold. In that dim light, the gargoyles squatted like toadstools.

Janet sipped coffee, rubbing her forehead. Her dreams had taken an odd turn again. More voices, only this time she could understand them: *Release me. Make me real. Release me.* She shuddered. Utterly creepy.

She found herself wandering into the living room. Her violin gleamed in the cloudy light. Well, why not? It was Sunday; there was no pressing work. And a settled melancholy was coming over her. *Neal.*

It felt good to work on the composition. To copy out her earlier work onto her new music paper and journey on through the long, gloomy phrases. The tune was getting darker as it progressed: long sighs that turned into musical sobs as she played them out, a steady, yearning misery that fitted well with the gloomy day. The musical phrases cried out longingly as she played them, joining chords, testing. *Give me back what I have lost. Release me from my misery.*

And then, as the day waned on, the composition was finally done. Janet centred the pages on the stand and, standing straighter, began to play from the top.

Each note sobbed; each chord sighed. As she played, slow tears slid down Janet's face, but not enough to fill the deep void of her sorrow. *Give me back what I have lost.* On she played, the day vibrating around her. *Release me from my misery.*

At last, the final note died in the silent house. Janet remained still, tears sliding down her cheeks. "Neal." It escaped in a sigh: the first time she'd spoken her lover's name since the funeral.

Not the one for her aunt, which she had attended in a distracted daze; but the one just before. The one she'd stood well back from, away from the notice of Neal's family—his parents, his children, his wife—and watched while they lowered her lover's coffin into the earth, grief churning with guilt.

His family and friends all knew how he had died. But none of them suspected that he had died because of *her.*

Afterward, when the mourners left and the gravediggers finished packing fresh earth in the hole, she'd come forward and fallen to her knees and then to her face, clawing at the soil, begging his forgiveness, begging the earth to give her back what she'd lost.

But the earth does not give back. It takes, it transmutes and births again, but it does not return what has become its possession. Neal was in the earth, and there he would remain.

"Neal," Janet repeated. *Give me back what I have lost.*

Release me from my misery.

Release me.

NIGHT FELL SLOWLY, gathering in trees and pooling between hills. A handful of leaves, snatched up by the wind, rattled against the window as Janet ate a desultory dinner in the kitchen. Halloween seemed to be coming early this year, she thought, listening to the wind. She wished it could drown out the tune in her mind. Strange: her own compositions didn't normally become stuck in her head . . .

There came a sudden thump.

Janet looked up, jaws freezing mid-chew. Was someone at the door?

The thud sounded again, but not from the front door. It was much nearer. It was behind the basement door.

Someone was coming up the stairs. A large, heavy someone.

Ice shot through Janet's veins. She jumped to her feet, backing away—only to trip over something large, heavy, and ceramic.

It was a gargoyle. And it wasn't alone. The kitchen was filled with them, all crowded on the floor, all facing the basement door. Janet stared, breath coming sharp and laboured.

Then the gargoyles moved.

They all took one step forward. She saw them lift their disparate legs, the pull of impossible muscles, heard the pottery *chink* of their joints. They all took one step forward, toward the basement door, while the thudding footsteps steadily rose and a red light grew around the door's edges.

There came a tug at Janet's jeans leg. She looked down to see the alligator-bat. *Don't just stand there!* it said. *Run! Hide!*

Janet was never sure, afterward, how she got out of the kitchen, but she must have, because she next found herself shoving a bureau across the door to the bedroom, the alligator-bat and the four room-guardians helping. "What is it?" she panted hysterically. "What's coming?"

The troll, of course, said Alligator-Bat. *Your spell set it free within this house. Get into the closet, hurry!*

Janet dived for the closet, easing the latticed door shut behind her, and it was a measure of her state of mind that she was actually relieved when Alligator-Bat crawled in with her, climbing into her arms. *The guardians will try to stop it,* it said, *but I'm not sure—*

It was broken off by a sudden deluge of noise from the

kitchen: a roar, followed by shattering pottery. Janet cringed, and Alligator-Bat clung hard, its cold talons digging into her flesh.

A moment's silence. Then the steps sounded again.

Janet trembled as they drew nearer and nearer. *Should've gone outside. Should've driven off in the car—*

There came a shattering thud at the bedroom door, followed by another, and another. Then a crash as the bureau fell over.

More thudding footsteps, and the bureau being kicked aside. She could hear the rasp of the troll's breath now, a constant stertorous noise. Its bloody glow filled the cracks of the closet door. Then the chinking noise of the guardians leaping forward, only to be met with more broken pottery.

Nearer the monster came. It was right outside the closet now: she could see the savage gleam of its eyes through the slats, the hulk of its great misshapen body. Patterned by the lattice, its sickly red light shone. In her arms, Alligator-Bat trembled.

Then, with a single movement, the troll ripped the closet door off its hinges and dragged Janet out.

She screamed, and she choked as the monster's foul stench of rot and fungus hit her. Her legs kicked uselessly as it lifted her off the floor. Its mouth opened, revealing a cavern of wet tongue and sharp teeth—

Little witch, it said, its words communicated through growls that resolved into meaning in Janet's ears. *Little witch who cast the spell and set me free. Can you understand me?*

Frantically, she nodded.

The troll turned and tossed her onto the bed. She scrambled up, crawling as far away as she could, pressing into the wall.

The troll's black eyes travelled over her contemptuously. *You,* it said. *You have not half the wit nor the power of your predecessor, but you have enough. One spell to set me free within this house. Another to make me real.*

"Y-you seem pretty real already," Janet managed.

I am real only to you. To all other mortals, I am nonexistent, barely able to frighten them from the shadows or trouble their nightmares. The troll gave a wordless growl of frustration. *And only within this house! I have no ability to leave this dwelling, to hunt frightened mortals, to slake my hunger or wet my teeth on their blood . . .* Its voice trailed off yearningly. *Only you can give that to me. Only you can cast that spell.*

"I can't." Janet's voice rose. "I can't cast spells!"

Liar. Fool and liar. You cast the spell that broke the seal holding me prisoner. "Release me," your spell said. And so I was released.

Janet gaped. She was responsible for this thing getting out?

And now . . . The troll stepped closer, and she cowered back. *You are going to cast another spell. The one that will make me real and set me free in the world.*

Its simian arm shot out. Janet screamed, but still the troll grabbed her and, holding her off the floor, it thundered back through the house, past the shattered bodies of gargoyles, and into the living room. Janet let out another cry as it dumped her before the music stand.

Play, the troll commanded. *Cast the spell.*

Janet stared crazily at the stand. She couldn't have lifted her bow in her present state, never mind played anything. "I can't."

The troll leaned close, and she almost fainted at the stench of its breath. *Play or die.*

Janet forced herself not to scream. "It doesn't work like that." She had no idea where she got the words from, but she spun them out frantically. "I . . . I have to compose the spell. Like I did before. I can't just play a new composition right out of my head. It takes time."

The troll paused. Janet pressed her advantage. "Give me a week to compose the new spell."

The troll let out a hiss. Janet held her breath.

Three days, it said at last. *You may have three days to compose the new spell. On the night of the third day, I will return, and you will play me real and play me free. And don't try to run, little witch,* it added. *I still have allies among the ghouls and gremlins, the oak-hags and goblins. They'll find you.*

No need to describe what would happen then. *Until the third night, little witch.* Then, turning, the troll stamped back across the house. Janet heard the basement door close just before her legs gave way and she fell gasping to the floor.

AFTER THE TROLL was gone, she spent the night curled in a rigid ball, rocking and staring in unthinking terror. Even Alligator-Bat, when it joined her in the living room, couldn't break her from her horrified trance. Then, as the sun rose, lightening the shadows and peeking between tree branches, the gargoyle had reverted to its inanimate state, freezing into its original position, eyes literally glazing over. *They must come alive only at night,* Janet thought, the world blackening around her. *The movies have it right, I guess.*

The thought made her giggle hysterically as she passed out.

When she awoke, it was midmorning and the house was a mess. Janet cleaned up, sweeping the shards of broken gargoyles into paper bags and picking up broken furniture and doors. Then, the house restored to some semblance of order, she proceeded to tear the entire place apart.

She wasn't sure what she was looking for. A book of spells, dusty with the magical lore of the ages? A letter her aunt had left her, telling her in detail how to get rid of trolls? A mystic sword of legend? But she found none of those things: just artworks and old furniture and outdated clothes and dusty paperbacks.

Finally, Janet sat down amidst the chaos. She propped her aching forehead in her hands, trying to think.

Spells. Magic. Trolls. Aunt Vera. Her composition. What did all of these things have in common? Janet took a deep breath, let it out again. She got up to find pen and paper.

Writing what she thought of as the main "actors"—*Troll, Seal, Vera, Gargoyles, Composition*—as headings, she filled in the columns below with as much information as she had. Which wasn't much. But it was enough for her to discern a pattern.

Art. She circled it. Vera had exercised magic through her art, making the gargoyles, the seal, and even Stephen's gremlin statues. Janet had done the same, composing and then playing music. So there wasn't going to be a spell book, no set of instructions on what to do next. Magic, apparently, didn't work like that. It must be triggered and exercised through—Janet groped for the right word—*creativity.* Creativity and originality. The troll had said so itself. *Compose the spell.* Janet smiled bitterly; it was hard to imagine the troll making sculptures or writing music. But maybe its magic was different.

Janet realized she was ravenous and went to cook something. Outside, the sun was setting behind the autumn trees as a cold wind rattled the baring branches. She'd wasted almost the entire first day of her three-day window.

Janet pushed aside the thought. There had to be some way out of this. But the troll had said running was no use, and she believed it. She would have to compose another song—another spell—that would send the troll rampaging through the world—

She bit back a sob. Crying would do no good. Logic might.

Magic. Art as magic. Magic through creativity. But the troll hadn't quite seemed to understand that, had it? It had dumped her before the stand, expecting her to come up with a spell right away—maybe because that was the way troll-magic worked. She'd had to explain that she needed time . . .

For the first time, a ray of hope broke through. She couldn't run, and she couldn't fight the troll. But maybe . . .

Grabbing her bowl of eggs and rice, Janet ran to the living room.

Night fell, and found Janet sitting on the floor in a sea of crumpled music paper.

Movement, and she tensed, lifting her aching head, but it was only Alligator-Bat, crawling across the floor. Janet anxiously glanced past it to the doorframe. "Will the troll come back?"

It might. It's trapped in the house, though. You should find somewhere else to sleep. Alligator-Bat cocked its head at her. *What did you do with the shards of my brethren?*

"Swept them up and put them in paper bags. I'm not sure what else to do . . . "

Bury them tomorrow. Not in bags or boxes: just bury the shards in the earth. They'll be reabsorbed. Alligator-Bat sniffed at the discarded papers. *What are these?*

Fighting tears, Janet explained the troll's ultimatum. Alligator-Bat sniffed some more. *But these papers won't work,* it said. *There's no power in any of them.*

"I know." Now the tears started rolling. "I've tried and tried all day, but I couldn't seem to—to make the power come like before . . . Do you know what I should be doing?"

Alligator-Bat gave a flowing sort of shrug. *I'm not a witch.*

Just an elemental, bound in this statue. I never understood how Vera's magic worked.

"Art." Janet stood up, the room spinning a little. "It comes out through art. But just a collection of notes isn't art."

From the basement, a growl sounded. Both froze.

Come on, said Alligator-Bat, crawling to the door. *We can't stay here.*

Janet spent the night in her car, Alligator-Bat curled in her lap, watching the troll's red light shine from window to window.

JANET HAD JUST finished burying the last of the guardian shards the next morning when Stephen's car rolled up.

"Good morning!" He hopped out, beaming; then frowned at her. "Are you sick or something?"

Janet hoisted a smile and stood on the patch of disturbed earth that contained the shards. "Oh, no!" she said a tad too brightly.

Stephen wasn't buying it. "Everything all right?"

"Yes." Janet barely refrained from continuing, *I just got finished burying earth elementals who died defending me from the troll that got out from under Aunt Vera's seal when I played the right spell on my violin, and I have two days to compose another spell that will set it free to eat people . . .*

"Well, you look awful." Stephen slammed the car door. "Didn't you get any sleep last night?"

"Not much," Janet admitted. She wondered exactly how to go about this. "Stephen . . . did my aunt ever tell you anything about her work?"

"Well, she showed me her stuff." Stephen pulled on his gloves. "And there was that thing about the gremlin. But you shouldn't hold that against her," he added hastily.

"I don't. I just wondered if she ever told you more about . . . that side of her work."

"Not really. I mean, she showed me things sometimes—like the troll seal—but she knew I didn't believe in all that, so . . ." He shrugged. "Why do you ask?"

"Just curious," Janet said airily. "I wondered if she ever told you anything about that troll."

"Just that she was sealing it up. And she hoped no one ever cracked the seal."

I'm sorry, Aunt Vera. "Did she say how to put it back? If it ever got out?"

Stephen stopped working to stare at her. "Where's all this going?"

"Nowhere. I'm sorry." Janet slumped down on the front steps, watching him. Of course he didn't know anything about Vera's witchcraft. He'd never believed a word of it.

"Stephen." She was surprised by her own voice. "I did a bad thing."

"Oh, yeah?" He barely paused in unwinding the hose. "What?"

Let out a troll. "I had an affair with a married man." It came spilling out. "I knew he was married, but I did it anyway. And then he . . . then he . . ." She swallowed. "He died."

"How?" Stephen stood frozen, the hose in his hands, his face unreadable.

"Car crash." Janet buried her face in her hands. "Because of me."

"Because of you?"

"He was driving to see me," she said dully. "It was a dark, wet night. The car slid out of control . . . I went to the funeral. I stood back and watched them bury him. I wasn't invited, of course. I saw his wife . . . his kids . . . ." She shook her head. "I did a bad thing, and then I lost him, and it was my fault, and I don't know how to make it right."

There was a pause, broken only by the wind.

Stephen spoke at last. "Say you're sorry."

"But she doesn't know . . . "

"No. Say sorry to yourself. You're the one you're hurting, after all." Stephen's voice was gentle, though his words were hard. "Find a way to make it right to yourself, before you try apologizing to his wife. Then maybe you can move on."

A moment's silence passed. In the trees, a bird began to sing.

"Yes," Janet said quietly. "Yes, maybe I will."

THAT AFTERNOON, JANET composed music.

Notes, phrases, and chords slipped from her pencil. She played them on the violin; she hooked phrase to phrase. Slowly, the new spell grew, as the first had.

She still wasn't finished when night fell. Placing the music sheets in a folder that she tucked into her purse, she drove away, Alligator-Bat at her feet, to eat in town before coming back to sleep once more in her car, her violin at her side, a blanket thrown over her, while the troll once more prowled the house, its red light glowing from the windows.

The next morning, the house was a mess—the troll had broken more furniture in its growing frustration—but she didn't stop to clean. Instead, she sat at the table, and the composition grew. She scratched, she played chords, she debated, she replaced.

Then, by late afternoon, she was done. The new composition rang true from start to finish, not a false note anywhere.

Wearily, she put the sheets away and caught a nap, curled up around Alligator-Bat. She woke as the afternoon waned toward evening, to change her clothes and eat something. Then she sat in the kitchen, facing the basement door, waiting.

She did not wait long. As soon as the last scraps of light slid away, there came the familiar thumping, the red light, and the door crashed open.

The troll filled the doorframe. *Well, little witch?* it demanded. *Have you the spell?*

In reply, Janet stood and went to the living room. The troll stamped close behind. Its glow sickened the hallway, and she felt its hot, fetid breath on the back of her neck.

The troll stood in the middle of the living room, almost absurd in the electric light, among the human furnishings, and glowered as she adjusted the sheet music on the stand.

Ready, little witch? it snarled.

She nodded levelly. "Ready." She propped her violin against her chin, raised her bow. The first notes sobbed out.

The tune started slow and sad. It sang of guilt, of wrong things done in foolishness and ignorance. It sang of mistakes, and it sang of deeds better left undone.

The troll stirred eagerly. *Good,* it growled. *Good!*

Janet played without pause. The tune sang on, and now it told of the hollow time after great pain, when the agony is ended but the wounds are not yet healed. It sang of guilt and self-recrimination, the misery of knowing you've done wrong.

Yes, growled the troll in delight.

Then the tune changed.

What? The troll snarled. *What is this?*

Still Janet played. She played of wounds healing, of the power of friendship to end pain. She played of green things, of the stirring of life even in darkness, seeds cracking open. She played of new beginnings. She played of self-forgiveness.

The troll howled, but the spell was wrapping tight around it, cords (*chords*) of magic. Hope filled Janet, her notes swelling. She played of rectifying one's mistakes and moving on. She played of fixing problems instead of stewing in guilt. She played of the defeat of darkness, both within and without.

The troll screamed, but its cry came to a gurgling, strangled halt. It was compressing, it was shrinking, its red light fading. Its limbs froze, its eyes glazed. As life triumphed over death in Janet's spell, as hope ascended despair and the song came to its victorious finish, the troll shrank on the carpet, an ugly ceramic statue, smaller than any of the gargoyles.

The silence was deafening. Cautiously, Janet lowered her bow and violin, but the troll didn't roar back to life. The statuette stood lifeless, a monster caught forever in an attitude of rage: imprisoned.

Movement, and Alligator-Bat nosed in. It sniffed the statuette. *That was well done, mistress.*

"'Mistress?'" Janet stood still, watching. "You've never called me that before."

The guardian inclined its head. *You've earned the title.*

Yes. Perhaps she had. Janet put down her instrument and went over to pick up the statuette. She moved slowly; she was tired, so terribly tired. The statuette was smooth and glazed in her hand. It didn't feel as though it had ever been alive. "I think I'll keep this on a shelf in full sunlight," she said. "Where I can keep an eye on it."

That's a good idea, mistress. Alligator-Bat cocked its head at her. *Will you be staying here then?*

A wry half-smile curved her lips. "Well, I can hardly sell the house *now*, can I? I'll commute back and forth between here and my apartment. I think I've got a lot to learn here."

She did indeed, she reflected as she placed the statuette on a shelf in full view. She'd have to compose a spell of hibernation or something, and play it all the time, so the troll remained inanimate. She smiled at the thought, and at all the other spells and songs just waiting for composition.

Perhaps she wouldn't go back at all. After all, she seemed to have found a very promising new career here.

The Giants

Gregory L. Norris

I.

I NEVER TOLD you about that day in the field?

I was a teen, used to walk places, burn off all that excess energy. Miles in every direction. Often right past the big field with the windmill in the centre. Now, by windmill, I don't mean one of those stone and wood giants from Holland, where the tulips used to grow. This was a tall, skeletal frame made from metal with a pinwheel on top. It was how farmers generated electricity until all those poles and power lines went up.

The school bus travelled past the field, so I knew the windmill was there, a colossus running taller than the rows of corn that grew in summers and even the surrounding trees, which were taking back the cleared land. It had always struck my imagination as being our small town's version of the Colossus at Rhodes or some other ancient wonder in ruin.

That late winter day I was heading to Barlow's Country Store farther up, which still sold penny candy and nudie books in the back on a rack beneath one of those telescoping round mirrors when the windmill drew me off the side of the road, into that desolate field. I remember moving closer and the hollow cadence of its pinwheel high overhead as it turned in the brisk March breeze.

Creak.

Creak.

After plodding across acres of hard soil and the remains of the corn stalks, nubs chopped off just above the frozen earth, I reached my destination. The giant towered over me.

Creak.

I looked up. The stark blue sky over my eyes distorted. The windmill's pinwheel turned slowly, as tall as the moon. Dizzy, I leaned against one of the posts holding up the structure. At any second, ground and sky were going to switch position, I was sure, as vertigo embraced me and my stomach tied itself in knots.

Creak.

Heat coated my skin—worked up from the hike. But in the minute that followed, the sweat cooled. When I blinked myself out of the trance, I was shivering and the creaking over my head had stopped. It was like the entire world was holding its breath.

Here's the thing—the wind was still blowing. I felt it on my skin and heard it moaning across that empty field with the voice of a ghost. The knot in my guts had conspired with the chill sitting on my flesh to freeze me where I stood beneath the windmill, but fresh fear got my legs moving back in the direction of the road far beyond those acres of dead cornstalks and roots.

Creak.

The turning of the pinwheel sounded at my back, only this time it was different.

Creak.

I hastened forward, aware of the shaking under my soles and how the sound now struck my ears like a succession of giant footsteps in pursuit. A second after that realization, I was running. Running and shrieking, because I knew that if I looked over my shoulder a giant horror would be chasing me.

Until the snows, I'd never been so terrified, so certain of my death. At one point, I realized I was back on pavement and running along the road. I chanced a look over my shoulder but nothing was there, and I was far enough away that I couldn't see the field.

I travelled past it for a few more years on the school bus, but I never went back. Right before we moved, they knocked down the windmill, dug up the cornfield, and put in a neighbourhood of battleship-size houses. I remember reading about the fires there right before the snows. That's where the first one was sighted. Where it clawed its way up out of the ground.

II.

"THERE *WAS* SOMETHING chasing me," Carmine said, his voice barely above a whisper. "And I think it was one of them. I know, it was daylight and they only come out after dark, but maybe it was, I dunno . . . a spirit or some kind of advance scout, out for a look."

The handful of young faces huddled around the fire listened without commenting. It was still daylight, what little of that now fit the definition, but all had learned to stay quiet.

Carmine cast a look at the cellar window, the only one of four not covered over with scraps of insulation. It was getting darker, which meant no more wood could go into the cast iron stove, and that they'd let the fire die out. Embers would have to suffice. Soon the giants would wake.

"Last chance at bathroom breaks," he said.

After the end of the day's stories, no hands raised.

"All right," Carmine said. "You know the drill."

Wordlessly, the four children climbed onto the mattress in the corner. Taggert and one of the mothers covered them in layers of blankets and over those laid tarp. The chill was already creeping into the cellar. Carmine stole a final glance out the uncovered window before jamming in the square of insulation and rags, sealing them off from the new night and any potential prying eyes.

He imagined the last of the wood smoke thinning, dissipating in the late afternoon wind, their location beneath the rubble of the old church secured as much as could be hoped for in this new insane world.

The adults, Carmine included, went to their corners and covered themselves in piles of blankets. Carmine sank down against the cement, his eyes drifting up to that window, now hidden behind camouflage, and his heart resumed its twilight gallop in anticipation. Soon, he sensed the quiver rising up through the earth, shaking the foundation.

Boom.

The giants were awake, walking about, and hungry.

Boom.

He remembered the first time he'd seen one of them striding out of the forest back at the start of the snow. Carmine assumed he was one of the lucky ones—normally, if you saw one and it saw you, you weren't long for this new reality. You were dinner. Though having survived the encounter didn't exactly feel like luck.

It was near the lake. It was snowing and late in the afternoon. The Souceys had taken a gamble—made a break for the woods, because way up there, at the end of the trees, was the interstate. Their dad was sure someone would give the family of four a lift to one of the refugee centres cropping up under the protection of guns, tanks, and fighter jets; sure they'd get there before dark.

He'd travelled with them as far as old Mrs. Patton's house, one of those moneyed manors with a circular driveway. Mrs. Patton lived alone after the death of her husband. They didn't have children, and she'd hated kids on her lawn or sneaking through her yard to swim on the lake. No worries that year—it was the end of June, snowing, and the lake had yet to thaw following a long and terrifying winter.

Mister Soucey, his wife, and the two kids—Carmine rode the school bus with Anne Marie—cut across the skim of new snow covering the old woman's lawn. If she was home and infuriated at such an invasion of her sovereignty, Old Mrs. Patton didn't cause a furore. Only one of her cars was on the circular drive— the giant, rusting gas-guzzler that had belonged to the late Mister Patton.

Boom.

The sound reached him through the cadence of his laboured breaths. For a terrible instant, Carmine was back in the cornfield and something was in pursuit.

"*Hurry,*" he hissed through his teeth as he scrambled to reach the car.

But the Souceys hadn't heard him. They were cutting across the road, still headed toward the woods and the interstate beyond.

Carmine ducked down but risked a look through the window. *Boom.*

The ground trembled beneath him. The tall pines, branches drooping and white, shook off their fresh coats of snow as the giant stepped out of the woods. Carmine held his breath. He'd seen them on TV before the airwaves steadily silenced. Up close was different. He froze, forgetting to blink as well.

It walked upright, cloaked in some kind of ceremonial robe or matted fur. It wasn't quite human in design, was as tall as the surrounding pines and coated in the new snow like them. It emerged from the woods and looked down on the family of four, now stopped and silent.

In the pall that followed—an absence of sound only broken by the wind's disembodied moan—he wondered if the colossus was a frost giant from ancient Norse lore or something demonic that had dug its way up from Hell.

Then the resuming footsteps, the screams, and the paralyzing twilight view through the dirty windshield as the giant made a grab for them, scooping the Souceys up, and fed.

Boom.

Carmine was back in the present. One of them was out there, close enough that its footfalls vibrated through the ground and former church's foundation. Someone sobbed and, at first, Carmine couldn't be sure it wasn't he who'd made the sound because he was back on the road, having escaped the cornfield and the windmill, moaning as he sucked down breath. Then one of the mothers admonished the child, and all again fell deathly silent in their secret refuge.

He heard the cracking of branches, more proof of its nearness, and several additional footsteps. But then those trailed off, and the giant moved on.

It wasn't that he slept anymore so much as passed out. Exhausted from the constant cold. The constant fear. The constant struggle.

When Carmine woke, one of the children was at the cellar window, peering out at another snowy, grey morning.

III.

THEIR NIGHT VISITOR had gotten close. Too close. Footprints between the trees and the wrecked church put the giant to within a hundred yards.

"Help me," Carmine said to Taggert.

It was daylight, the usual murk; even so, they worked quietly using handsaws to turn the oak branches into lengths suitable for the fire. The wood was dead, long ago giving up the ghost of its green. They hauled back enough to keep the fire going to warm the cellar.

On the return trudge, his pack loaded with wood, Carmine froze.

Creak.

Through the camera of his mind, he was again in the desolate cornfield. But it was only the forest, branches stirring in the cold wind, he told himself.

Taggert huffed, "Carmine."

The other man was a dozen steps ahead, the foundation and rubble another twenty or so beyond that. It wasn't much of a home, but it was all they had.

He remembered how he'd run that day, and also the Souceys attempting to reach the imagined safety of the interstate before dark. Carmine ordered his legs to resume hiking and hastened to catch up with Taggert. Back then he'd thought he was the lucky one, but now he knew better. The Souceys' struggles had been over in an instant. None of this shivering, starving, never-ending drudgery. No, the next time one of them came striding out of the trees and its eyes locked on him, he wouldn't run. Instead, he'd dig in his heels, close his eyes, and wait to be taken out of his fear and suffering.

Sleep, he told himself. That's all he needed. Only Carmine knew that sleep was an illusion and that once he closed his eyes he'd be back there in his dreams, standing beneath the windmill.

A Golem's Progress

Tamsin Showbrook

SOMETIMES, YOU LIKE to find a shady spot under a tree and just sit, reconnect. The government encourages it, and who are you to argue with our elected officials? You like the mottle-barked plane trees in the centenary park best. The thick haze in the air is no better here, but the trees are worth the walk through it. Their tangled roots are like varicose veins bulging from the earth, and when you stand up, you can feel their impressions in your thighs and calves and the dark heat of wood and earth humming in your body.

It's only taken a few minutes for the feeling to disappear as you've paced past the railings around the old Whitworth art gallery on your way home. Your guilt at being away from your creator has become too much. Like all golem, your first function is to protect him, and he's old and getting frail.

Today, at the base of the recently added Queen Elspeth II memorial—a surrealist mishmash of bronze polyhedrons that's obliterated most of the old speakers' corner—a young man is standing on a stack of pallets and sermonising in the murky sunshine. A steady stream of people, heading for the latest pro-leave gathering, placards in hand, pass close by but don't stop. Over their chatter, you catch snatches of the speaker's impassioned words: "Retrograde step . . . They say we're lost in a mire of over-regulation, but . . . Your lives. Your children's lives . . ."

Yesterday was the hottest day ever on record in Manchester—35.7 degrees Celsius at 2:16pm. The washing, hung out in the stunned air, was stiff as a board in half an hour. Father's underpants had the texture of Ryvita.

The sparse park grass has faded to grey-brown and the earth around it is crazed and eggshell pale. You shouldn't come out barefoot anymore. Father gave you a pair of Mother's old trainers and a pleading look during the one o'clock news last month, and you tried them on to keep him happy, but they've just sat in the entrance hall of the terrace since. The way they held your toes made you feel like stones were pouring into your abdomen, and the uppers rubbed your heels. You imagined fibres worming their way into your flesh.

"You could wear socks?" Father's eyes pleaded as he proposed this solution. He held out a flaccid blue pair, but you shook your head and—

The speaker, eyes wild, face pink with sunburn and rage, blocks your way.

"Look!" he demands, pointing to the tree nearest the statue.

That tree.

The tree guarded by a police officer. The tree no one must take pictures of since the first press conference. A drone was shot down last week, trying to do just that. It burned a man's head and neck when it landed on him. He ran screaming down Wilmslow Road and a barista ran out of a coffee shop and dumped a jug of water and ice cubes on him. Later, the film appeared online and the mayor was livid. The outside world could not see this.

"No one wants to see! You don't want to see!" the speaker rages on. You follow the line of his pointing finger to the huge, open, weeping canker on the otherwise healthy plane's trunk. The bolus of wood was excised and sent to a nearby university building, one with mirrored windows and guards on the door. Not before everyone saw it though. The canker hadn't been caused by fungus or wasps or a genetic defect. Instead, running through the bolus, were dark clots of microplastics. The same thing had been happening for a while to golem—it's happened to you, and you were repaired—but this was the first tree. That people knew of.

The tree has been left standing. "Why cut down a perfectly good tree?" the First Minister said when she visited. She appeared on the telly just after you'd put the trainers on. Feet squirming, you watched her stand under the plane tree's broad shade and deliver the speech, flanked by armed guards.

"This government is doing everything it can to deliver on its promises. Our commitment to improving and protecting our environment—your environment—is unshakeable, unlike that of the community we may be about to leave. We can do this better alone. This tree will stand. It will serve as a symbol of the indomitable spirit of the Engle people against all the odds. Don't let Scotia and Wales and the Europa nations fill your heads with lies about their intentions. They, let us not forget, are the people who want to give our golem human rights, making a mess of our society. They are also the people who want to make their problems with waste our problems.

"This tree can heal. Our waters can heal. Our land and all who walk it can heal."

She placed one hand on the empty canker and raised the other, folded tight into a thumbs-up. Camera flashes, by turns, drained what colour there was from her steely smiling face. "Peaceful protests will not be stopped," she said in response to one of the reporter's questions. "Peaceful protests are healthy: they allow the people to release their anger in a measured way . . ."

By the end of her speech, Father's face had started twitching like he might cry again, so you kept the trainers on your sockless feet to avoid upsetting him further and ignored the lurching avalanche in your abdomen until he switched the telly off and left the living room. Even though you're afraid he might do something stupid, like Mother—because of everything that's happening, that keeps happening—you haven't been able to make yourself wear the trainers since. And at the moment, this gesticulating, pontificating young man in your path is stopping you from getting back to him, to make sure he's okay . . .

The speaker is still raging.

"How can *you* not care?" he asks. "This affects you and every other golem much more than people like me. When you can't be rebuilt anymore because of this . . . shit . . ." He wipes his eyes, his whole face. "Those idiots over there . . ." Wildly, he gestures at the gathering crowd of pro-leavers. ". . . they'd have you tethered to your creator, or so sick with pollution there'd be no point to your life, or just dead full stop. Do you want to die?"

"Don't be ridiculous." Your voice, raspy with heat, surprises you and him. He takes a step back.

"Yes, I *can* speak. I know that's unusual. I know most creators can't do that for their golem, but mine can and did."

Other people are staring now. None of them will touch you; you know this. The certainty of it beats inside your chest where a heart would be. You are registered family. The shapes of Mother's lips on your left wrist and Father's on your right, prove it.

"I have no political voice though," you say, "like all golem. We rely on people like you for that. Don't attack me; help me. Help us all."

The sun beats down on the silence between you both. He squints. You don't need to. Your eyes are dry and feel as though they may flake again later, but you've never blinked. You've never felt the urge, even though Mother said the right words— new words of her own creation—for that when you were moulded. It takes two people to make a golem like you, to take a lump of earth and craft it, add to it, day on day, month on month, year on year. To get the words just right every time. You are a precious DIY toy. Not worth stealing though; like every golem, you'd crumble if you were too long away from your creator. No person could start a going concern on a craft website with golem. Many can't even make it out of their homes without their creators.

"You're incredible," the speaker breathes. He shakes his head and marches back to his pallets. It's then that you see he has a golem. It sits, holding a placard up to the height of what might be Queen Elspeth's knees. The workmanship is crude, the eyes blank, the face is creased into the same determined expression on its creator's. A shadow; nothing more. It has no mouth, no ears; one leg is a little longer than the other. You give it a few months at most, especially if this heat continues. Maybe the speaker will do better next time. People attend classes; Father has told you this. But very few ever master the art in the way he and Mother did together.

If you pass, you don't know if he'll make a replacement. He's said he won't. Without Mother, he says, there's no point. She knew the words; she could say them correctly. They streamed from her like morning light through winter air. He says. Besides, his hands are palsied—you're his last.

Your head pinches in on itself as you continue to stare at the speaker's golem. Father discusses the issue with you sometimes, over the morning coffee and ten o'clock news tea and whisky that define the opening and closing of his days and yours. You should have rights, he declares. Even the ones without your craftsmanship are entitled to know what it's like to be a person. There are more laws protecting dogs than golem. You know many of the people with placards are jealous as much as anything else; the more humanity hurtles forward, the more polluted the ground beneath its feet becomes, the fewer the people with the talent and skill to craft their own golem. The less good earth there is.

And you're a machine to them. Some golem are security guards; some are domestic help; some are children's entertainment. None are paid. In the whole of the world, there are maybe a few hundred like you: truly conscious companions to their creators. You would like your opinion to count; you'd like things to change. Father has asked you to try to stay calm. The second vote will change things, he promises. This time, the people will definitively vote to stay in Europa.

A sluggish stream of people crawls along the pavement through the heat. Some are on their way to the pro-leave march; others do their best to avoid them; others glare.

Some cast you looks as you pass. Some have golem that glance as well. You're as used to this as you are to the smog. The plane trees *are* worth it.

A huge man wheezes towards you, face screwed up at the traffic and accompanying fug of particulates. He catches your shoulder as he passes—so hard you feel a crack form inside— and glares at you.

"Earthfuck," he mutters, rubbing his arm. "Where's your creator?"

You don't have to reply, so you simply walk on. He can't do anything—the police, hidden in their airconned cars at the roadsides, would take a very dim view and hurt him far worse than he's hurt you. Another golem passes, one who you recognise as belonging to a neighbour, who uses it to walk their tiny dog. As ever, it's oblivious to your wave, and the dog pulls it onward through the people.

The crack rubs out inside your shoulder, sandy grounds and miniscule beads of plastic filling the void as your arms swing, because even the earth in the back garden is full of it. You developed a cyst just before Mother passed. When it split open, a nugget of compacted plastic dropped out. Mother let out a yelp.

Victoria Park is a quick stroll up the road past the hospital where both Father and Mother used to work as surgeons. Father's friends can't understand why you both still live there. One said "it" takes Manchester back at least a century, makes it into Dickens' Coketown, and Father had to explain that she meant the wraith-like fog that licks at the house and coils around the trees nearly every morning. It disperses to the fine sepia haze that was still hanging around Oxford Road and the park most days. But sometimes in winter it sinks razor-like canines into the air and won't budge.

Manchester fog loves you. It glides across your surface and seeps in with a delighted sigh whenever you go for milk or Father's paper in the morning. It curdles in your torso and limbs, thickens your movements, and only when you sleep does it drain back into the air.

FATHER SAYS HIS eyes and lungs suffer with it. "Why don't you move to the countryside?" his friends ask. "Life expectancy's so much better there. You won't see 2030 at this rate." Father shrugs. The perfectly restored terrace is Mother though: her things, her glow in the mahogany stair rail and the Minton tiles. Their wardrobe still smells of their clothes together, even though he gave the last of hers away two years ago.

Just as you open the door, you feel your right cheek split. The heat's proved too much after all, but Father will fix it, sit you in the garden under the rowan tree while he finds just the right handful of soil.

Inside, The Stone Roses, Mother's favourite, drift down the hallway. You still find people's music confusing. The earth has its own: a rhythmic thrum, expansions and contractions, layers that shift with weather. As you walk towards the kitchen, your cheek feels like it's healing a little in the cooler air and the tiled floor soothes your feet.

The wireless speaker is on, in its usual place beside the spatula tin, but Father is nowhere to be seen. You listen for movement above. Nothing. Through the garden window, not a single leaf stirs. The sparrows who normally festoon the feeder on the rowan tree are absent again. They will be, Father assured you yesterday, hiding in the hedgerows and the canopy of the copse at the end of the garden. A shame, he sighed, as it gives the cats more chance to plot when they stay still. The neighbour's cat, Tiger, is curled in the rowan's shade, tail snaked between hummocks of desiccated yarrow and couch grass.

You turn to face back towards the shaded hallway. "Father?"

The mercury in the antique barometer next to the doorway sits low in its glass tube. A storm, you remember; Mother told you that means there's a storm on the way. And a sense of anticipation, she'd said, smiling. You will have the feeling that something is about to happen.

Father doesn't reply. Maybe he's gone out somewhere nearby, but he feels close. You check the garden again. Tiger flicks an ear at a stray fly, but there's no sign of anything else. *I Wanna Be Adored* finishes, to be replaced by *Waterfall*.

"Father?"

You decide to search the house, following your instinct. When you were first created, Mother and Father would play hide and seek with you, giggling "warmer" and "colder" as you clomped around in search of them. You didn't need the temperatures called; you could sense where they were. Trails of slowly cooling ground would be left in their wake and your own feet would be inexorably drawn to them, like magnets to railway tracks. When you wander back down the hallway, they lock onto a trail leading up the stairs.

It takes you to the office, where you see Father collapsed, next to his tall bookcase. He told you that if this ever happened, you were to call 999, so you do. As a shallow fissure forms across your chest, you tell them what's wrong, that you can't tell if he's breathing, and then you sit down next to him and don't move until the ambulance crew come up the stairs and find you.

The crack in your chest is deeper by now, creeping towards your lungs. If you're not repaired soon, you'll lose your voice.

A woman with kind eyes checks Father and says he's unconscious, most likely from heat exhaustion. He'll need to go to hospital; he's eighty-one and something like this can be serious.

Her co-worker scowls. "What were you doing?" he asks you.

"I don't understand." Your lungs heave like a broken accordion.

"You should have been keeping an eye on him; what's the point of him making you otherwise? Especially as you've got a voice. He made you; it's your duty to protect him. Why didn't you remind him to drink water regularly?" He points at the full glass on the desk. It sits next to Father's laptop, which is displaying a letter he was writing to *The Times*. He's been working on it since yesterday and the content is very similar to what the speaker in the park was shouting.

"Father said I could go to the park."

"You what?" he sneers.

"Al," the woman snaps. "Leave it alone." She turns to me. "I'm Morag. We'll take you with us. Your creator will probably want to see you when he wakes up. Unless he has anyone else?"

You shake your head. "Mother died last year. They didn't have children."

"Do you have a name?"

"Rowan. Like the tree in the garden. Father told me they grow everywhere. People believe they protect them against evil."

Morag is lifting Father onto a stretcher, strapping him down tight. "And what's your father's name?"

"Harris. Harris Iqbal."

AN ASTRINGENT STENCH of disinfectant pervades the ambulance. Father remains grey-faced and unconscious under the cold overhead light, as a heart monitor chirps alongside him. You want to place your hand on his, but you've become so dry, you leave a trail of fine clay powder on whatever you touch, and the ambulance is clean. Very clean. You count the things made of plastic until it breaks a hundred and a voice interrupts your thoughts.

"How old are you?" Morag asks, one eye on Father's monitor.

"Four hundred and fifty-seven days."

"An old man yourself then?" She smiles.

"I'm not a man."

The smile flickers. "No . . . No, I suppose not. I made one, you know: a golem. With my mum. She taught Creation at Moston High School. People told her it was a Mickey Mouse subject—like PSHE—but she loved it and the kids did too." Al snorts, but Morag continues, "Your creator sounds very trusting, like her. Public spaces are dangerous for you at the moment though, especially with your crafting; it'd only take one idiot to get carried away and forget about the police, and you'd be a pile of—"

"Shit!" Al groans from the driver's cab, as we're thrown deeper into our seats.

"What is it?" Morag calls.

"Bloody protest that was kicking off in the centenary park. They said it might turn nasty. Gods, we're only a couple of hundred yards away from A&E too! Traffic's all backed up and they're walking between it."

"Are they pro or con-leave?"

"Pro, obviously. The cons have some bloody consideration." He puts on a mocking whine. "'We, the pro-leavers, like our fucked-up environment, here on our teeny tiny island. We don't like to share our responsibilities.' My Gods, someone should put can-ties around their necks and inject them with microbeads; see how *they* like it. I mean, those idiots in the European Parliament *are* going too far, saying that golems should have the same rights as us, but how did it all get mixed up with economics and the plastic crisis? Did any of them *listen* to the shared responsibilities and benefits declaration?" He rests his head on the steering wheel a moment. "No kids this time, thank God. D'you remember that boy last time? His eye?" His reflection blinks in the rearview mirror. "You *don't* want to see what they've got on the placards, especially with that back there."

You know from Morag's wince that "that" is you, and you know what the placards will show, because you've seen them on the TV. There will be dismembered golem, obscenities directed at golem, golem on leads like the dog you saw with one earlier. So far, no one has dared destroy an actual one. At least, not in public. The idea of it as a sin still runs deep in society. It's whether people's fear of what's happening to their own planet can drive over the old ideas completely.

Several shrill alarms begin to compete with the sound of the ambulance's siren.

"They're smashing windscreens. The regular police are tasering all they can, but there's not enough of them." Al turns to face us, his forehead creased. "What do you want to do, boss? They could start on us."

Morag's lips purse. "Riot police'll be here soon. They'll sort it."

"What, like they did in April? The second vote's in two days— these guys don't want to see it happen and they mean business. There's a couple with golem in manacles and 'property of' written on their chests."

"We sit tight. We can't go anywhere with a patient on a stretcher. And that crowd could trample Rowan if they realise it's not got its creator with it."

You remember the large man from earlier and rub your shoulder.

"Are you all right?" Morag frowns. "You're cracked all over. Can you feel the gap in your chest? There's a seam of something inside it too."

"Yes. I'm afraid I'll lose my lungs and my voice."

She looks on the verge of tears. "I'd repair you if I could. You're very special." Then she adds hastily, "All golem are special. Will some water help your shoulder at least, even if it's not your father who pours it? We could—"

The rhythm of the monitor's beeps changes and Father stirs. Morag peers at him. "He's waking up, Al. Drip's working."

"That's one positive at least."

The ambulance sways a little, like someone or something has shoved against it outside. Morag closes her eyes and you see her lips move. As the ambulance shakes again, she reaches into her uniform and takes hold of a silver circle around her neck. Mother and Father were never religious, believing the power to create ones comes simply from the Earth itself, not any kind of divine power like the ancient Noorgods. Morag's finger and thumb rub the tarnished metal, while her free hand goes to Father's arm; his eyelids are twitching now.

"Harris? Harris, can you hear me?"

Your chest beats a little harder as Father takes a deep shaky breath and blinks. "Where am I?" he croaks.

"You're in an ambulance, Harris, on the way to the hospital. You have heat exhaustion."

His eyes focus and fix on her. "Where's Rowan?"

"I'm here, Father."

He turns to face you, reaches a hand out and takes yours. "Did you call them?"

"Yes, Father."

"Well done; you amaze me every day." Then he frowns. "You look terrible; you spent too long in the heat again. I wish I could fix you." He reaches across, places a hand on your chest. The gap can't close without earth, but it's soothed a little by the cool touch of his palm.

"I'm so glad you've woken up."

His face glows weakly with a smile and he repeats, "I wish I could fix you . . ." Then he frowns again. "We're not moving."

"No, Harris," Morag says, "I'm afraid we're stuck in a march."

Unable to pale any further, Father mutters, "Which side?" The ambulance shakes again, more violently. "Oh," he whispers, then his gaze settles on you again. "I wish . . ."

A knock on the back doors cuts him off and Morag jerks to face them. "Shit," she breathes.

The knocking becomes louder and faster. A woman's yell follows: "Let me in! I've got kids! Let me in, please!"

The ambulance rocks from side to side again and the lights flicker. Morag's jaw tenses.

"She's not lying," Al calls back. "I can see her and the kids."

"We sit tight." Morag's voice is stone, but it trembles at the edges as though struck with a hammer. "Let the protest pa—" Father's eyes have closed again and the monitor is agitated. "Shit! Al, he's crashing!"

"Where the hell did that come from?" Al leaps from his seat into the back, and all you can do is watch as the two of them try to resuscitate Father, with the ambulance still being shoved and the lights still flickering and the crack in your chest deepening. Your lungs become useless—you can't draw air into them anymore—instead, it swirls uselessly in the space like wind through a wrecked house. No more voice.

You sit silent, your strap rubbing at your bad shoulder and your broken chest, as Morag and Al continue their work, shouting commands at each other. The ambulance rocks again, the monitor's beeps become one long low note and Morag and Al's grim faces sway.

Outside, the noise of the crowd swells. It's like the roar of the bees Father keeps at the bottom of the garden, when he approaches to take their honey. You want to cover your ears with your hands, but you don't dare in case they crumble under the weight.

Morag stares at you. "Rowan, I'm afraid Harris is dead. His heart must have been weaker than we thought. I'm so sorry."

Opening your mouth would be useless, and you can't reach over to him. Now that he's dead, you will be too, soon, and your arm could easily crumble as you raise it, or it may already have fused to your body, because you're earth and you'll be reclaimed. You can't feel whether this will happen now or later, because you're numb inside.

Morag comes around the gurney and places her hand on yours. "Do you understand?" she asks.

Nodding, you turn your eyes towards your chest.

"You can't talk anymore?" Her thumb rubs yours lightly and she starts—a chunk has fallen away under the pressure. "I'm sorry. We can't help you."

You are earth. You are of earth and one day you'll return to earth. The first words you ever heard, echo in your head. Your fingers are dust and flakes of hardened mud, and now your vision is going: your view of Morag has crazed and fuzzed. The last thing to go, you know, will be the inside of your head, the vast network Father and Mother crafted inside it. It weighs heavy on your shoulders.

"Morag," Al calls, "you can't help it. You know this always happens; we just have to wait for the crowd to pass and we'll get this poor guy to the mortuary."

"I know," Morag sighs. The shape of her moves back towards Father. As she reaches him, your left ear canal collapses and your right auricle slides down your neck. The one benefit is that you now can't hear the crowd outside.

So this is it. Your life ends this way. If you'd known this, you'd have stayed in the park with the speaker and his dumb ghost of a golem. Maybe you did make the wrong choice. But if you'd stayed, you wouldn't have been here for Father. There was no way to win. It wouldn't have mattered how many times you got to choose.

Time passes. You're not sure how much, but you can no longer see or hear, and your body, you're sure, is no more than a heap of dirt in the seat. In your head, the pathways Father built are slowly collapsing. All that's left now is the last song you heard, looping, holding the last of you together and memories of a tree, and a cat, and hide and seek. You were supposed to protect and you didn't.

Dimly, you're aware of a pressure on what's left of you, then your body's falling into darkness. Later, there'll be air and sunlight—earth must be returned to earth. You have to believe that, with what's left of the honeycomb of your head, which someone is now lifting, cradling and carrying somewhere.

SOMETIMES, YOU LIKE to find a shady spot under a tree and just sit, reconnect. The government encourage it, for your physical and mental health. And who are you to argue with our elected officials? Their electors. And what is a protector, after all, without their health? Your creator encourages it, so you resist the guilt you feel whenever you leave the home to visit the centenary park and sit beneath the planes to which you've been so strongly drawn since your creation.

A little way off, surrounded by blue railings bearing a plaque, is the stump of a large tree that one of your creators told you was once important. It signifies what we've done to the earth, she said. We were all angry for lots of reasons, and the earth took the brunt of it. It's cleaner now and that's why you exist, made of earth from the garden of an ageing paramedic. You're her eleventh golem, and the first to be able to choose to wander free of the house or to pass the understanding tests and be eligible to vote.

"Off you go then, Rowan," she said, smiling.

She chose your name in memory of someone she knew a long time ago. A bad time, she'll say, shaking her head. It's not all passed, but we're on the right path.

The sky is blue, the air is clear, and the planes are heavy with fresh leaves. Soon, it'll be too hot for you to come out during the daytime—there's nothing that can be done about that at the moment—but for now, you're going to enjoy the feel of the tree's roots against your legs, and the warmth in the spring soil, and the peaceful hum of the park.

Maggie of the Moss

Sarah Van Goethem

THE CHILD COMES out of the forest fifty-two years after she disappeared. Hannah sees her first, as she always knew she would; she never stopped looking. She knew the Moss Folk would give her child back eventually.

Through the frosted panes in the winter she watched the frozen woodland until the blanket of snow melted into the spring rain pools, the weeds tightening themselves around the perimeter in the heat of summer. It's always been now though, in the rusted throes of Autumn, before the farm is set to a cold slumber once again, that Hannah expected Maggie to return.

A bell is ringing somewhere, but Hannah ignores it. She's waited so long for this moment, so very, very long.

ON THE NIGHT before Maggie's third birthday, as Hannah rocked her daughter in the bentwood wicker rocker, a single quick crack sounded from the forest. Hannah knew the shot had found its mark; spirits flew up and out of the forest in splashes of jade and emerald lights that bathed Maggie's skin in an eerie green glow. Hannah crossed herself before hauling her daughter off the porch and into the house. She dunked the child in the tub, scrubbed her from head to toe, washed her thick brown hair in mounds of lavender-scented shampoo and tucked her safely into bed.

Afterward, Hannah lay beside her daughter, her pointer finger tapping three times, light as a feather, on her daughter's arm. "That means I love you," Hannah explained.

"I."

Tap.

"Love."

Tap.

"You."

Tap.

Maggie giggled and tapped on Hannah, too.

Then, when Maggie fell asleep, Hannah went to the kitchen and baked a pink champagne cake. She drank two glasses of Dom Perignon while she iced the cake with rosy buttercream frosting. She kept an eye on the window, but the spirits had settled. Only the stars shone in the dark sky, and she thought maybe it would be okay.

It was almost midnight when Hannah stood by the open window and rang the small hand bell.

Several minutes later, the door swung open. "You rang?" Howard called, amusement in his voice.

He stopped at the laundry tub and Hannah floated into the entryway barefoot, weightless, the way she imagined the spirits in the forest. She watched the blood trickle off his knife, swirling crimson where she sometimes soaked her panties if her period surprised her. She wouldn't need to do that for awhile.

"Got a buck," Howard said, and Hannah had a flash of him making an incision in the belly, all the way from the neck to the anus. Next, through the belly muscle, sliding two thick fingers inside to lift the muscle away from the stomach organs. "Tons of meat for the winter."

"I asked you not to." Hannah's voice was level, but she felt the crack that threatened. It was inside her, between them, left in the night sky in a trail of faint green dust. "Not in our forest."

Howard scrubbed at his hands, his flannel shirt rolled up to the elbows, all logic. "We gotta eat, Hannah."

"The Wood Wives . . ." Hannah slugged back the rest of her warm champagne. She'd tried to explain this to Howard, but he didn't understand. He was born here, not across the salty ocean, not in Germany, where the *Moosleute,* the Moss Folk, were well-known. Before she'd been forced to board the ship that brought her here, Hannah had run wild in the depths of the Black Forest, where she'd stumbled on one of the moss maidens, with limbs of knotty bark and lichen for hair. It was blurry in Hannah's mind, but she knew this: a hunter had come and the unearthly woman, of an age Hannah couldn't place, had whisked her away and tucked them both into a tree marked with a cross, a safe haven. "Did you at least mark a cross?" Hannah asked, her throat tight.

Howard was near her now, his still-damp hands caressing her face. His eyes were bright blue, the same colour he'd bestowed upon their first daughter. "Yes, Hannah-banana, I carved a cross on a particularly large one, with a wide trunk and a great cave of a hole for all your wee folk to hide." He was making fun of her, but she didn't care, so long as he'd done it. Then, his lips were on hers, and he smelled of wood smoke and earth and the bar of soap at the laundry tub. He had a way of making her forget everything she was about, of making her notions seem far-away and silly, something she was supposed to leave behind, like childhood.

"Maybe I'll start ringing the bell when I want you," he joked with a wink. He led her upstairs and took off her dress in the moonlight, making her remember she was a woman, a wife, not a spirit from the forest. But when he bent to pull off his own pants, her eyes travelled out the window. She saw the pile of guts near the woodshed and wondered if the cross was enough.

HANNAH STARES AT the child through her fingers which are pressed to the glass, skin like crepe paper now, nails hardened and jagged. Her breath comes in a jolt, like something she's forgotten to do. She struggles to see Maggie; her eyesight has dimmed to shades of muted greys and browns, blurring into circles like Maggie's pinwheel in the wind.

Maggie is standing like a tree in the yard, still and rooted, staring at the house as if for the first time. Hannah thinks Maggie can see her gawking and she pulls back abruptly, as if she's been caught at something. She cowers behind the faded gingham curtains, the ones she hung the year they moved in. She never changed them. Or anything else.

And then, in a shock of adrenaline, Hannah shuffles out through the entryway, her house shoes clomping on the porch steps, the ripped screen door slapping behind her. She grows lighter as she walks across the grass, shedding a weight she barely remembers acquiring, it's been with her so long.

The child doesn't move, only stares at Hannah with widened watery eyes rimmed in white. Hannah slows her pace, afraid to startle her. She longs to wrap her arms around the girl and crush her to her chest, to inhale her and consume her and take back all the years of suffering. But it's been too long, all the years snatched away, and she restrains herself.

Hannah is surprised to find she's kneeled; she didn't know her knees could bend anymore. The usual shooting pain hasn't come, only a warmth that cloaks her from her feet to her scalp. Hannah sees her own wrinkled hand extend, reaching, but Maggie jerks back, and Hannah's hand finds its way to her own face, pushing back strands of loose grey hair.

Of course, Hannah thinks, feeling her coarse hank of hair. While Maggie has been trapped with the eternal Moss Folk, time has stroked Hannah's face and hair and body into something unrecognizable to her. Hannah is no longer the young mother with the skin as smooth as flower petals and hair the colour of harvested wheat, though in this moment, she almost feels as if she is again.

"It's me," she whispers. "Mama."

Maggie blinks, her eyebrows furled into a frown that squeezes Hannah's heart. Hannah has imagined this day a thousand times, but always, Maggie remembers her. She isn't prepared for this, for the forgetting. She wasn't prepared for it with Howard, either.

"Please," Hannah says, and she tries again, her hand outstretched, palm up. "Please come in the house with me." *Then, you'll remember,* Hannah thinks. *I've kept it the same.*

"Mama." The child turns, pointing at the forest. She grabs Hannah's hand, tugs at her. The word, *Mama,* slices into Hannah's heart.

"I'm so sorry," Hannah says. She's been wanting to say that forever, it's been a bitter taste in her mouth for years no matter how much water she drank.

The child clings, her hand cold and clammy, and Hannah

holds tight; she isn't letting go this time. Hannah's other hand finds Maggie's fragile shoulders and strokes her wet back. Hannah didn't notice it was raining; it's been the driest year she can remember. She tries to think if Howard has been obsessing over the drought-stressed crops and the cracked soil, but it doesn't come to her.

Hannah also doesn't remember the dress Maggie's wearing, something long and linen, earthy, plastered to her now-lean body. Hannah knows she disappeared in the birthday dress she made her, a bright concoction of flounces and ribbons and a velvet sash.

Gaudy, Howard said.

Gorgeous, Maggie squealed.

Maggie had so many words, where are they now? *Perhaps she's just in shock*, Hannah thinks. To spend half a century in the forest, only to be spit back out . . . Hannah doesn't want to think about it. Even the one night she spent had left a mark, a strange blister in her memory, a tug-of-war of sorts. Had she wanted to come back? Had Maggie?

"Let's get some dry clothes, shall we?" Hannah asks softly. The child is still stretching toward the forest as if she can't let go, and Hannah takes a tentative step toward the house. She'll have to do this slowly, methodically, with patience.

"Mama." The child's lip trembles and Hannah can't bear it. Her resolve cracks.

She pulls Maggie close, into the soft flesh of her middle, and strokes her wet hair. It, too, seems leeched of colour, paler, like her skin and eyes. She smells moist, like wet wood, like the inside of a hollowed-out trunk. Hannah squeezes her eyes shut and thinks of the rain pools in the woodland, with their carpets of dead leaves and florescent green moss, their reflections of the branches and sunlight above, masking the world beneath.

Maggie has come back from that world, and Hannah will never get enough of her now. When she squirms in her arms, Hannah finally releases her and opens her eyes. She staggers back, the world is so bright; a raging crimson and orange fire lit over her forest, the cloudy sky an intense white.

Hannah hears the offending bell over the rustling of the leaves in the trees. It's coming from upstairs—a call from Howard. He'll be wanting something, tea, or a carrot muffin, or the newspaper. *Tea,* Hannah thinks. He'll likely forget he wanted it by the time Hannah gets there; she remembers the doctor saying something about short-term memory failing. Long-term though—Hannah's fake teeth clench in anticipation—is still fine. He won't have forgotten Maggie.

THEY HAD MAGGIE'S favourite lunch—grilled cheese sandwiches with piles of ketchup. Afterward, Hannah poked three pink candles into the cake and Howard lit them. Maggie blew them out with a spit-filled breath and they all laughed.

Howard gave Maggie a handmade doll cradle, pieces of pine that he'd expertly crafted after Maggie was in bed at night. Hannah had painted it, a folk-art display of multicoloured leaves, a tree bent sideways, branches lunging everywhere. Hannah had also made a tiny patchwork quilt and a matching pillow.

Maggie laid her one store-bought toy inside—her Baby Dear doll, with the crinkled lips and the puffy cheeks—and covered it up, all gentle and protective, the same way Hannah did with Maggie.

After Howard left to harvest the beans in the back field, Hannah and Maggie sat on the porch and drank lemonade. Hannah mixed leftover champagne with hers. The air was still warm, but leaves fluttered down like confetti when the wind breathed and Maggie danced her way to the big maple tree, where she set about making a pile. Leaves clung to the lace of her birthday dress and she giggled.

"I'm a tree, Mama. I'm part of the forest."

"But you can't be," Hannah protested, playfully, "because you're my little girl."

At that, Maggie ran back up the steps and plied Hannah with kisses, tapping three times on her arm, before returning to her play.

Content, Hannah rocked herself into a sleepy trance, still tired from her lack of sleep the night before.

When she finally awoke, the light was all wrong. It came in from a crooked angle, kinked like her neck. Maggie was no longer under the tree, the pile of leaves forgotten.

Hannah searched the house and found Baby Dear missing from her cradle. She searched the barn next and slithered past the pile of guts, rotting by the woodshed. Then, she knew. She'd let down her guard and she would pay. She turned her eyes on the vibrant forest, radiant in death, bathed in a green aura.

Hannah went to the maple tree in the yard and with furious fingers dug apart the pile of leaves to expose the clawing roots of the maple. Sure enough, a mantle of moss clung, a velvety-green strip so vile Hannah retched into the leaves.

INSIDE, HANNAH PULLS on Maggie, her grip soft, yet persistent, a tether to keep Maggie from vanishing again. She stops in the kitchen, where steam seethes from the kettle. She shuts off the orange burner and pours Maggie a glass of apple juice, her favourite, and takes out the package of windmill biscuits she always has on hand. She used to make gingersnap cookies, but this is the best she can do now.

Maggie doesn't touch either. "Mama says not to take food from strangers," she whispers.

Strangers.

Hannah flinches, until she realizes this is exactly the thing she used to say to Maggie, the words she would drill into her head if they went to town. *Don't take things from strangers and don't go with anyone you don't know.*

"That's right." Hannah remembers to put the plastic cap on the bottle of juice, before she hears the incessant bell ring again.

"What's that for?" the child asks. She seems to be warming up, more talkative now, and Hannah feels a swell inside her, like a giant wave waiting to crash on the shore.

"That's Papa," she says. "Remember?" The child shakes her head and a twig falls from her hair and lands on the tablecloth. Hannah retrieves it and twirls it between her fingers. "You will," she promises. "Come, we'll get you cleaned up in your room."

Hannah is usually winded by the top of the stairs, but today she breathes easy. She turns left in the hallway and goes past the first open door, the room that belongs to Kathy, and stops at the last closed door. She turns the knob slowly, her eyes on the child. Will she remember?

The door creaks open, revealing the blue walls, painted the colour of the sky, and the pink ruffled bedspread. The cradle sits in the corner, with Baby Dear propped up the way Hannah had left her, her slits of eyes waiting for Maggie's return.

Sure enough, Maggie's eyes light up when she sees her.

"Go on," Hannah encourages, smiling.

The child goes over, but stops at the window. Hannah isn't worried; out this side of the house only the field is visible, with the never-ending rows of withered buttery corn. Maggie's attention goes back to the doll and she leans in to scoop it up.

Hannah wipes at her cheeks, wondering when the tears came; she didn't feel them. She goes to the closet and selects a cream-and-brown day dress, another of Maggie's favourites that had matched her hair beautifully. But as Hannah holds the dress up, a coldness seeps into her bones; the dress seems washed-out now, an odd contrast to Maggie's now-lighter hair. She swallows, quietly tucks the dress into the back of the closet, and selects another. This one, the colour of robin's egg, will match the diluted blue of Maggie's new eyes.

Maggie is still inspecting the doll, taking off its socks to look at its tiny toes. Hannah inches forward, her nose in the dress, the smell of the laundry soap and lavender, of Maggie, no longer an assault. Now she can put the smell back on the girl to whom it belongs.

The bell rings again and this time Howard yells, "Hannah-banana, where are you?"

Hannah is annoyed, but the child laughs, a strangle bubbling that she stifles with the palm of her hand.

Hannah loves the sound more than anything. "You always did think that was funny, didn't you?" Hannah says, clapping her hands. "Hannah-banana?" To Howard, she calls, "Hold your horses. We'll be right there!"

"We? Has Kathy come?" Howard is confused, but he'll see soon enough.

"No, it's a surprise!"

Hannah thinks of Kathy, though, as she unravels the old-fashioned garment from Maggie's small body. Kathy is younger than Maggie, only a baby. No, wait. That isn't right. Kathy is over fifty herself now, with greying hair and crow's feet and spider veins that bleed onto her legs in patches. What would she think to meet her older sister, the one she never knew? Hannah can't think about that now, it makes a strange guilt rise up her throat. She refocuses on peeling back the wet dress.

Hannah stops when she finds Maggie's strawberries, the

puffy red swells on her back, gone. The doctor said the hemangiomas would likely fade and disappear over time, but Hannah thought she would see it happen. The smooth porcelain skin she sees now feels like a violation, something Hannah wanted, but is sorry she asked for.

She changes her thoughts again, opens the blue dress, and slips it over Maggie's head. It spills around her like a carpet of bluebells in the spring, which is, in Hannah's opinion, the prettiest of wildflowers in the woodland.

The child is still, almost too still, as Hannah guides her arms into the sleeves. "What girl . . . who does this room and dress and doll . . . belong to?" she asks.

Hannah reaches for the brush on the dresser and wipes away the dust. "Why, you, of course," she answers, but her voice wavers.

Everyday, she is afraid Howard will forget her. Then, she is afraid she will contract what Howard has, as if the dementia is contagious. Worse, if that happened, she would've forgotten Maggie, and forgotten to watch for her.

She hadn't considered that Maggie might forget her.

She combs through Maggie's snarled bleached-out hair, dislodges a few more twigs, and untangles a strand of grey lichen.

The bell rings again (Howard has forgotten they are coming), and they are ready.

It was Hannah who found Baby Dear, though there had been close to fifty people in the search party, all combing through the forest and fields. Hannah crept into the places they didn't, into the nooks they thought vacant, under the mushroom caps they thought too small to bother with. Baby Dear was resting in a knoll where two maples had grown together in a lifelong embrace, married to each other in veil of vines. Hannah lay down between them with her head on the pillow of moss, and begged the Forest Folk to give Maggie back. But only the incessant jab of a nearby woodpecker and the murmur of voices from the other searchers greeted her.

Hannah pressed her palm to her belly where new life was growing, and offered a deal: this baby for Maggie. A trade.

The storm blew in fast, cold air that met the warmth of the

forest, whipping leaves and branches into frantic miniature twisters. Hannah thought she felt herself emptying, thought she heard Maggie singing in the torrent of rain.

She upped the stakes: they could have her, too. Hannah and her unborn, for Maggie. Two for one.

Hannah saw them hiding, their grey skin camouflaged in the brown bark, their tiny forms hunched in the foliage. They were different than she expected; they'd changed shape, grown hostile. She knew they were listening though, maybe even considering her offer; a price had to be paid, after all, for what Howard had taken.

But then Howard was there, pulling Hannah up, holding her in his arms, his tears mixing with the rain like a river in her neck. Howard drew her back and kept them both, Hannah and her unborn. He unknowingly sacrificed Maggie.

She wanted to be mad at him, but she couldn't; she was stronger than him. He didn't know any better. He needed her.

They sat in the shelter of the trees, Howard's arm around Hannah's shoulders, Hannah clutching Baby Dear. They watched the downpour raise the levels of the never-ending rain pools and, when it finished, Hannah saw her own reflection in the water. She thought she looked a little like a Moss Maiden, the pretty one from years ago, with blonde hair, not the grey bedraggled ones she'd seen today.

Hannah made Howard carve a cross in each of the conjoined trees. Then, she let him lead her back to the farmhouse. But part of her stayed in the forest, left behind, waiting for Maggie.

HOWARD IS IN bed, his t-shirt loose about his bony shoulders, a singular patch of dandelion fluff on his head. Hannah stares, confused. He's so old. She goes to him and runs her hands over the wrinkles of his shirt, as if she can smooth away the years. He can't look like this, not for Maggie.

Howard senses her excitement. "What are you about today, Hannah-banana?"

A giggle.

Hannah steps aside, lets Howard see Maggie. Hannah presses a hand to her heart and wills it to slow, gentle and measured, like the molasses she uses for her gingersnap cookies. She winces as she watches the slow blink of Howard's bright blue eyes; Maggie's used to be that bright, too.

"Who is this?" Howard asks, and Hannah hands him his glasses.

"It's Maggie." The name sounds so right on Hanna's lips she can barely contain herself. She sinks into the bed at Howard's feet, overwhelmed.

"Maggie?" Howard looks confused, and Hannah musters patience. She often finds herself angry these days, mad at the forgetting. "*Our* Maggie?"

Hannah nods eagerly, takes Howard's hand. Her words come in a whisper, "She came out of the forest . . . like I told you she would."

Howard slides his glasses on, his jaw slack. "No, Hannah."

Hannah licks her lips, feels the cracks with her tongue. "She's back, Howie."

Howard rubs a hand to his forehead. "But Hannah, it's not—"

"Howie. Look at her." Hannah wields an arm to point at Maggie, but the child is at the window, staring out at the forest. "Dammit."

"Mama," the girl says, fingertips pressed to the glass.

"That's not Maggie," Howard tells her. "Maggie wasn't blonde like you, Hannah. She had brown hair, like me."

Hannah wants to claw at him, to rip what's left of his memory out of him. "The forest took it," Hannah explains. "She was one of them, the moss people. She's just changed, is all." Why will he never see, not even now?

"No, Hannah, no." Howard's fingers dig into hers, forcing her to look at him. He shakes his head, sad, as if it's Hannah who's forgotten everything and not him.

"Mama." Maggie bounces now, and there's the sound of tires crunching in the laneway.

A door slams, and Hannah goes to the window to see. Below, there is a police car, with two cops and a young woman. Hannah only knows one of them, Officer Brady, grown almost as old and gnarled as Howard and herself.

THE YOUNG POLICE officer assigned to Maggie's case was clean-shaven and small. *Barely out of diapers,* Howard grumbled, but Hannah didn't mind. He had a freshness about him and something to prove, a drive that compelled him to keep opening the file long after the trail went cold.

When the initial search produced Baby Dear in the forest, and Betty something-or-other down the road (Hannah hadn't put much effort into getting to know the neighbours) claimed to have seen a strange (strange meaning unknown to her, as she knew everyone) truck parked beside their farm the same day, Officer Brady became convinced Maggie had been kidnapped.

Hannah didn't say anything for months, as she lay in bed.

She finally confessed, when she rose again, with her hands clasped over her swollen belly, that she knew he was right—but only partly. Her Maggie *had* been kidnapped. But not by human hands, no, but by creatures of the forest, *wilde Leute*, the guardian spirits of the trees.

"They won't harm her," Hannah said. "The Moss Folk are all women, young and beautiful and withered crones, they will all keep her safe as long as the forest is left alone." It almost sounded like a rhyme, the way it came out, and Hannah hummed a little.

Officer Brady had a way of absorbing information, of cocking his head just enough that he might hear not only the words that were said, but the ones that weren't. "The . . . Moss Folk . . . they're . . . young *and* old? Is it not one or the other?"

Hannah arched a brow; she wasn't sure how to answer. She was impressed Officer Brady knew what she was talking about at all. Most people here didn't. Most people everywhere couldn't see what was right under their nose. "Is any woman just one or the other?" she asked him finally.

Officer Brady could smile with his eyes, and Hannah thought if she ever had a son she hoped he would turn out like this young man. Though he wasn't much younger than Hannah, Hannah felt much older now. Flattened and trodden on, ripped apart yet somehow still together, wizened, yet pitifully hopeful.

Hannah picked up some knitting from a basket at her feet. "She'll be returned to me," she told him; for some reason she wanted to comfort him, the same way she did with Howard, to give something to those who couldn't see what the Earth was made of. "But for now, Maggie is of the Moss."

THE DOORBELL RINGS and Hannah jerks away from the window, realizing too late Maggie is waving, flailing her chubby hand.

The child is out of the room before Hannah can stop her. Hannah listens to her footsteps on the stairs, soft padding she thought she'd never hear again, and then the old familiar door creaks open and there's the sound of kisses and crying and a name, over and over again, *Penelope.*

Hannah's throat constricts like the knotted brambles in the forest, but Howard is there. He pulls Hannah up, into his now scrawny arms, the same way he did all those years ago. She weaves her hand under his baggy shirt and presses her palm against his chest—the place the cross is.

"Oh, Howie," she says, but he shushes her and pets her head and calls below to tell their guests they will be down shortly.

As they leave the room, the light catches against the brass hand bell on the nightstand and Hannah remembers—the bell *is* for her.

It's the way Howard brings her back to him.

"THANK YOU FOR taking care of my Penelope," the woman says when Hannah and Howard are back downstairs. "I'm so grateful it was caring folks who found her." The woman gives a shudder, thinking of what could have happened, and Hannah wishes she could trade places with her. She wishes she was the mom who got her child back, who only had the fear for an hour or two, and not the rest of her life.

There is a hand on Hannah's arm—Officer Brady's. "Hannah." She sees his eyes can still smile, though the skin around them is sagging.

Hannah also sees truth there—he knows what she has done.

Hannah looks at the little girl, leaning into her mother's waist. Maybe she isn't Maggie . . . "Would you like the cookies and juice now?" Hannah asks.

The girl looks to her mother, who nods permission. Hannah takes the child back to the table and studies her while she nibbles and slurps.

"There was a pioneer fair today, over in the park. *Penelope,*"—Officer Brady stresses the name— "slipped away and found her way into your forest."

"Hmm," Hannah says. "Who is your new partner?"

"What? Oh, that's Joe. New guy. I'm showing him the ropes."

"You were new once."

Officer Brady nods, paces to the window, and looks outside. Hannah follows him and sees shapes and outlines coming from the forest.

"Why are there more people in my forest?" Hannah latches onto Officer Brady's arm. "What have you done?"

"We had to look for her, Hannah." His voice is low; he doesn't want to frighten the child. "For *Penelope.*"

Hannah feels herself falling, into the same crack from years ago.

"Hannah, there's something else. Come and sit." Officer Brady takes her arm, leads her to the chesterfield, sits her beside Howard. Hannah has never seen him fidget like this, his hands kneading his thighs like bread. "While we were searching for Penelope, a body was found."

Hannah feels Howard's hand slide into hers, and knows Officer Brady is still talking. His words drift in the room, landing on her at random. "*We don't know for sure . . . probably your daughter . . . rain pools all dried up this year for the first time in a century . . . closure . . . so sorry.*"

Hannah pictures Maggie, all soft-skinned, with coffee-coloured hair and strawberries on her back, curled into a bed of moss in a rain pool. Hannah sees how it happened now, how Maggie left her bones and flesh behind and flew upward in a flash of green.

Hannah is oddly calm; she was always right.

The other child, the one they call Penelope, comes into the room. She's still holding the doll. The doll that Maggie will never play with.

The mother is insisting Penelope give the doll back. She urges her daughter forward to stand in front of Hannah. "Thank the lady," she says, "and then we'll go." The woman shifts her weight awkwardly; she's gotten more than she bargained for today. She thinks she can run away, forget it all. Hannah knows better, knows the woman will never forget this day.

"Thank you." The child reluctantly holds out the doll.

Hannah squints; the child is in the line of the window, surrounded by the light. It leaves her face shadowed. Hannah can smell her—the ginger on her breath, the lavender on the dress. Above the child's head, Hannah sees a halo of green. "You keep it," she says.

The child's hand finds Hannah's arm, right before her mother snatches her away. But Hannah knows without a doubt what she felt—three taps.

Children of the Colossus

Tim Ford

THE THING YOU have to know first about New Refuge is that we was scared. We was so a-right scared of just about everything: of the God-Kings coming after us that fled their crazy war, of the Gods they right selves, because even if we didn't believe in the war that pitted one against the other we sure'n believed in them that built the world. I think we was scared of each other, too, even if we did pack up our things and ship out on four of their big war machines and cross the ocean together.

It split families apart, it did. Hard people who thought the war could be won, even after twenty years of forcing soldiers to kill, then forcing farmers to kill, then forcing teachers and doctors and anyone else could hold a sword and shield and march in a line to kill. The hard people called us soft, and they was right, we were too soft for that world, too much mud against stone. So we left them, and hard people and soft people were on opposite sides of marriages, or siblings, or even kids against they parents.

Split like that makes people distrustful. So we was scared of each other.

When we found New Refuge, and we built up a home for our own selves, away from the God-Kings, then we were scared to lose it. We had hope you see, and hope can be great and terrible

213

and terrifying.

Terrifying like the face that rose up out of the ocean, right off the nor-nor-west side of New Refuge, some three hundred miles away, just visible from up on the island's mountain.

When that face first come up, and one of my friends—ol' Follett, you seen 'im around, with the wispy strands of white hair and the skinny limbs—spotted it with his telescope, it was like we was put right back on the front line all over again. People cried. Some prayed. Me'n a bunch of others, though. We got real curious.

We didn't know if it was one of the Gods, come to punish us for skipping out on their righteous war. Maybe it was a magical thing, conjured up by a God-King to drag us back just to lop our heads off. But we was going to find out.

So we took a boat out, six of us, including me n' Follett, to go say hi to the big stone face what was sticking up out of the ocean with a frown on his brow and a spark in his eyes.

Up close, little ones, let me tell you: any woman would've been a-right to be afraid. I was. But then Follett said to me, "It's right wonderful, ain't it, Maleta?" And he was a-right to be struck dumb with awe.

No flesh nor blood nor hair on it, to be sure. It was stone, greyish and white, with a furious-looking brow of deep-hewn angles. The nose was a right brute piece of slab that protruded out to a jutting flat ledge, and on each side of it were deep pits like bowls. Those were the eyes, and they were a-glow with some kind of inner fire, coulda been gems, coulda been magic, I couldn't say. The mouth was cut right deep, but thin and straight, like the pursed lips on a papa who caught his kid picking pipe leaf and he ain't sure to be proud or scold him.

And that face were the tip o' the iceberg; the top of the colossus. It weren't just a face. It were a full man, toe to tip, walking across the ocean floor same as you or I might walk across a creek. We could see the shoulders, and the beginnings of the chest and stomach, but beyond that the water was too dark to make out the bottom. But we knew, we all did, we felt it, that there were feet down there, taking him stride by stride towards New Refuge.

"They's trees, too," Follett said, pointing down into the water.

He was right. Big piney trees and leafy trees, bushes too, and grass, all over his shoulders, down his chest as far as we could see.

"They grow underwater?" I asked.

"No way no how," Follett said. "You oughta know that."

He was right. I worked the land of the God-Kings before I became a sailor, and them trees weren't the type to grow underwater.

"He's coming from the sea," I said, more to me than to Follett. "But he ain't *of* the sea. He's of the earth, he is. Colossus."

"What's that?" Follett said.

"A word I heard from a priest in a story. Seems . . . right."

"Well we best try to get the measure of your colossus, Maleta."

We tried to take the depth of the water with a reader on a string, but couldn't hit the bottom. Every step that colossus took our little boat was tossed about like a cork in a maelstrom. We didn't rightly know what to do besides that, so we went back and told everyone what we saw.

There was more cryin'. More prayin'. But some said we had to take more action. One of the cap'ns who brought us out to New Refuge from day one, Casten, he took in what we said and got a real serious gleam in his eye, serious like he was trying to match that big stone face look for look. "We still have the cannons," he said. He was a-right about that, all them ships we had come in on were still loaded for the God's War, and if we were supposed to be fighting gods with those tools, sure'n we could pop those guns at a big stone colossus.

Well I thought about what I'd seen out there, and about feeling like a cork in a maelstrom, and my heart, little ones, my heart seized right up and I thought to myself, "Casten's right." But soon as I did, I swear to you that such a shame came over me, such a shame as I hadn't felt since I looked my mama and papa in the eyes, threw down my sword at their feet and said, "I will not be part of this any more." This time though, I was shamed that I might be picking it back up. So I spoke up.

"It ain't hurt a-one of us yet, cap'n," I said. "We went out there close enough to spit on it, and it paid us no mind at all."

Casten turned that stone face look of his on me then. "You

were floating at eye level," he said. "The New Refuge settlement is on the ground. The ground which it will step on." He spoke then like I'd heard generals and admirals speak, and my guts chilled. "Are you saying we should just let that happen?"

I felt like I was standing on one toe. "No," I said, "I sayin' we just don't know what it wants. Didn't speak a word back and forth between us. Might be it don't even see us as anything worth bothering about." It was my turn to try to chill his guts right back. "And I thought we come here not to do more violence."

Casten ground his teeth like a mill. "I understand your reservations," he said. "But I did not come out here to see this home destroyed. I saw things you women from the country couldn't possibly understand. If you're afraid of doing what needs to be done, I promise you I can do it myself."

Well, he had me caught, I hate to say, same as my papa and mama nearly had before I left. "I's no coward," I said, with ice in my tongue.

"Good."

So we loaded up again, not just me n' Follett and our little boat, but every dang ship and boat we had brought out to New Refuge. We packed 'em in with all the powder n' shot we still had left and waved goodbye to the little huts we'd built, the grass baskets we'd weaved, the wild pigs we'd penned up. Not a one of us could say for sure if we'd be back at New Refuge ever again.

We pointed our bows out to that big stone face, and we set off.

The colossus was making good time towards New Refuge. Slow as his steps were, each one of 'em must have been the length of a pasture, and it took us a lot less time to get out to him again. Casten spread us out, in his words, "to maximize our firepower." On his signal flare, we'd all fire off at the same time to give the biggest wollop we could.

I was on a gun, primer in hand. No way no how was I gonna let someone else have that spot, not after Casten laid me out in the settlement like a child in the school room. Then I looked up at the face, and dang if I didn't feel that same hurt, seeing that flat-mouthed, glowing-eyed, innocence staring straight past us all without a care in the world.

"Why you come here," I whispered. I wanted to shout it out loud, wanted to talk, but the boats were all around and I was just a part in a big machine now. "You ain't of the sea. You're of the earth. What you doing in the sea?"

Sure as I'm standing here talking to you, little ones, I swear to you: the colossus raised one hand up out of the water, and pointed back behind us. It pointed at the island. At the mountain.

Casten popped the signal flare, and all the thunder of mankind ripped across the water. I dropped my primer.

Smoke filled the air, and my eyes burned. Someone else, I never saw who, grabbed the primer from under me and fired off my cannon, too. I couldn't see a thing, or if the colossus was still up. I grabbed the railing and tried to blink past the tears in my eyes.

The air cleared up.

And the face was suddenly a lot closer.

We hadn't put a dent in it. It came onwards. The ships in front, mine included, tried to come about, but it was no good. Stone face met wooden ship, and wood lost. The beams cracked and flew apart, the sails ripped to shreds, and we dove for the water, far as our legs could take us, trying to get clear of the face.

I was underwater.

Under the surface, the burning pain from the smoke was cleared away, but now I had the light sting of salt instead. It faded away, and I could see more of the colossus. It was . . . beautiful. It strode on through the sinking ships around it like a queen walking through falling banners. I gulped on my last breath and pulled for the surface, breaking out of the water to suck in stale, burning air.

After the first shots, the ships that weren't smashed apart by the passing colossus had given up. They scooped us out of the water, and maybe luck was with us, or maybe one of the Gods we'd abandoned somehow still had us in their palm, but one way or another not a single soul drowned.

We picked up our broken supplies and broken strength and sailed past the colossus, back to New Refuge.

"We move," said one of the captains. "We pack up and just move. We found a new home once, we can do it again."

"With fewer ships, and less supplies?" argued another captain.

"We aren't going anywhere," said Casten. "We are going to take that thing down."

"How? We unloaded every gun we had on it and it brushed us aside like we were flies."

Casten got that same stony face look he had before, and for all that I say about the man, I will say this: he were right smart. He pulled out a chart we'd done up of the island and the sea all around, and jabbed a finger at a spot close by.

"Here," he said. "That reef we found. Deep enough for our ships to pass over, but shallow enough that when that thing crosses over, it'll be sticking up a lot more out of the water."

"What's your point?" said the other captain.

"My point is that it'll be vulnerable then. Its legs will be out of the water, if I've estimated right. That's a weak spot. We take our anchor chains, lash them together, and pull them tight across our remaining ships."

"We trip it?"

Casten smiled. "We trip it."

I stood by, waiting for someone, anyone, to say something. It were a good plan, to be sure, but there would be someone, I thought, who would speak up, keep them talking. Long enough that they wouldn't be able to do it. Or someone else would come up with something better. The moment went on, though, and I knew weren't a one going to say nothing. They were scared. That was New Refuge.

"Then if we're all in agreement . . ." Casten said.

"I wanna say something." The words tumbled out of my mouth into the room, and all eyes were on me.

"I don't think we have time for—"

"We're building a new world here, Casten," one of the other captains interrupted him. "One where everyone gets a say, no matter what their rank or birth." The captain nodded her head at me. "Speak up, Maleta."

I swallowed hard. "It's like you saying, cap'n," I said. "This is a new world. New Refuge. We come here to get away from the Gods War. All that violence and killing. Yet first thing we can think to do to this . . . colossus . . . is shoot it with our guns. When that don't work, we find another way to hurt it."

"You tried communicating with it and it didn't answer you," Casten replied.

"Well why can't we just let it be? Ain't paid the slightest to us."

"It tore through our fleet!"

"It walked through 'em. Sure'n we lost some boats, but alls here n' breathing, my own self among 'em. Fact is, it breezed on through us like we'd do in a swarm of gnats. If it meant to harm us, seems to me it could've done for us all then and there."

Casten snorted. "You can't possibly know that."

"I know that I ain't here to fight. I know that that ain't me. That ain't my nature. I's from the God's lands, but I was never *of* them, you ken? We all was. Not now. And that giant out there, that colossus, it ain't *of* the sea. It's of the earth. You see it on its back, on its chest, its arms. I can see it, feel it."

"What difference should that make?"

My throat was tight. I might've had people thinking for a minute there, but they was looking at me then for an explanation. Even Follett, bless him, had a pain in his frown that cut me across the cheek sure as if he'd slapped me. I looked down. "Same difference it made that we had to find an island before we could be home," I said. "The earth is home."

Casten shook his head. "I think we've heard enough."

The captain who had spoken up on my behalf squeezed her mouth shut and nodded in agreement.

A few hours later we was back on the water. This time, we had a chain strung out between our boats. Half of them angled out to the right of the oncoming colossus, the other half on the left. We had to time it just right, pulling the chain between us with our sails unfurled, crossing the colossus's path just as it would stand atop the reef.

Little ones, I am not ashamed to tell you that I prayed we would fail.

I prayed that the ships might time it wrong.

That the chain would fall, or break.

That the colossus would jump over the chain, or be too strong for it.

None of that happened.

I forced myself to watch.

When the colossus stepped up onto the reef, it rose up out of the water for the first time, only its ankles still covered by the waves. It had no sex, no clothing. Its muscles were thick-packed mud jammed in with gravel. Its joints were mossy-covered granite, scraping and screeching something wonderful. Each of its hands could have held a castle. When it stood tall, it pointed, back towards New Refuge, a hand of stone reaching out for the beach and the jungle.

Then the chain snapped into its leg.

It all must have been over in moments, but each of those moments stretched on for me into yesteryear. The pointed hand pitching down, the fingers splaying out to try to catch itself. The face with its same constant look smashing down into the water, which was all too shallow for it at this point. Worst of all, I saw the ankle snap open in the side, as the shift in weight were too much, and the outer layers of thick rock split apart to reveal soft clay underneath.

Casten saw it too.

"There!" he yelled to the fleet. "Fire into there!"

Our ship was the only one with a good angle. I shook my head and threw down the primer. It was picked up by eager hands. Follett's hands. He looked me right in the eye and primed the cannon. The shot sailed into the opening that had been left by Casten's damned chain.

The colossus screamed. Little ones, I will never forget that sound. It was the sound of a roaring quake, like all the echoes in every canyon everywhere were booming out all at once.

It lay down and was quiet. But then, oh then, I swear by all of my years and by all of my heart, it looked right at me. At me, among every ship and every sailor, its glowing ember gaze burned right into me, and it pointed, again. It pointed at the island, with its beach and its jungle, and above that the mountain.

I didn't understand it all. But I put my hand on my heart and nodded once, if only to tell it it was going to be ok. Then it put its head down, and those glowing eyes went dark for good.

Everyone celebrated that night. Follett asked me for a caper round the fire. I gave him such an earful it would turn butter sour, and left to go look at the colossus's body in the bay. Even with the tide, it stuck up out of the water to a huge height. I thought about how far it must have come. How desperate it had seemed, pointing up at that mountain. Something stirred in me, thinking on that mountain.

How could we have known? We were from the God lands. We didn't know what a volcano was.

When the top of that mountain blew off ten days later, and ash and rocks rained down and blew our settlement to the four winds, I knew there was only one way to go.

I pulled myself and as many as I could find together, including Follett and the captains, and I led us right down the dead gullet of the colossus. Inside, the air was mossy, and dank from the tide. It was dripping wet, and we were cold and terrified.

Outside, though, the rocks bounced off the hide of the colossus, the ash fell down like snow, and even the damnably hot lava cooked up the ocean around us, but couldn't get through.

We lived.

And so we have for two more generations, little ones.

People ask me, elder Maleta dear, did you know the whole time? Why didn't you say more?

Truth is I didn't know. I still don't.

Could be the colossus was a messenger of the Gods. Could be it was a wayward spell from the God-Kings, all of them long-dead now, having murdered each other to the last back in the old lands. It could even be that New Refuge itself called the colossus here, trying to keep us safe from the volcano. So I tell the ones who ask that I don't know nothing worth putting me up on no pedestal of leadership, and some things we'll never know for sure.

I do know this though.

I know that the earth is old, impossibly old. I know that stones don't hold grudges, don't run in cycles of violence and misery. I know that we don't live in the sea, or in the air. We live in and on the earth.

So my little ones, when you think on why we live in the body of a creature that we never got to speak with, and never fully understood, and find yourselves thinking badly on that poor thing's fate, I can tell you this much: we honour the earth with our lives. Now go on and play, my little ones, and let old elder Maleta rest. Earth is home, and I'll be called back to it soon, too.

Earthbound

V.F. LeSann

I'D BEEN TWO glasses of something the consistency of motor oil and one blue-vitriol cigarette deep, when I finally stopped wrestling with the fact that I was going to need a dragon to pull this off.

I was staring down the barrel of thirty: a dragon rider without a dragon, and with my doomsday clock ticking dangerously close to midnight, I couldn't decide if the entire notion was bullshit or if I'd fucked up somewhere along the way. The unlit runes on my face sure seemed to indicate the latter. Either way, I couldn't pull off the crazy plan I was hatching on my own; I needed to up my odds. There was only one drake who fit the bill, and I was just desperate enough to go into his lair and ask him a favour.

The only problem was we hated each other.

I picked my way down into the abandoned parking garage with a frozen turkey banging against my thigh at every step. The turkey was a last minute addition to sweeten the deal so he heard me out instead of eating me; some might call it a bribe, but those people ran in better circles than I did.

Rasikh was exactly what I needed—even though he was prideful and surly, he had a flexible moral compass and a chip on his shoulder as hefty as mine. And, in his defence, I hadn't given him much reason *to* like me. But today the charm was dialled up to eleven.

Time and weather had turned a multi-car crash on the exit ramp into an ugly abstract sculpture, the torn metal bristling with rust, sealing the underground parking garage like a tomb. I wound my way through the fused metal, grimacing as the jagged steel nipped at my jacket, thankfully not breaking skin. The stink was so thick down here it made my eyes water, a bouquet of rust and oil and rot.

I could hear Rasikh before I could see him. The deep, slow whoosh of his breath could've been the wind hissing through the echoing space. The skin-prickling rasp of metallic scales sliding over concrete could've been some old abandoned thing settling . . . which, in a sense, it was.

Be nice, I reminded myself. *Be polite. Be flattering. Be confident. But not too confident.*

"I can hear you . . ."

The low growl froze me in place turning my insides as cold as the ragged metal around me. Some dragons were talented at playing human. Rasikh was the opposite of that.

"Congratulations, your ear-holes work," I blurted, belatedly reminding myself to be nice. "It smells good in here. You must've lit some candles or something . . . I mean, not that it didn't smell great before . . . shit. Hi, it's Caja, remember me?" Seas and skies, I was off to an awful start.

"My sense of smell also works. And you stink the same," he said, the baritone rumble suffused with dry humour.

The next squeal of grinding iron shook me to my molars. Fear squirmed in my stomach, but I continued downwards, hopping over the crushed hood of a mangled convertible. At the base of the crash-choked ramp, the garage opened up into a long hollow studded with columns. It would have looked like some sort of fairy-tale hall carved by dwarves if the pillars weren't still faintly marked with things like P4 and PASSHOLDERS ONLY.

I squinted, straining to adjust to the dim strobe of the few fluorescent bulbs that refused to die. Chunks of the floor were torn up in mounds, shredded by long claws of something that ripped up fucking concrete for kicks. There's no fear like knowing you're in the presence of a grouchy dragon, who you may have pissed off, and not being able to find him.

"Fair enough," I called, "but I brought you a peace offering, if you'll hear me out." I hoisted the shopping bag, waggling it a bit so the thawing meat rustled within.

A low laugh poured out of the shadows.

I could feel my pregame buzz burning off as adrenaline coursed through me. Luckily, this wasn't my first rodeo and I held it together. Being marked as a dragon rider meant I'd grown up around them, and this wasn't the first time I was seeing Rasikh either, so I didn't piss myself when he stepped into my limited range of sight.

If he was going for a dramatic entrance, he nailed it. He pulled himself up from a pit at the end of the garage, clawed hand over clawed hand, and started towards me.

I'd seen dragons so gorgeous they made me want to die. Rasikh was not that kind of dragon. His scales were rust-eaten, falling away in places that glowed with a dark sickly red, and he slunk low to the ground, dragging himself forward with jagged sickle-like claws that punched through the surface of the floor, sending up flashes of sparks. His head was a skeletal nightmare, lips pulled back from dark, stained fangs, long narrow snout questing forward, pure lizard. And his eyes, sunken, clouded orbs, were no less frightening than the first time I'd seen them.

I shifted my weight, scuffing my boot against the floor so he could hear me and wouldn't run me over. He stopped far short, forked tongue snaking out to taste the air.

"Frozen turkey?" The scales along his nose bristled. "You come into my den, fling insults around like confetti, after leaving last time like your tail was on fire . . . with cheap, freezer-burned turkey?"

My temper came up strong, tearing down my sense of self-preservation like a riptide.

"I figured it would be a nice change from whatever gutter-meat cordon bleu you're used to eating," I said with a cold, painted smile.

"Failed dragon riders, mostly," he snarled back. "Why are you here?"

"Oh, you're a comedian now?" I bit my tongue, holding back further snark—I didn't need to find out the hard way if he had a breath weapon.

I'd been called a failed rider so many times I'd lost count but it still hurt like a slap. My heart was pounding with offence rather than fear now, but I decided throwing a frozen turkey at a dragon would be a poor life choice. Instead, I shook the meat out of the bag and let it roll across the concrete towards him. "I hear some smugglers caught wind of a deposit of lux, outside Abraxas," I said, not burying the lede. "First new discovery in almost a decade, right on our doorstep."

Rasikh's facial scales smoothed as he listened. "How nice for them."

"Nicer for us if we can get to it first."

"You have a death wish," he said, lip curling back further. "Everything about you suddenly makes much more sense."

"No, I've got a plan," I insisted, "They'll hit it hard and fast: excavators, gun turrets, poison sprays, the works. And the Avian Guild will be dispatched to counter them. The two of them going toe to toe? It'll be a mess." I smiled, dropping the notion that'd brought me here. "And none of them will be expecting someone to snatch the lux from below."

"That's barely a plan," he muttered, but his smirk had disappeared.

"It's a pretty good plan," I said with a laugh. "Wasn't it you who was bragging you could move through the old tunnels, that the underground was your playground?"

"It's not bragging if it's true," he murmured, but there was no heat behind it.

"Think what we could do with even a bit of lux." It was better than gold, the new-age diamond. Every alchemist needed it, everything ran on it, and once the old bones of the extinct Apex dragons ran out, we'd have none. We'd backed our world into a corner with our dependence on magic, and now the finality of our most precious resource was going to clothesline us back into the dark ages.

The path was so damn clear in my mind, every door opening to me with even a single crate of the stuff. I could clean myself up, buy some new gear, and finally bribe my way into the Avian Guild where solid dragons were still looking to bond with riders. I'd be able to show regular drakes I was someone worth bonding with, even at my age.

Rasikh was still silent, probably indulging in some lux-fuelled fantasies of his own.

"Well?" I coaxed.

His head rose, serpentine, blind unblinking eyes staring through me. "The tunnels are my playground, not yours. I could get it myself."

"Like hell," I said. "Maybe you're the king of the underground, but it's a big city up there and I only said it was outside the walls. So, unless you're planning on digging a moat around all of Abraxas, you can't find it without me."

His snarl echoed through the concrete, and he surged forward, gnarled teeth snapping near me. I fell to my knees, hands pressed tight against my ears.

"Fine," I bellowed against his maelstrom roar. "Fucking eat me then! You eat failed riders, you've got one right here. But I'll tell you what, I'm not going to taste near as good as whatever the hell you can buy with that money."

The room fell silent, and he twisted his head, aiming an ear-hole towards me.

"Neither of us can do this alone—so either we're stuck together, or broke. And I know my preference." I shoved myself back to my feet, my breath seething through my teeth.

I stared into the cloudy globes of his eyes, neither of us blinking, both of us scowling. His head lurched again, and I jumped back towards the cars, bracing for the pain of teeth.

I landed well, eyes trained on him—like I'd been taught—and watched his serrated teeth crush the turkey with enough pounds per square inch that my bones ached in sympathy.

His tongue licked the edges of his black lips. "Let's talk."

LIFE IN THE city was harder than Rasikh understood down in his dark dungeon, and topside, he would've been no better than me. But down in the grimy tunnels beneath Abraxas, I had nothing on him.

"I will not wait for you," he rumbled, swivelling his head in my direction. "You will have to keep up with me."

"No problem," I said, forcing the last buckles on my jacket to fasten. "But when you have to stop because you don't know where the hell you're going, I'll just be back here. Y'know, waiting."

Snorting, he lumbered into the darkness. The night glasses I'd pulled from the same bag as my training armour were better than nothing, but not by much. It felt weird suiting up in my old gear for more reasons than because it didn't fit me the way it used to. About a decade out of date, but it would have to do, since the coordinates had cost me my next month's rent. The world around me shifted from pitch black into shadowy grey. I started forward at a jog.

On cue, Rasikh took off at speed. His body slid and wound like a snake, filling tunnels and moving around corners like they were straightaways. His claws made gravity a non-issue; where there was an impediment he'd scrape up the side of a wall and use the ceiling as his floor, skirting over it like it was nothing.

Me, I thought I'd have an easier time than I did. Those obstructions he cruised over took me minutes to scrabble around. If I was lucky, there'd be a path through the rubble I could squeeze through, but mostly it was climb or bust.

None of my years in the baby ranks of the Avian Guild had prepared me for this. This was the land of the forgotten, where the rats and garbage thrived. Twenty minutes in, I slipped and stumbled into a puddle of I-don't-want-to-know-what when I finally tapped out.

"I need a break," I gasped. "Hold up. I need, like, three . . . five minutes." I flopped onto my back, my pride left somewhere in the first pile of shit I'd sunk my boots into. I spent more time under motors than I did training these days. "Big guy, you there?"

I assumed he was long gone, but then I heard the whoosh of his breath just ahead of me. Or was it behind? I was all turned around, disoriented in the endless shadows.

As if trying to make me grateful for small blessings while I had them, my glasses flickered off and plunged me into total black. "Shit," I snapped, ripping them from my face.

A slight burst of sparks from claws striking stone barely lit the shape of Rasikh as he nosed into the space beside me.

"Humans are so fragile." His inhalations were quick, the whoosh sounding more like puffs of angry wind than a living thing. He was *panting*.

"You were running," I exclaimed. "You jerk!"

"*You* were being cocky," he said, air rumbling through his

chest.

I screamed in frustration, dragging my hands down my face. "This is no fucking time to show off! I literally, *literally* have everything on the line here. By the seas and skies, you're a piece of work."

"You are too sensitive," he said.

"I'm exhausted and sitting in fuck-knows-what! I think this is the right reaction given the circumstances."

Rasikh didn't argue. I could hear the swish and grinding of his tail flicking with agitation. More sparks shot up behind his silhouette like a firework backdrop.

I staggered to my feet. "Listen, we both want to win, and I *can* keep up if you're not running like a maniac."

"I am better at the tunnels than you."

"No shit," I said. "Detective Dragon right here."

Another hiss slipped through his gnarled nostrils. My eyes were adjusting to the darkness, but everything was still just shades of black, like a load of darks in the laundry, the spectrum of hues of your teenage goth years. I could make him out though, and saw his head tilt, his brow-scales wrinkling.

"Your glasses are not making noise anymore."

"They're dead. Another mystery solved by Detective Dragon."

Another sharp exhale followed by an audible grimace.

I stole a moment to catch my breath with my hands on my hips, studying his large, not-put-together-right edges. "Does it hurt when you breathe?"

I'd assumed the after-sound was part of whatever helped him breathe, like the last sigh of a blacksmith's bellows, but it wasn't. It was a whimper that followed his laboured breath. Like the soft whine of a kid who just got through a fight and realized when she touched her cheek that it was actually broken.

"You may not ride me through the tunnels," he snapped. "Your glasses are dead, and our fool's errand is done."

I shook my head, rummaging in my bag. "I can keep up if you do me a solid." I pulled out my welder's goggles. "I brought these in case we had to use heat blades to extract the lux, but if you drag your tail, I can follow the trail of sparks. I have a blowtorch in here for extra light, but I don't want to waste the fuel."

"Why do you have a torch?"

"How the hell did you think we were going to get through the Apex's bones?"

Rasikh scoffed. "I would tear them off the corpse."

"Nah, lux is in the marrow. You have to burn through the bones to get it. Smash the bones, lose the lux. The catch, you ask? That sparkling answer to all our problems is flammable as fuck." I flipped the strap around my finger, smiling. "Lucky for you, you have a *bona fide* welder right here. Certified and everything."

His body churned in the dark, his edges melting into murkier shadows. "I thought you just stunk like steel."

"Nope—that is, in fact, my job, not my natural musk." I sighed, rubbing my temple. Our initial meeting had jumped from awkward hellos, to a competition of who could sling the best insults in Draken, with none of the "getting to know you" stage in between.

"Why don't we take our little partnership here down from *How to Insult a Dragon* to something more buddy-cop style, like *Fly Hard*," I said.

"I don't fly," he snarled.

I backpedalled, remembering the contorted rust-coated exoskeleton on his back that must've once resembled a massive set of bat-like wings. "Sorry, I'll come up with something better. All I am saying is, if we'd done this right, we would've gotten through the basic questions right out of the gate."

"I'll start. Hi, I'm Caja and I fix shit. Twenty-nine years old. I grew up in Abraxas. I'm a mechanic, own my own shop, and I have a weakness for cake with caramel in it. I drink, smoke, and sleep around in equal parts not enough and too much. Not married, no kids, no family." I paused, peering at him through the darkness. "Okay, your turn."

He was silent a few moments, his tail no longer flicking in agitation, but moving in mesmerizing figure-eights to a metronome beat, contemplative. "I am called Rasikh," he said at last, "I am not from Abraxas. I am not a mechanic. I am not sure how I feel about caramel. I also have no family. No children, no mate."

Sighing, I secured my goggles on my head. "Well, that's a start. Can we try this again at a sane pace?"

His answer was something I'd learned to expect from years

working with dragons. Spinning, he dragged his tail and showered me in a semicircle of sparks before trotting off down the tunnel.

I kept up pretty well, and though I wasn't going to call him on it, whenever Rasikh got too far ahead, he slowed down. Sure, he made a show of smelling something, or pretending to inspect the wall of the tunnel with his claws, but it happened suspiciously whenever I started falling behind. After a full hour of jogging, he stopped long enough for me to fall in beside him. The shadows around me looked identical to everything else.

"Where are we?" I asked.

"Just beyond the edge of the city—no one's land. The tunnel ahead has fallen."

"All right." I reached into my bag and attached the wristband with the coordinates to the hypothetical lux deposit. The screen stayed in night-mode, emitting gentle red lights in the shape of a compass.

"There will be no stone for my tail to make sight-light for you if we are leaving the tunnels," he warned.

"Got it covered, Razzle Dazzle. I get some ambient light off of this thing so we should be fine." The red gleam of the wristband caught on the overlapping edges of his scales and the dagger-sheen of his claws, the sketched outline of something monstrous in the dark.

"So, I've got the map here . . ." I rotated left and right, spinning in a circle. The dial spun with me, but the arrow remained constant. Perfect, easy guidance.

"Detective Mechanic strikes again." He laughed in his throat, the guttural sound echoing through the tunnel.

"I don't like that for the name of our premiere," I said absently, my attention focused on the map. "Like I was going to say before your one-dragon comedy debut: north and south, or left and right for directional cues? And . . . let's just agree to be nice during our first road trip. Some kinks will undoubtedly have to be ironed out."

"How lucky I am made of iron, then. I understand bearings."

"Perfect," I grinned, securing my goggles for the impending spark show. I could see in the dusk that the tunnel ahead was indeed blocked. Giant pieces of carved stone concaved inwards, bound together with tangles of roots, impenetrable.

"We need to go northwest and drop down fifteen feet. So, if we backtrack we can probably find a tunnel to loop around . . ." I paused. Rasikh was already on the move.

His front claws latched into the wall of the tunnel. Buried up to his fingers, he tore the entirety of the stone outwards, sending showers of dirt and rock out in his wake. He moved fast, burrowing into the earth like a demon-mole, leaving me to give chase. Rasikh was digging through the side of the world as fast as I could run.

The tunnel he dug was Rasikh-sized so I had no problem moving through upright, and despite the ruckus of his digging, he responded to my verbal cues like a champ. We went down, deep into the world—if I'd been claustrophobic, well, let's just say I was glad I'd passed containment training with flying colours.

Breaching the soil, we came in through the roof of another stone-crafted tunnel that made the ones under Abraxas seem like they were made for worms, and this one for an anaconda.

Rasikh took the plunge first. The dim light of my wristband glimmered off his outstretched skeletal wings as he dropped. They likely splayed open out of instinct, like a phantom limb, but they seemed to keep him on the better side of a tumble. About halfway down, a wave of darkness swallowed him whole.

I, on the other hand, intended to embrace my inner grace as I descended and drove an anchor into the clay-dirt, hooking my carabineer to my climbing rope. "How deep is it?" I called down, looking behind me as I steadied my footing, testing the anchor.

"More than five of me on hind legs. Are you able to do this?" Rasikh asked, his voice rumbling like a demon speaking up from hell.

My brain envisioned an upright Rasikh and tried to do speedy math, pulling out as much rope as I had; two hundred feet would have to do. "We're 'bout to find out!" Testing my weight a final time, I hopped off the ledge, rappelling down into the gaping tunnel.

Three seconds into the fall, my wristband beeped, boasting a forty-eight percent charge as it went dead, plunging me into an obsidian freefall. "Shit!" I tightened my brake hand and lurched to a halt. The rope creaked in the presiding darkness.

"Caja," Rasikh called, his voice echoing around me. "What's

happened?"

"My light went dark and I'm somewhere three-quarters of the way down? I think? I don't know if my rope reaches the bottom—and here I was planning an aerial twist at the end." The darkness seemed to pulse around me with my racing heart.

The dragon grumbled in his throat. "Talk, and go slow."

"I don't have echolocation, Razz!" I yelled, the tremor in my voice unmasking my attempt at calm. "Not a bat!"

"You have been blind for two hours!" he snapped. "I have been blind much longer. Go slow, and speak."

"Fuck, fine," I grumbled, loosening my brake hand to descend. The drop suddenly seemed much faster than before and I winced, jerking to a stop again.

"Caja, speak."

My muscles were locked with fear. I didn't know if the ground was fifty feet away or five, and the last of my rope could zip through the carabineer and drop me at any second. I steadied myself, grabbing my courage by the collar and dragging it into the front row.

The guy had a point, this was his strong suit, not mine. I didn't know what to say, or what to talk about—which was strange for me. So, I started to sing, *"Busted flat in Baton Rouge, waitin' for a train . . ."* Each time I let myself drop, my voice spiked, hitting a higher note, but I kept singing.

Finally my feet touched something and I held my breath, testing the surface with the tips of my toes until I was satisfied it was solid. I blew out a sigh of relief, lowering to a secure standing position.

"That was a nice song," rumbled from beneath my feet, the vibration shaking through my boots.

"Seas and skies," I swore, jolting. "Razzy, am I standing on you?"

"Of course. Sit and I will lower you."

I unfastened my climbing gear and fed the rope the rest of the way through. To my horror, there were only a few feet left before I would've had a seriously sudden drop. "Thanks," I murmured, taking a seat on warm, iron scales, careful not to touch the jagged edges.

The wind lifted my hair as we lowered down. When his front claws clacked against the floor, I slid free from his brow.

"The navigator's dead," I told him.

"Your human machines are so weak," he scoffed. "So much trash." The sentiment threw me hard, coming from him, and I was addressing the big metal elephant in the room before my brain caught up to my mouth.

"Are you a machine, Razzy?"

Dragonscale was tough, but it didn't spark on stone, and I would know the smell of soldered metal anywhere. Maybe he thought I was too stupid to know the difference, but the guy was *rusting*.

There was a long moment of silence, scarier than a roar.

"No," he said, "I am alive."

Well, I was in this deep. "Are you . . . a cyborg? I mean, there's a gear in your jaw. I saw it when you were roaring at me."

There was the growl I'd been expecting. "No," he snapped. He blew out a breath and I could hear the hydraulic hiss in it. "There was human, a long time ago. He made me stronger. Gears in my jaw, yes—my bite is the strongest of all dragons my age and size. My iron scales could tear our foes to slivers. I was tireless. I was . . ." His lungs wheezed, broken scales leaking air. ". . . I was magnificent."

I sat frozen, picturing him as he must have been. A mechanically enhanced dragon. *Damn.* "What happened?"

There was a long pause and I thought he wouldn't answer. "Your kind is so . . . fragile." He shook his head, his jaw striking sparks off the floor. "Put on the protectors on your eyes, you are no good blind. Let's find the treasure. Forget your machine . . . I can smell the rot from here. It is this way."

He spun, showering me with sparks as he galloped down the hallway, lighting the way for me again.

My hand went to the dark line of runic marks running down my left cheek, my own version of rusted scales, a brand of disrepair showcased for the world to see. Dark husks devoid of the magic of the bond, the shifting colour meaning you'd exceeded your potential, that you were magnificent. If he'd stuck around two seconds, I might've told him that.

In the flashes of light I could see the faded beauty of the tunnel. It wasn't concrete like the last one; this one was shinier, polished. Gilded carvings decorated the enormity of the cylindrical tunnel from roof to floor. I caught brief glimpses of bas-relief scenes etched into the walls, daubed with faded colour, a history of tooth and claw and fire. A sense of existential vertigo crept through me; this shit felt older than merely "old". Rasikh seemed to feel it too, slowing to a walk.

We trudged along, finally coming to a large set of ornate brass doors. I reached out to touch Rasikh to stop him, but whatever senses he'd honed in the absence of his sight was warning enough. He stopped when I did.

Rasikh flicked his tail side to side without me asking, sending up enough sparks I could see the workings of the mechanisms. I slung off my backpack, pulling out my toolkit. The light provided by the tail-embers was behind me now, so I dropped my goggles to my neck and got to work.

"Good thing the Apexes got humans to do their dirty work, or this may have been a much bigger job. Literally." I pulled my putty from its container and ran a small strip around the edges of the lock frame, careful not to slip into any carvings or ancient Draken runes.

"What is *dirty work?*" he asked, his nostrils flaring, taking in the new scent of my gear.

"You know, the crappy things you have to do for yourself, unless you're rich or tyrannical dragon overlords with a serious god complex. Executions, laundry, *definitely* dishes, cooking, flaying the rabble . . . the usual stuff. And, in the case of this despot, opening doors." I grinned, grabbing my spray bottle and held my breath. "Don't snort this, and you can kill the tail-lamp."

The spray hit the putty as the last sparks dimmed, bathing my workstation in a teal glow

"What is that stench?" Rasikh hissed, coiling backwards.

"Good old synthesized bioluminescence. Ravers use it. You know, like algae?"

"It's awful," he sneered, tucking his nose under his front feet.

"We need light and as little heat as possible—so the mechanisms won't react from the nudge of my weld," I said, already getting my picks and soldering materials into the lock mechanism. "Most Apexes were fire drakes, so their traps were activated by intense heat . . ." My voice trailed off as I secured my welding goggles and put the second fire stick in my teeth, bracing as a flurry of sparks spilled from inside the mechanism.

"How do you know these old things?"

I grinned past the stick in my mouth. "One of the perks of having me along," I mumbled, contorting myself with another pick and firestick. "We potential dragon riders get hauled off to an academy to learn dragon shit until we hit voting age. And lucky for us, I majored in the archaeology of the ancients. Don't tell my old profs, but I always fancied myself a treasure hunter." I shrugged and lit the next stick, welding two more gears in place. Another weld and I held my breath, listening for the click of activated clockwork. Three seconds later, I let myself breathe. "And that is how it's done!"

I grabbed the two protruding lock picks and turned them counter-clockwise. The internal mechanisms gave a happy click as cogs and gears ticked, bolts and pins released, and the great door unlocked, breaching the seal that barred the door centuries ago. I stepped into the chamber, holding my blowtorch like a lantern.

It was common knowledge our city was built on the corpse of an old one as literally as it was figuratively. You could still match the roll of the S-bend in the Apex's spine that made up Abraxas, concrete and iron towers soaring between the spaces in the dragon's ribs. But it was a very different thing to see the skeleton of an Apex dragon unceremoniously rotting in its throne room.

This one didn't hold a candle to Abraxas for size, and the body was more serpentine, like Rasikh's. But the designs and runes woven into the bones were the unmistakable internal birthmarks of a pure-blooded Apex. Inlays of silver and obsidian decorated the skeleton in shapes like the march of termites through driftwood.

Long-dried blood still stained the ornate tapestries lining the floor. A massive head about the size of a tank tilted to the side, throat bared, neck broken. Primitive weapons, shotguns and spears, were strewn nearby. The room was trashed and scavenged to boot. The lack of bounty wasn't the end of the world. Only a fool broke into a dragon horde to steal coins or candlesticks; the real treasure was in the bones of the dragon itself.

"Holy shit," I breathed, old survival instinct advising me to keep quiet for fear of waking the sleeping monster.

Something crashed behind me and I felt like my bones jumped out of my skin. Spinning around, brandishing my blowtorch, I watched as Rasikh stumbled over another pile of expensive garbage. His feet scrambled in a panic and he went in reverse at top speed, slamming into the wall adjacent the doorway, his sides heaving.

"Whoa, whoa," I yelled, cringing at the jingle of crystal and glass above us. The high ceiling still dripped with elaborate chandeliers and a crumbling mosaic I couldn't make out. "Razzy, stay still, there's shit all over the floor. This guy didn't go down gentle—the room's trashed."

Rasikh scurried to his feet, the stress of his rapid breath grating his iron scales on the golden walls. His lips pulled back in a snarl, but I spoke first.

"I should've said something instead of just waltzing in here," I said, "It was ignorant, I'm sorry."

The swell of his breath eased and his snarl regressed. "I was not going to be angry at you. I was mad at the things, and my feet for moving too fast."

I smiled, relaxing. "That's fair by me. I'm gonna need your help though. Some vertebrae will be in our weight category, but they're way out of my reach." Rasikh was good for keeping my eyes from turning into dollar signs, a reminder that it was going to be a harder road home the more lux we took.

Clearing the floor, I did my best to make a path for big ol' Razzy to wander over to the Apex, and slid on my work gloves. "Can you boost me? I can work at the top of the ribcage."

He obliged without comment. It was easy enough to steady myself once he got me up there, but when I got situated and trained my blowtorch on the space between the bones, the room rumbled.

Pulling my fire back, I stared, unsure if actually defacing the remains had triggered some ancient curse.

"What is it?" Rasikh asked. He'd been feeling around at the skull of the corpse, nose to mirrored nose with it, but paused to turn his snout up towards me.

"I don't know. I tried to torch the first bone and it sounded like I set something off. I'm going to try again." This time, with more caution, I set the flame to the bone. Nothing. Shaking my head, I got to cutting, using the fire like a knife, letting the blue flame be my fingers. Within minutes I'd breached the deepest layer of bone and the opalescent lux oozed out of the slice, flecks of crimson fire glowing on the dark backdrop like a midnight opal. I pulled the torch back, not wanting a kamikaze spark to flambé our profits. My breath was coming fast. Lux, real lux, right under my nose for the taking. It gleamed like the answer to every problem.

"Razzy, we're going to be rich!" I exclaimed.

Rasikh was pacing in the hollow of the chest, sliding over the ribcage like iron waves of the ocean. "You are a very good mechanic," he said.

I grinned, not wanting to get sappy and admit mechanics were only a fraction of what it had taken to get us here. Getting back to work, it was about fifteen minutes to dislodge each vertebra. I filled what I could into the shop boxes I'd brought in my backpack, then Rasikh took to bagging and I did the hacking. We were three cervical bones in when the clinking of the chandelier pulled me out of my zone.

The dangling crystals swayed in time with an unheard tune, tinkling together like fairy wings. I furrowed my brow and watched them, the glimmers of light from my torch-light refracting into swaying rainbows on the golden walls. A sprinkle of dust fell from the base of one of the ornate fixtures that helped the chandelier encompass the whole of the roof like a diamond spiderweb.

Rasikh froze along with me, his skinny snout pointed towards the same place I was watching.

The room breathed, and another spray of dust showered from the sky.

"Get down from there," Rasikh warned, scrambling up the ribs and stretching towards me. Another breath, and then a shriek as the roof hurtled down in pieces.

I screamed, throwing my arms over my head, shielding myself while Rasikh latched his fangs into my jacket and pulled me off the spine just in time to miss the first chunk of gilded stone that plummeted into the Apex corpse. The old bones shattered, exploding into pieces.

Rasikh curled his way back inside the ribs, following his same path down when another chunk smashed into him. He dropped me and the ribcage crumbled down with us.

We fell in a maelstrom of gold, bone, and lux, crashing to the floor. I fell on Rasikh, his jagged scales slicing me on my left side. I slid up to the softer scales of his chest as he flipped like a twisting crocodile, and his body concaved onto me, the weight of him bearing down as the rest of the mess exploded on top of him.

He roared in pain, his scream drowned out with the rush of noise streaming down from the surface. I knew the sound of warfare and dragonfare, and this was all of it. We should've had time and warning before these assholes made it to the chamber if they'd been moving carefully, but I guess they were adopting the "if I can't have it, no one can" mentality. The skeleton was ravaged. There wouldn't be any salvageable lux by the time this was over.

"Hang on," I yelled. The prismatic rivulets of raw lux seeped down through the gaps in Rasikh's iron skin and pooled on the floor around me, sizzling and sticking to everything it touched. The seams of ooze wormed their way to the giant dent in the floor where I was trapped.

Rasikh cried again, and my attention was torn from my own welfare to his. This shit was all over his scales, burning him alive, and the rest of the room was crushing him. I screamed, some primal desperation boiling in me, in time with another death-wail from him.

I pounded my fists, trying to squirm out from under him to help somehow. I could feel his panicked gasps and the whimper that drowned out the sounds of battle and any logical thought fled my mind. A single compulsion was all that was left: Rasikh was in pain and I wanted to fix it more than I wanted to live. Every breath and step he took was pain, every damned day. Someone had let him fall into disrepair, left him a mangled mess like an abandoned wreck, like he didn't matter. He didn't deserve to hurt like this, and I was going to fix it no matter what.

My name is Caja, and I fix shit—this damn dragon wasn't going to be any different.

I dug in my nails and pulled, dragging myself right through the corrosive puddles of lux, under the shelf of his massive jaw. Where the lux crept through the seams in my armour, my body felt like it was on fire and my mind warped with the pain until I thought I could feel phantom limbs searing—tail and maw and revenant wings. Then the pain settled under my skin into something bearable, deep into my bones, and the ache drummed in time with my heartbeat.

Glancing upwards through the shattered ceiling, my vision cleared and my breath steadied. I saw glimpses of dragon battle and the velvet smoke plumes from giant excavators. And worse, much worse, I could see smugglers bristling with weapons, starting to crowd around the edges of the hole in the ceiling. If they didn't get their lux, maybe an iron dragon and an idiot mechanic would make decent consolation prizes on the black market.

"How are you with fire?" I yelled.

I waited a one-two beat for an answer before calculating I was the more flammable of the two of us. Spying my blowtorch nearby, I lurched for it and grabbed it with both hands. Spinning the flint and pressing the trigger to release the gas, the torch burst to life. I squirmed back under Rasihk and put the fire to the pool of lux. A textbook page burst into the forefront of my mind: standard traps in an Apex's lair had everything to do with defence, weapons, projectiles, movable walls . . . and floor.

The lux ate the fire like a starving vampire and the entire room was blazing in seconds. Giant demons of flame raced up the walls until the room was an inferno. I tucked under Rasihk, curling in against the heat, shoving my hand against his throat to let him know I hadn't left him. "Hang on, big guy." I didn't really know what I was doing—I couldn't move him, let alone with the debris and bone piled on him—but I had to try something.

Slowing my breath, I listened. I didn't need to see the erupting flames to know the way out of the room. "Okay, when I say . . . I need you to try to follow me. I'll keep talking, okay?"

I pulled the fire resistant shirt over my face to protect from the heat. Then I heard it, the staccato clicks of mechanisms triggering and gears whirring.

"Stay down, no matter what!" I yelled. The first blast sounded, followed by seven more: projectile weapons. I could hear retreat orders being called by the Guild and smugglers alike.

Then the room shifted, as two adjacent walls started to close in.

Rasikh was shuddering now, a growl rumbling in his chest. "The walls are closing!"

"I know," I called back, remembering where I saw the change from tapestry to floor. "I need you to reach forward until you don't feel the carpet anymore, then dig those fucked up claws in like our lives depend on it."

He stretched his pained claws forward and shoved his hooks into the floor up to his scales.

I heard another grinding gear from beneath us. "The floor's going to give way and take all that shit off your back. Hang on, now!" Digging my fingers between his scales, I clung on as the floor gaped open beneath us.

We swung down like a hinge, Rasikh's claws still on the topside of the throne room. I could hear the splashing and hissing of the rubble that had been piled on us falling into some toxic trap below.

"Can you pull yourself up?" I scampered up his mandible to the right side of this gamble, bracing my boot against his straining claws like I could somehow keep him from falling. "C'mon, Rasikh, pull! Use your tail."

The room was hotter than hell, old gears groaning as the walls closed in, knocking every memory from this room into the abyss below.

He heaved and scrabbled, digging his way up the wall. I stayed with him the whole time, sneaking peeks through my shirt to dart around the flames, staying in line with his nose for scent and, by the seas and skies, I remembered to keep talking.

Once he was out, I led the way with my hand on his snout, skirting the edges of the path. Everywhere with carpet had turned into the gaping maw that was eating the room, and the walls were pushing everything in to be consumed. Rasikh snaked along, following my lead while still shielding me from the flames, and I followed the map I made in my mind, hoping for accuracy. Any errors and we would plunge into the acid bath below.

I barely realized we'd made it out of the throne room, my skin still blistering with residual heat. Pulling my shirt off my face, I darted to the door, spinning my lock picks as Rasikh cleared the room. The two grand doors slid together, sealing the chamber and chaos inside. The last thing I saw before they closed was the skull of the Apex dragon, dragged backwards by the length of its spine, slipping over the edge into the darkness below.

And then it was just us again, alone with the sound of our panting breath. As my eyes adjusted, I found the faint sheen of Rasikh's shape beside me, his snout questing for me. Wordless, I put my shaking hands out, sliding them over the smooth scales of his muzzle.

"Tiamat's teeth," Rasikh groaned, sniffing at my backpack. "All of that for nothing. No treasure, barely any lux . . ."

"Not nothing." I ran my fingers over the places where the molten lux was cooling on him, filling in the gaps where his iron scales had rusted away, sealing the broken places with something tougher than dragonscale, hardier than iron. I realized I was grinning stupidly, a lump in my throat and my eyes hot. In the sunlight, my boy would sparkle like a dark jewel. And it was about time he got some sun. Razzle Dazzle indeed.

I peered closer, catching a faint glow reflected in the dark scales, a vertical row of runes sliding from green to blue to purple. And above them, my own startled eyes. I brushed my fingertips over the line of my markings, now alight, my heart pounding.

"Not nothing by half," I said, with a shaky laugh. "So . . . how the hell are we getting home?"

Biographies

Rhonda Parrish
Editor

Rhonda Parrish is the editor of many anthologies including, most recently, *Fire: Demons, Dragons, & Djinns; Grimm, Grit and Gasoline;* and *F is for Fairy.*

In addition, Rhonda is a writer whose work has been in publications such as *Tesseracts 17: Speculating Canada from Coast to Coast* and *Imaginarium: The Best Canadian Speculative Writing* (2012 & 2015). Her collection of true Edmonton ghost stories, *Eerie Edmonton*, and her YA paranormal thriller, *Hollow*, are forthcoming in 2020.

Her website, updated regularly, is at www.rhondaparrish.com

Jane Yolen
Grin of Stone: A Political Rant

Jane Yolen is the author of over 376 books in almost every genre. She is a Grandmaster of SFWA (Science Fiction/Fantasy Writers of America, SFPA (Science Fiction Poetry Assn), and World Fantasy Assn. Her books and stories and poetry have won 2 Nebulas, 3 World Fantasy Awards, 3 Golden Kite Awards, two Massachusetts Book Awards, The Boskone Skylark Award, and dozens of others. Six colleges and universities have given her Honorary Doctorates for her body of work. She was the first writer to win the New England Public Radio's Arts & Humanities Award and the first woman to give the Andrew Lang lecture in St Andrews University in Scotland, a series that has gone on since 1923. One of the awards set her good coat on fire.

Chadwick Ginther
The Enforcer

Chadwick Ginther is the Prix Aurora Award-nominated author of the *Thunder Road Trilogy* (Ravenstone Books) and *Graveyard Mind* (ChiZine Publications). His short fiction has appeared recently in *Fire: Demons, Dragons, & Djinns, Over the Rainbow: Folk and Fairy Tales from the Margins*, and *Abyss & Apex*. He lives and writes in Winnipeg, Canada, spinning sagas set in the wild spaces of Canada's western wilderness where surely monsters must exist.

Kevin Cockle
Wings of Stone

Kevin Cockle is a speculative-fiction author with over thirty short stories appearing in a variety of anthologies and magazines. His novel *Spawning Ground* is narrowly believed to have invented the micro-genre of "occult game theory", and was published by Tyche Books in 2016. In 2019, Kevin, alongside co-writer Mike Peterson, won AMPIA's "Rosie" award for the feature-film screenplay *Knuckleball*, breaking a persistent streak of long-list nominations, honourable mention citations, and other close-but-no-cigar metrics.

Damascus Mincemeyer
Soil, Native and Otherwise

Exposed to the weird worlds of horror, science fiction, and comic books as a boy, Damascus Mincemeyer has been ruined ever since. He's now a writer and artist of various strangeness and has had stories published (or soon-to-be published) in the anthologies *Fire: Demons, Dragons, & Djinn* (Tyche Books), *Bikers Vs The Undead, Psycho Holiday, Monsters Vs Nazis* (Deadman's Tome publishing, books for which he also provided cover art), *Hell's Empire* (Ulthar Press), *Crash Code* (Blood Bound Books), *the Sirens Call* ezine, and the magazines *Gallows Hill* and *StoryHack*. He lives near St. Louis, Missouri, USA, and can usually be found lurking about on Twitter @DamascusUndead.

Laura VanArendonk Baugh
Land Girl

Laura VanArendonk Baugh loves writing fantasy of many flavours, as well as other genres and non-fiction. She began this story after spending a day on East Falkland photographing penguins and recalling similar landscapes in Ireland and Northern Ireland, with rather fewer penguins. She lives in Indiana and enjoys Dobermans, travel, chocolate, and making her imaginary friends fight one another for imaginary reasons. Find her award-winning epic fantasy and other work at www.LauraVAB.com.

Catherine MacLeod
The Stone Alphabet

Nova Scotia writer Catherine MacLeod loves ginger tea, television soundtracks, and overheard conversations. Her publications include short fiction in *Nightmare, Black Static, On Spec, Tor.com*, and several anthologies, including *Fearful Symmetries, Playground of Lost Toys*, and *Licence Expired: The Unauthorized James Bond*. Her story *Hide and Seek* won the inaugural Sunburst Award for Short Story.

Mara Malins
Winner Takes All

Mara Malins battles spreadsheets by day and fiction by night. She lives in Manchester, England, with her menagerie of three cats, two turtles, a social media loving partner, and a disobedient garden. If you want to know when her next fiction is released, or see thousands of pictures of her cats, find her on Twitter at @maramalins, Goodreads on Mara_Malins, or check out her website at www.maramalins.com

Steve Toase
Kiln Fired

Steve Toase was born in North Yorkshire, England, and now lives in Munich, Germany.

He writes regularly for *Fortean Times* and *Folklore Thursday*.

His fiction has appeared in *Shimmer, Lackington's, Aurealis, Not One Of Us, Cabinet des Feés,* and *Pantheon Magazine* amongst others. In 2014 *Call Out* (first published in Innsmouth Magazine) was reprinted in The Best Horror Of The Year 6, and two of his stories have just been selected for The Best Horror of the Year 11.

He also likes old motorbikes and vintage cocktails.

You can keep up to date with his work via his Patreon www.patreon.com/stevetoase, www.tinyletter.com/stevetoase, facebook.com/stevetoase1, www.stevetoase.wordpress.com and @stevetoase

Suzanne J. Willis
Goblin Harvest

Suzanne is a Melbourne, Australia-based writer, a graduate of Clarion South, and an Aurealis Awards finalist. Her stories have appeared in anthologies by PS Publishing, Prime Books, and Falstaff Books, and in Metaphorosis, Mythic Delirium, and Lackington's, among others. Suzanne's tales are inspired by fairytales, ghost stories, and all things strange, and she can be found online at suzannejwillis.webs.com

Blake Jessop
The Poacher and the Priestess

Blake Jessop is a Canadian author of science fiction, fantasy, and horror stories with a master's degree in creative writing from the University of Adelaide. You can read more of his speculative fiction in Rhonda Parrish's first elemental anthology, *Fire: Demons, Dragons, & Djinns*, and DefCon One's *I Didn't Break the Lamp: Historical Accounts of Imaginary Acquaintances*. He tweets @everydayjisei.

Buzz Dixon
Mike's Massive Penis

A long-time writer in TV, films, graphic novels, comic books, video games, short stories, and novels for the YA market, Buzz Dixon's credits include such animation classics as *Thundarr The Barbarian*, *G.I. Joe*, *Transformers*, *Jem*, *Batman*, and *Tiny Toons*; the films *Dark Planet* and *G.I. Joe: The Movie*; creating the Christian manga category with his hit *Serenity* graphic novel series; work for Disney and Marvel Comics, the Terminator 3 video game among others; and short fiction published in *Mike Shayne's Mystery Magazine*, *National Lampoon*, *The Pan Book Of Horror Stories*, *Analog*, and other publications. His new YA adventure novel, *Poor Banished Children Of Eve*, will be published shortly. A husband, father, grandfather, and litter box cleaner for a cranky old cat he inherited, Dixon can be found on his blog www.BuzzDixon.com, Facebook, Instagram, and Twitter.

David L. Craddock
Where Green Things Grew

David L. Craddock lives with his wife and business partner in Ohio. He is the author of *Stay Awhile and Listen*, a three-part series that chronicles the history of World of WarCraft developer Blizzard Entertainment and Diablo/Diablo II developer Blizzard North; and *The Gairden Chronicles*, a young adult fantasy series published by Tyche Books. You can find him online at davidlcraddock.com, facebook.com/davidlcraddock, and @davidlcraddock on Twitter.

Rose Strickman
Troll Seal

Rose Strickman is a sci-fi, fantasy, and horror writer living in Seattle, Washington. Her work has appeared in anthologies such as *Sword and Sorceress 32, That Hoodoo, Voodoo That You Do,* and *UnCommon Evil,* as well as online zines such as *Aurora Wolf* and *Luna Station Quarterly.*

Gregory L. Norris
The Giants

Gregory L. Norris is a full-time professional writer, with work appearing in numerous fiction anthologies, national magazines, novels, and the occasional TV episode (and, so far, one produced feature film—*Brutal Colors*, which appeared on Amazon Prime in 2016). He once worked as a screenwriter on two episodes of Paramount's *Star Trek: Voyager* series and is a former writer for *Sci Fi*, the official magazine of the Sci Fi Channel (before all those ridiculous Ys invaded). Three times now, he's garnered mentions in Ellen Datlow's Best Of The Year books, and two of his paranormal romance novels were published by Home Shopping Network for their "Escape With Love" line, the first time HSN has offered original novels to their global customers. He won Honourable Mention in 2016's The Roswell Award in short SF fiction, and last year saw the publication of *Into Infinity: The Day After Tomorrow*, which he was hired by Anderson Entertainment in the UK to pen based upon the classic Gerry Anderson TV movie (and which he watched when he was eleven). Next month, his original sequel, *Into Infinity: Planetfall*, releases with a third novel planned for the franchise in 2019. Follow his literary adventures at: www.gregorylnorris.blogspot.com .

Tamsin Showbrook
A Golem's Progress

Tamsin Macdonald lives in Stockport, England. As well as being an English tutor, she's mum to two boys who will soon be taller than her (not difficult). Her stories are mostly speculative in nature, because they just turn out that way, and she's had quite a few of them published and shortlisted in competitions.

Sarah Van Goethem
Maggie of the Moss

Sarah Van Goethem is a Canadian author who resides in southwestern Ontario. She spent lazy childhood summers on the farm, reading on the old tire swing beneath the maple tree, believing in fairytales.

Her first YA novel was in *PitchWars* and her second novel was longlisted for the Bath Children's Novel Award. She's also won various awards for her short stories, and her most recent, "Accidents Are Not Possible" will be in the *Grimm, Grit and Gasoline* Anthology published by World Weaver Press.

Sarah is a nature lover, a wanderer of dark forests, and a gatherer of vintage. You can find her at auctions, thrift stores, and trespassing at abandoned houses, all of which she tweets about @Sairdysue

Sarah is represented by Dorian Maffei of Kimberley Cameron & Associates Literary Agency.

Tim Ford
Children of the Colossus

Tim Ford is a Calgary-born writer and journalist of mixed race heritage. He has had bylines in publications including *Beatroute Magazine* and *Livewire Calgary*, and has written plays for stage and radio, including the first live radio play performed in 80 years in Calgary, *Dead Air*. His fiction has appeared in publications including *Neo-Opsis Magazine* and *Crossed Genres*, and his story "The Fivefold Proverbs of Tseng Xiaquan" was included in the Aurora Award-nominated anthology *Shanghai Steam*. Tim is accompanied at most times by his perfect fur baby, Bailey, the legendary corgi-pitbull cross. Follow him (and Bailey) online at www.thecanerdian.ca

V.F. LeSann
Earthbound

V.F. LeSann is the co-writing team of Leslie Van Zwol and Megan Fennell, united for greater power like Captain Planet, and sworn to tread the wobbly line between grit and whimsy. Having already launched mermaids into outer space and sent a demon to the glaciers of Iceland, "Earthbound" might solidify their reputation as the worst possible travel agents a cryptid could hire.